Ricochet River

RICOCHET RIVER

by
Robin Cody

ALFRED A. KNOPF NEW YORK 1992

THIS IS A BORZOI BOOK
PUBLISHED BY ALFRED A. KNOPF, INC.

Copyright © 1992 by Robin Cody
Map copyright © 1992 by Claudia Carlson

Library of Congress Cataloging-in-Publication Data
Cody, Robin. Ricochet river / by Robin Cody. — 1st ed.
   p.   cm.
   ISBN 0-679-40431-7
   I. Title.
   PS3553.0336U6   1992
813'.54—dc20   91-19408
                                                            CIP

Manufactured in the United States of America

First Edition

To Bob, who knew the rivers,
And for Betty, who had the words

Ricochet River

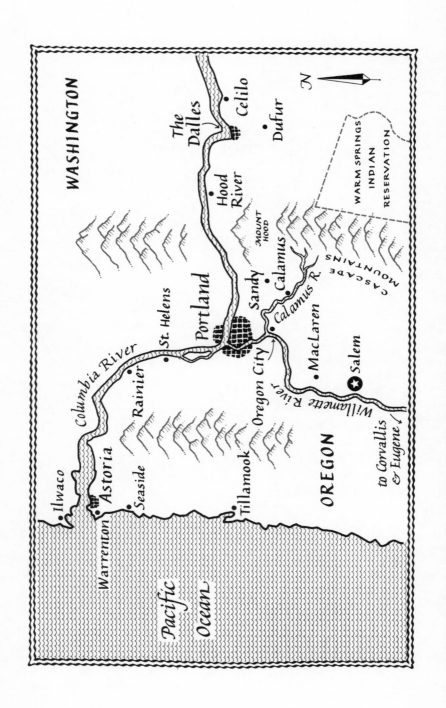

ONE

~~~~~~~~~~

THE RAP ON JESSE—one of the raps on Jesse—was that he
wasn't very smart. You'd try to help him out sometimes. Like
down at the lake one time we had Link's boat out, checking
the crawdad trap, and I said something about déjà vu. I'd
just had one.

"What?" Jesse said.

"Déjà vu."

Jesse gave me his dumb Indian look. "Whatever you say,
Kemo Sabe."

"Déjà vu," I said. "It's that eerie little brain-tick when
something that just happened has happened before. Only it
couldn't have happened."

He stared at me, his brown eyes empty. I was rowing.
Jesse had one leg draped over the stern, trailing a bare foot
in the water. I tried again to explain it. "Like something trig-
gers this brain-whisper," I said, "that you've been in this
exact same place and time before, even though you haven't.
What's happening has already happened. Déjà vu."

He didn't seem to get it. Skip it, I figured. I took a couple
of pulls on the oars and then left them out to drip on the glassy
surface of the lake. That's the best part of rowing—the glide.

Little drops from the cars plinked their circles on the water mirror. At the outer arc of each growing circle, black upside-down fir trees wriggled up into the ground-ceiling as if to find their roots and shake them loose.

"Vujà dé," Jesse said. He, too, was watching the water circles when I looked up.

"Déjà vu," I corrected him. Some people can't get anything right.

"Vujà dé is the opposite," said Jesse, who wasn't very smart; everybody said so. "Vujà dé is that weird feeling you're the first one out here. Nothing in the world has ever happened before."

THE FIRST time I saw Jesse was the summer before our senior year.

The wind that July was blowing the wrong way, whipping hot and dry off the flat skillet of eastern Oregon, over the Cascades and down into Calamus. When the east wind lasts for more than a week or so, as it had this time, they shut the woods down. The last of the log trucks came snorting through town, and the mill was on graveyard. Folks were on edge. Somebody had shot out the eights on the Entering Calamus sign—Population 9 ● ●.

I was on my way to baseball practice. After work, at the dam, I rowed up to the house and then walked toward the ballfield through the center of town. Truth is, I'd been feeling pretty significant lately. Me being Wade Curren, the ace pitcher and shortstop. We'd had a good summer season, and this was the last practice before a big playoff game with West Linn. I ambled up Main Street with the glove in one hand and my Reidell spikes—the only pair in town—slung over one shoulder. It wouldn't hurt for the star to be a little late for practice.

Up on the flat, I picked up a sound like rifle shots. That was strange, it not being deer season. I quickened my pace, past the Methodist church and a tidy row of houses. The diamond came into view around the corner of the school. Players circled the mound as if it were a bonfire. In the catcher's box, Schrenck held up his glove.

A poof of dust rose from Schrenck's mitt. And the following *crack* of leather on leather shot clean and crisp through the outfield heat waves.

I hurried on over to the diamond.

On the mound, pitching, was a guy about our age—a skinny left-hander with this goofy grin. He was an Indian, I could see right away. His tight skin glistened like oiled mahogany. Taller than me but not by much, he wore no cap. His hair flopped to his shoulders, straight, not exactly black but the darkest shade of red, dry and shiny in the late sun. On his fingertips he rolled the ball slowly, showing us, maybe, it was a real baseball. Then he threw again. He whipped that loose left arm as if he had two or three rubber elbows in it.

Crack, the ball slammed into Schrenck's mitt. He even got an echo off the right-field bank.

I shifted position to get a better look.

He wore black brogues and argyle socks, not even close to the right stuff. Stiff new Levi's. His long-sleeved white shirt still had its store-bought creases.

I nudged Henderson and asked him what the story was.

"I dunno, man." Ray scratched his head. "This guy shows up at practice and says to Palermo can he work out with us."

"What's his name?" I asked, as if that would help.

"Just moved in, he says. Jesse."

"He lives here?"

"Jesse Hall or somethin'. Yeah. Just moved to Calamus."

His white shirt was too wide in the shoulders, too short in the arms. With each pitch, his bronze left arm shot out the cuff like the cartridge in a spring-loaded pen. Then it came back into his shirt with an easy shrug of his shoulders.

I sat on the grass to lace my spikes.

Schrenck pulled off his catcher's mitt and dangled his left

hand, a red puffed carp. Palermo stepped out to address the group, his eyes bulging as he opened his mouth to speak. Nothing came out. He cleared his throat, hocked, spat an oyster on the grass and tried again.

"Senough," he coughed. "Less hit. Let's hit."

We pounded gloves and shuffled spikes and spat on the ground, but the huddle around this dark stranger just expanded a step or two instead of breaking up. Who would throw batting practice? Not me. I was pitching tomorrow against West Linn. And nobody was anxious to step in and hit against this Indian guy.

Coach Palermo, thinking everything was clear, bounded toward the bench with his clipboard. Hired fresh out of Lewis & Clark, Palermo was going to be our high school baseball coach. He had those muscle-bound legs where his kneecaps were dents instead of bumps. But one of his first summer-ball moves was to boot Mitch Jukor off the team for drinking beer. Which didn't sit too well at the barbershop.

Palermo noticed nobody was moving.

"Jesse," he said to the new guy. "You throw. Just get 'em over."

The Indian nodded, grinning through too-white teeth. With his glove he wiped a shock of hair from his eyes.

Others broke for their positions, the nonstarters heading for a safe place in the outfield. I took a couple of steps toward shortstop. But Larry was already there, calling for an infield ball. My only move was to run in and grab a bat. Be aggressive. That's what they tell you.

I picked out my Nellie Fox 33 and watched the Indian throw a couple more pitches at the same blistering speed. Left handed. I'm a left-handed hitter. I stepped in and got set.

The pitch was an aspirin tablet, a strike.

I looked over at Palermo.

"Batting practice," he shouted to the mound. "Throw easy. Just throw the ball right."

Jesse looked baffled—throw the ball right? He looked at Palermo and then nodded. OK, you're the coach. He switched his glove to his other hand. Then he wound up with a mirror image of that hose we'd all seen and whipped another bullet. Right-handed!

I was stunned.

The pitch was a perfect strike, but I bailed out. Schrenck, too, reacted as if the guy had pulled a bazooka on him. Sitting flat on the ground, he reached up to snag the ball.

"What the fucking Goddamn . . ." Palermo sputtered, waving his clipboard. Palermo had a language problem. "Stop this . . . foolin' around." He wiped his mouth with his forearm. "Throw the ball right, doggone it. None of this funny stuff."

Jesse's grin flickered and almost left. He shrugged and looked around for an interpreter.

I volunteered: "Throw easy," I said. "Easy does it. It's just hitting practice."

He looked grateful for that. Actually the guy was real relaxed and friendly-looking.

I stepped back up to the plate. He wound up with the same fluid motion, and I felt panic rising. The pitch was not full speed, but my weight was on my heels. I waved at the ball, lofting a soft pop-up to third base.

Earl called too loudly for it. Larry, at shortstop, said, "You got it, lotta room," as if it were the last out of the World Series. Earl grabbed it, and they tossed the ball around the infield. Which didn't seem all that necessary. For hitting practice you don't toss the ball around the infield.

ANOTHER thing about the Entering Calamus sign. There's only one. Jesse, who's been around, picked up on that right away. The only Entering Calamus sign is on the Willamette Valley side, from Portland.

"Any normal town," Jesse says, "you got at least two Entering signs."

Which is true. OK, sure, you can drive through Calamus and on up the river road for logs or fish or deer or huckleberries. But everything dead-ends in the woods. The roads peter out and stop. So if you arrive in town from up the river, Calamus must be the last town you were in. You should know where you are.

I mentioned this to Lorna.

She didn't think it was remarkable. "Gad," Lorna says. "They ought to put up a Leaving sign."

So AFTER Jesse's first practice a bunch of us piled into Larry Wirtz's '51 Chev and drove downtown. Larry parked diagonally in front of Jake's, which is two doors on Broadway. One door is by the red and white barber pole, screwing itself upward. The other goes to the restaurant, which is also known as Jake's, formally, or just the barbershop. Jake's used to be all one establishment, but the board of health made Jake separate the barbershop from the restaurant part. Thin red strips of plastic now hang in the connecting doorway. The plastic strips don't hurt the acoustics at all. Anything good in either place, you can usually catch it.

The barbershop, when we got there, was full of idled loggers, but the soda fountain hadn't picked up yet. Lorna, in her white uniform, sat at the counter reading a fat dog-eared paperback. It was another of those Russians. Dostoevski. I think she thinks if you can't pronounce the names it must be good.

"What's this one about?" I asked her.

"Axe murderer."

She looked up, a little put out at our arrival. But even when she's annoyed—which is often—Lorna's eyes are a gift. They are a milk-chocolate brown with light gold specks. In the deep parts I can swim laps.

"Another mystery?" I said.

"No mystery. He did it right away. This pathetic old lady? Bashed her head with an axe. It's kind of a backward book."

She folded it up and put it in the menu rack.

I joined the guys at a booth.

As if we might order something she couldn't remember, Lorna came over with her check pad in one hand and a stubby yellow pencil poised in the other. It was cherry Cokes and lime phosphates, the usual, except I ordered a blackberry milkshake because I was trying to bulk up for football.

"I got the late shift after this," Lorna told me. "Mrs. Swenson's got cramps."

Which meant we couldn't go to the show tonight. I'd forgotten we were supposed to, so it's a good thing she said it.

To tell you the truth, Lorna is no Grace Kelly. She has this hair that to be polite about it you might call unruly. And a bit of a complexion problem, not too bad. But she takes a tan well and she has those terrific eyes. And she reads books, although her tastes run more to morbid than mine. I don't know. Her flyaway, light-brown hair is best when she corrals it into a pony tail, like when she's working. I tell her she should fix it that way all the time. But does she listen to me? Sometimes.

She stuck the yellow pencil over her ear and turned toward the soda fountain. And that, too, her walking away, is one of Lorna's best parts. Now that they're wearing skirts above the knee. Before she turned the corner, a collective nod spread around our booth. Nothing said, you know, but I got it. Truth is, Lorna has definite ideas about how far you can go, and it's not far.

Anyway, the topic in our booth, of course, was the Indian. We'd seen he could hit, too, and he had that dark gift of speed. "What a ath-a-lete," according to Wirtz. But more than that he had a way of carrying himself, or just being there—him and his eerie grin—as if he belonged.

"You don't suppose he's eligible, do you?" I said. "I mean for playoffs. Just got into town and everything."

"Why not? If he lives here."

Well, that was a good point. Except I figured there must be a rule or something about rosters. If he hadn't played all summer, how could he be eligible? We had submitted birth certificates. Would an Indian have a birth certificate?

I wasn't saying all this, just thinking it.

Lorna brought our drinks. I gulped too much shake too fast. A cold fist inside my head tried to smash out between my eyebrows. I swiveled my neck.

Pretty soon who should come in but this Indian guy. He let the screen door bang behind him because he didn't know how to do it. We tried to ignore him, standing there trying to figure this place out. What we should've done, at the end of practice, was ask him to come with us. A new guy and all. But nobody had. And now it didn't seem correct to ask him over to the booth, where we were about finished.

Jesse spotted us and came right over, leading with those white teeth.

He plunked himself down next to Goode, who scooted over to make room. There was this nervous, "Hey, how ya' doin'," and "Good to see you."

"What's good to eat here?" he said.

The guys said nothing much was, which isn't true. I don't know why people have to be so negative. They got to arguing about what, if anything, was good to eat here.

So I asked him, I said, "What are you doing here?"

Might as well come right out with it. He looked surprised, like maybe I was deaf.

"Gonna get me something to eat."

"No," I said. "I mean in Calamus. Who are you?"

"Ah," he said. "Jesse Howell. I'm a Klamath. From Celilo. Came to Calamus from Warm Springs."

I knew those places, east of the mountains. Celilo was a big falls on the Columbia River. Warm Springs is a reservation, on the road to Bend.

"Peace," said Jesse. He stuck out his hand.

"Peace," I said. I mean what do you say? Like I should have doffed my cavalry hat, set my Winchester aside. I shook his hand, which was leathery and warm, with long fingers. There was this crooked grin about him, like now I should explain what *we* were doing here. His eyes had black-water depth that wasn't unfriendly but made you nervous. He was a good-looking guy, no getting around it.

I tried to think how to rephrase the question.

Schrenck punched the jukebox selector and out came "Running Bear." Which is this incredibly dumb Johnny Preston song about brave Running Bear and Little White Dove. I tensed up, but Jesse winked at Schrenck—he got it; he thought it was funny. Schrenck went *oom-pah-pahing* to the Indian chant in the song.

Lorna came over.

Jesse ordered the cheeseburger deluxe with everything. "Plus also a Coke."

"Plain Coke?" she said.

Lorna gave me the old sideways eye. She ran her tongue past her chipped front tooth. Which I forgot to mention is another thing good about Lorna. That broken front tooth. You'd think . . . I mean it's actually a defect, but it's kind of exciting. Anyway Lorna eyed me like I was supposed to introduce her, but I didn't even know this guy. Jesse.

So it was a plain Coke.

Lorna stuck out her lip and poofed the bangs off her forehead. She turned to go behind the counter. Jesse's eyes got big. He kind of went limp, like he might slide off the seat and under the table. He said, in Lorna's direction: "Not bad. Not bad at all. That's worth at least two canoes and six blankets where I come from."

From the look on Jesse's face, I guess he thought it deserved a laugh.

Around the booth there was this ugly silence. Everybody looking at me, like what was I going to do?

Situations like this you see all the time in movies. Some drunk insults your woman and you deck him with one punch—*pflatt*—or send him spinning out through the swinging saloon doors. But when it actually comes up . . . The trouble is, thinking about it. You have to just do it, not think about it. Will it hurt my hand? What if he gets up?

By the time it dawned on me this was real life, my timing was way off.

Rising, I caught the under edge of the table at midthigh, toppling lime phosphates and cherry Cokes but not the table, which was anchored to the floor. A glass broke and somebody shrieked. When I got free of the booth, Jesse, too, was standing, with a bewildered look on his face. His hands were up in the air like he was being arrested and didn't know what for.

I swung on him with all I had.

I may have blinked.

The next thing I knew, overhead lights spun by at a crazy angle and I was seated on the pink-and-white tile floor. Jesse had ahold of my right wrist, as if he'd *caught* the punch I threw at him. Which is exactly what happened, I guess. He caught my punch and just let my momentum take me to the floor. I fingered the tiles, perforated with the spikes of caulked boots. Blood pumped to my head as I jiggled through an inventory of my body parts. Nothing seemed missing or damaged.

Quite a crowd spilled from the barbershop section. I guess it was clear I'd been attacked by this long-haired savage, this stranger. Frank Jukor got him in a full nelson and jerked him around so hard I thought his head might fly off before they got a chance to lynch him. But Jake, the old wobbler, pushed through the crowd waving his barber shears.

"Get the hell out of here," he shouted at Jesse.

"Goddamn Indian, anyhow," said Jukor, releasing him.

The screen door banged shut behind him, and there was a lot of heavy breathing inside the barbershop.

"Should of give him a haircut," Jukor said, and a lot of others wished they'd thought of that.

TWO

～～～～

"Coyote was out looking for something to do and he heard this big dance going on," is the way Jesse tells it. Jesse has these Coyote stories. Coyote was this goofball Indian god. He made mistakes, was always screwing up.

"Down at the lakeshore everybody was dancing and moaning," Jesse says. "Coyote was a terrific dancer, so he went on down there. *They'll be glad I showed up*, Coyote thought."

They danced all night, swaying and dipping and sighing. Coyote had a high old time, but he had trouble keeping up. These people about tuckered him out. His feet got bloody. He wouldn't admit it, but Coyote wished the dance was over.

But they're sure glad I came, Coyote told himself.

When the sun came up, Coyote could see these dancers weren't people at all. He was dancing at lakeshore with a bunch of cattails, swaying in the wind.

Since Lorna was tied up that Friday night, I stuck around and got a haircut. Friday night, generally speaking, is logger night at the barbershop. Although the woods were shut down, most of them were in uniform. The cotton striped shirt and suspenders. Canvas pants cut off and frayed at midshin. Except they wore moccasins or loafers, instead of caulked boots, over thick-ridged gray wool socks. If there was any doubt you were among loggers and mill workers, you could count fingers. Calamus is way short on fingers and thumbs.

Those who had seen the fight—such as it was—said I had done honorably, although fighting was out of character for me. Which is true, but you hate to admit such a thing before you even have a real fight.

The surprise for me was that a lot of folks in the barbershop knew Jesse. Or knew of him. Knew his mother. Come to find out, Jesse's mother had lived in Calamus a long time ago. Before Jesse was born, or thereabouts. Reno was her name. I gathered Reno had been plenty popular around town. Vern Maxwell, in Jake's barber chair now, had seen Reno at the Silvertip last night. She and this kid, Vern said, had taken a room above the poolroom. Vern reported how *respectable* Reno looked, the way you might mention about somebody just home from the hospital how good he looks.

I began to get the idea.

"Damn fine dancer, she was," said John Hamline. "Reno was kicking up her skirts in Calamus for two, three years, I recollect, before she up and left."

"Pregnant was what they said."

"That was the scuttlebutt."

"A Celilo, wasn't Reno?" said Jake, who should've retired long ago. Jake shakes so bad you take your life in your hands when he grapples the straight razor. His big daughter, Mack, mans the second chair and actually runs the place. Jake is so slow your odds are about seven to three, when it's crowded, of getting Mack and a decent haircut.

"Maybe she was a Yakima, somethin' over east there, but she *went* to Celilo Falls," said Vern.

Celilo Falls is over on the Columbia River, by The Dalles. It is—it was—a big fishing place. The Indians netted salmon from the rocks. I'd seen it, before they put in the big dam.

Now Celilo is a wide silent lake where the village used to be. They moved the Indians out, I guess. I'd never thought about where the Indians went.

I got Mack when it was my turn for a haircut.

"Them Celilos got a pile of money, I hear," said Reese Ford. Reese, a younger guy, was a recent celebrity at the barbershop. Convinced that his wife was spending her afternoons with Jack Martin, Reese had taken his chain saw and *brrrrazzzzzed* his way into Martin's house, and then the bedroom.

But anyway, a lot of others in the barbershop had heard about the money for the Celilos. Somebody thought it was $60,000 apiece if Reno and the boy were truly displaced. Nobody could say for sure, and of course Vern hadn't asked Reno about that, he'd been so surprised to see her.

The idea of paying Indians got them going about knotheads in government. The only thing worse than a Republican general as president was these stiffs who were running for it, Nixon and Kennedy. There wasn't much more to learn, though, about the Indian.

It was dark when I left.

After I got past the lights of town it was dead quiet along the lake road except for the warm-air buzz of insects, and frogs on ditch duty. The wind had died, as the east wind does at night. There was no rustle in the high branches of firs. I smelled smoke from the slash burner, but the mill itself wouldn't whine to life until graveyard shift. And if you ever want a cure for feeling significant, try walking the lake road at night under the cover of fir trees, some of them three hundred years old, older than Calamus. Older than America, even, their thick trunks silent but rooted three centuries in place.

Makes you feel like that Alice, in Wonderland, growing small.

BIG GAME, big crowd.

When I got to the field on Saturday, a dozen or so cars

already lined the edge of the bank by the diamond. More rigs wheeled in, staking claim in a row of chrome-rusted grills down the right-field line. A dirt road runs parallel to the first base line, and the most god-awful wrecks in town always grab that elevated bank. Pickups, crummies, panels. If a normal car ever makes it into that row it stands out like a fresh strawberry in hash.

Clayton Edwards pulled up in the Hudson Hornet he'd slashed out the back of to make a small open-bed truck, an old purple number that kept coughing after he shut it off. He cranked the emergency brake and got out to kick a neighbor's fender, to guffaw and punch shoulders like he hadn't seen this guy since grade school.

The east wind had shifted, overnight and without rain.

Heat stayed but the colors changed, became sharper. It was like stepping into one of those fake Western scenes where the sky is too blue and the green jumps out at you. Fir trees jigsawed against the sky above that lineup of rusted metal on the road. The diamond itself was the one corner of cool green grass on the stretch of yellow-brown stubble between the grade school and the high school.

One thing we have is a good diamond.

Duncan, my dad, honchos the field. He and Wilbert Forrestal, who has the Feed & Seed. Duncan works in Portland, but he grew up in Calamus. He used to log, before he went to college, so folks don't hold college against him. When I arrived at the field, Duncan was out there bent over his tape measure and string. As if the ground might have shrunk or buckled overnight. One time in Babe Ruth ball one of the other fathers, helping, took the lime spreader and laid out on-deck squares instead of circles. Duncan was shaken. The color left his face and the focus unraveled from his eyes. He got a grip on himself right away, and of course Duncan wouldn't come right out and tell this dope what he'd done. But square on-deck circles, for crying out loud. Can you imagine?

By the time Duncan finished pounding spikes and tying

down the bases, most of our ballplayers had arrived. But we had only one baseball, heavy as a river rock, to toss around. I got a pepper game going.

Off in the heat squiggles, beyond center field, came Palermo carrying the ball bag and equipment. The Indian was with him. In uniform. Spikes, too. Palermo had found him a pair of baggy white pants with our green pinstripes and a cream-colored top with no pinstripes.

The West Linn bus pulled in and poured out the visitors. They had sharp new uniforms—also green pinstripe except theirs were trimmed with yellow, which only made our uniforms look worse. The crowd buzzed and fussed, and people behind the backstop were talking much too loud.

"Big muthahs!"

"Feller's got a *muss*-tash! Now tell me he's seventeen. Brung his wife and kids to the game with 'im."

My own theory is that the other team always looks bigger, whether they are or not. Calamus folks have watched us for years. What they see is not really us, right this minute, but part that and part a collection of smaller people by the same names they saw last year, and the year before that, all the way back to little wiggly things in diapers. We come out smaller.

But it's true, these West Linn guys were studs.

Palermo got to the bench and broke open the ball bag. He dumped the used balls and kicked the best of them toward us. Then he reached down to unpack a new Wilson. I expected him to toss me a new ball, saying, "You ready, Ace?" or some such thing. I like to rub up the game ball. Scrape the seams with a thumbnail so they stand up better off the white.

Instead of tossing me the ball, Palermo turned to Jesse. He was telling Jesse about keeping the ball low, one of his favorite topics. He paused.

"Mr. Palermo . . ." I began. The minute I said Mister, I knew it was wrong. He flared up like a wounded grizzly.

"I'm running this fuckin' team!" he shouted. Palermo

caught himself and gave a quick look behind him. Players were frozen in mid-throw or -catch. His face expanded and the artery up his neck stood out. "Wade, you'll play short-stop like I told you."

But he hadn't told me. Maybe he thought he had. I looked around for help. Ray and Earl stood on either side of me, studying their cleats. Schrenck stared at the fir trees.

Earl tossed me a baseball so I would have something to do, which was good of him, and I moved into the row of guys warming up. I thought Duncan or someone would notice I was warming up for infield, not sitting on the bench where the pitcher should be. Nobody seemed alarmed.

West Linn took infield first. They looked tough, all right. When they were through, they came off the field punching gloves and slapping each other on the butt. From the bleachers came a kind of worried sucking sound. As we trotted onto the diamond there was a hesitant, embarrassed sprinkle of clapping, but it built into a full wave. We were a little tight. Earl grabbed the first easy hopper at third and fired it into the grill of the Hulls' DeSoto behind first base.

"I said home, dammit. Bring it in." Palermo pulled a second ball from his tight hip pocket.

I kicked one, too. I wasn't trying to look bad, either, although I'd thought of that.

In the bleachers was a better dressed and more prosperous bunch than on the bank, like folks that go to the Methodist church compared to Church of Godders or Seventh Day Adventist. Judge Moore, the doctor, stood at the backstop wearing his madras sport coat and fat unlit cigar. Duncan sat with Virgil Beasley, Ed Lawrence, and a group that could have been a Kiwanis meeting. Link sat in the bleachers—that's Lincoln Curren, my grandfather, Link—with a clutch of his cronies. Link wore his red logger suspenders and had his honey jar open. Link eats the honey and we hit better.

And over behind our bench was that smug Indian, throwing his strange easy heat, popping the catcher's mitt with that same sharp crack. After each pitch, he waved off a swarm of pop-eyed little kids, like brushing away gnats.

Heads turned in the bleachers. Infield was forgotten now, though it had become crisp and snappy like we can do it.

JESSE got through the top half of the first in good shape. I mean why wouldn't he? Maybe it surprised me because he'd seemed almost unreal when he was wearing those brogues and new clothes at practice. Yet he threw just as well in the game. Jesse's only trouble was his cap wouldn't stay on his head when he released a pitch. The umpire got sore about it, said it was distracting. Palermo went out to the mound and gave him Palermo's own melon-head cap, which came so low on Jesse it looked like he couldn't see. The West Linn coach said *that* was distracting, which I don't blame him.

Jesse had no nerves. He just rocked back and threw as if to drill Schrenck into the backstop. He got the first two batters on infield taps and struck out the third.

We got a standing ovation as we trotted off the field, and the guys slapped Jesse on the back as if the game were over, him with that odd smile, always grinning.

I grabbed a couple bats and rested them against my crotch, folded my cap and slipped it into my hip pocket. I'm the lead-off hitter. But then I hadn't heard the lineup this time. I'd better check. The scorebook lay open on the bench, so I eased over to sneak a look. My name was in the top box, all right. Jesse was hitting second.

H-O-W-L is the way you spell his name, if Palermo got it right. Not Howell. Jesse Howl.

Their pitcher, a tall lanky fellow, took his warm-ups. He was all elbows and knees, with wire-framed glasses and a jerky motion. He threw hard, but the ball came in straight and he was over the plate. As I tossed the extra bat aside, I was tempted to act hurt. But sulking doesn't come easy at a time like this. Cheers came down from the bank and out from the bleachers as if nothing were wrong. I settled on a tough frown as I scraped in the box. A good sharp hit to start things off would show them, I thought, as the first pitch came in.

Strike one.

A good lead-off hitter lets the first one go by. Make the pitcher throw a strike. Get a look at his motion, the ball, the background. I stepped out of the box to rub dirt on the bat handle and to knock my spikes clean, although the last mud out here was a dim memory.

The next pitch was wide, but the one after that came in pecker-high, over the heart of the plate. I was ready. The ball was suspended there, frozen clear and hard as I leaned in to meet it. And it's a funny thing—you can tell right *before* you hit a ball whether you've rung the bell or not. The staccato crack of the bat and the feel of hard leather on wood, almost no feel at all when it's right, is just a replay of what you already know must happen. The ball jumped off the bat in the same line it had been thrown, through the pitcher's arms and elbows, miraculously not hitting him.

The ball shot into center field, clean-springing white on the green grass.

I rounded first, taking a larger turn than necessary, and scooted back. The crowd loved it. There was all this honking and carrying on in the cars, right behind the West Linn bench. I flipped the batting helmet to the batboy, pulled the cap from my back pocket, smoothed out the crown and fixed it on my head. I glared darkly at Palermo in the third base coaching box, but my heart was not dark.

Jesse stepped in to hit, right-handed.

He stood straight and calm, with no hitching or rubbing or any of those things that make you look like a ballplayer. Palermo didn't have the bunt sign on, which is just as well. Jesse hadn't looked over at him. He just stood there, strangely confident, fixing his dark happy eyes on the pitcher. And grinning. The pitcher threw over to first base a couple of times for no apparent reason—I wasn't going anywhere—before he delivered.

And on the first pitch to him, while I was still figuring my new batting average in my head, Jesse leaned forward and flicked his wrists, as easy as you can imagine, and sizzled the ball past my ear like a hot clothesline.

The ball took one quick skip to the right fielder, who knocked most of the juice out of it. It got a step or two past him, not far. I steamed around second toward third. As I rounded second base, though, Palermo raised both arms to hold me at second. I put on the brakes, but my legs got tangled up.

So there I was in no-man's-land, no outs, too late to get back to second. I stumbled on toward third.

I looked at Palermo to see if I was supposed to slide, but his eyes were glazed. He looked right through me. I was about to hit the dirt when Palermo snapped out of it. He wheeled his arm, screaming silent directions against the roar of the crowd. He wanted me to keep right on going, to score.

To score!

Home plate looked a mile away. I pounded toward it in a mad swirl of crowd noise, screaming and honking. A quick glance fieldward failed to pick up the ball—or Jesse—but then I saw the catcher already had the ball. All mask and shin guards, he was waiting for me. Now this is when, in my experience, I usually wake up. *Ah, it was just a bad dream.* Except this time I didn't wake up. The catcher got closer and bigger and closer until I got clobbered *from behind.* Knocked me headfirst into the waiting catcher. My own view of this play, already limited, ended with eyes closed, a mouth full of dust, and ears ringing with crowd noise and cars honking.

THE WAY they tell it at the barbershop, and they never tire of telling it at the barbershop, Jesse drilled that single to right and just kept running. Until he caught up with me at home and launched me into the catcher, and the catcher out of the play. When the dust cleared and the ump saw that the catcher held the ball, he chalked it up as one out—me—and one run scored—Jesse.

"Now *that's* a sewercide squeeze, if I ever seen one!"

"Just one run, but them West Linn fellers never stood a snowball's chance in hell after that."

"That right fielder picks up the ball and is gonna go for you, Wade, at third, could of had you, too, except he sees Jesse take that big wide turn at first so he changes his mind and throws back to first, gonna nail Jesse."

"But that Indian he just kept runnin'!!"

"So this gawky first baseman gets the ball, sees it's too late to get Jesse at second, checks you, and this first baseman flings the baseball to the catcher, it's not gonna be *his* fault. And here comes you and the Indian like a Harley after a Schwinn, and pretty soon it's all dust and feathers, ass over teakettle at home plate."

"All that honkin', folks goin' plumb crazy!"

"I thought your granddaddy was gonna bust a gasket. Swallered a gob of honey, we had to whack his lungs back to work."

I reminded the barbershop storytellers that I'd stumbled, out past second. It wasn't that Jesse was that much faster than I was. But this sort of detail isn't the stuff of story. And the "suicide squeeze" rose straight to the status of story at the barbershop. I didn't think it was quite that brilliant an event, although it was a good one.

I guess sometimes—or at the barbershop—reality has to adjust to story.

Jesse had pitched a two-hitter, struck out twelve. He switched to pitching right-handed in the fifth inning, when we had a 6–0 lead, just for the fun of it. Those are facts, and they fit the story. Other facts—for example, that West Linn appealed and it turned out there *was* a rule about playoff eligibility (we had to forfeit)—didn't fit the story and were never recalled at the barbershop.

Anyway, Jesse Howl had come to Calamus. With that crash at home plate he made his impact on the town, and of course on me. It would be a while yet before the town made its impact on Jesse.

THREE

Up on Day Hill Road, on the other side of the lake, is a turnoff where Lorna and I park. There's a view back down on Calamus.

From Day Hill, woods hide most of the lake. Which technically is not a lake. It's a reservoir behind the dam, about a mile downstream from town. What we call the lake is actually a quiet, deep-green pause in the Calamus River, filling the old whitewater canyon before the river flattened out and turned blue, as it still does below the dam. The canyon is narrow. The lake is a long green bean with five or six bulges. In most places, like in front of our house, you can skip a flat rock halfway across the lake—that's how narrow it is.

Across the lake, the town of Calamus perches on the west slope of the Cascades. The next big goose-drowner rain might wash it into the Willamette Valley, where a town belongs, or slide it sideways into the lake.

The smell of smoke from the slash burner mixes with diesel fumes as log trucks, hidden from view, approach Calamus on the river road. The trucks downshift and belch black smoke over the treetops until they pull into Calamus, and into view, to dump a load at the millpond. With a good early start they do two cycles a day, up the river and back. Two round trips.

JESSE and his mother moved into a room above the Silvertip Tavern. Bachelor loggers live at the Silvertip, or old boozers who like to be close to the source, I guess. I'd never seen those upstairs rooms, but from the outside it's a dump. The Silvertip is one of those night buildings that sags at the edges in daytime. Brown paint peels off the windowsills, and the venetian blinds have slats missing.

I was interested, naturally, because of Jesse, but it's tough to gather information when you're looking for it. Reno Howl didn't appear to be a whore, if that's what you're thinking. A little plump but not sloppy, she wore tulip-color clothes that looked expensive and fit right. She had skin darker than Jesse's. Reno's face was more Indian than his—high cheekbones, tough-looking pretty with her long shiny black hair and gold-loop earrings. She didn't seem old enough to be Jesse's mother, but it's hard to tell with Indians. It was when I saw her move—walking across the street in a light rain, dodging puddles—I knew she was Jesse's mother. Or sister. Had to be. Just from the serene and catlike way she carried herself.

So anyway Jesse and I had only a nodding acquaintance that first week or so after the baseball wreck. Until one morning at the dam they told me to run a fuel pump up to Austin Hot Springs. A camp tender had broken down. Chuck Betts tossed me the keys to one of the pickups. Which amounted to a free day, a paid trip up the river. I was feeling pretty fortunate.

When I picked up the fuel pump at the Chev garage, Jesse was shuffling up Main Street. I helloed him and said would he like a ride up the river?

"Ho," Jesse said. He hopped right in.

The pickup was celery green with the Northwest General Electric logo—NWG and a white lightning bolt—on both doors. Jesse carried "Stagger Lee" into the cab with him in a little transistor radio, which he didn't shut off. It occurred to me that passenger service, here, was not correct. Me being on duty and everything. But it was too late.

We were on our way.

Jesse wore regular jeans and faded blue T-shirt, not those new clothes I'd first seen him in. And a Cleveland Indians baseball cap, cattywampus on his head. He propped his radio on the dash, opened the glove case, and found a pair of golf balls.

"What we got here is a Maxfli 3," he said, "and a—what's this?—a Tittly-est."

"Titleist," I said. "That's a Titleist."

"Ah. They spelled it wrong," he said. "Where we going?"

"Up the river," I told him. "I have to deliver this fuel pump." Truth is, I don't know a fuel pump from a carburetor, but I pointed to it with some confidence. Having a job, having something to deliver, can do that for you. "Up to Austin Hot Springs," I said. "You know where that is?"

We'd left town and were headed up the Calamus River Road.

"I don't know where anything is," he said. "I don't know where Calamus is. Jungle, this place," he said. "All these trees, too much brush. You can't see where anything is."

"Not like Celilo, I guess," which was true. You drive out the Columbia Gorge toward The Dalles, eastern Oregon, and the trees get thinner and shorter and scattered and then they just disappear like they got sucked into the thirsty earth. You can see as far as you could ride a horse in a day. Sagebrush and wheat country. Desert.

"This your lunch?" said Jesse, opening the brown bag on the seat. He inventoried the contents. A big navel orange. A cheese and lettuce sandwich in wax paper. A baloney and lettuce sandwich that he couldn't be sure was baloney without opening, which he did. And a big slice of berry pie in its wedge-shaped plastic container.

"This pie looks good," he said. "I was on my way to the store. How long is this going to take?"

"Take half the day if we don't hurry."

Jesse repacked my lunch. He pulled the fire extinguisher from its clamp beneath the seat and read its directions aloud. Was he proving to me he could read?

"If you see a fire, I want you to stop," he said, waving the fire extinguisher. "And we'll douse that sucker."

For the first time since we left town, Jesse looked outside the cab. On the passenger side is a drop so sheer you could spit a seed out the window and—if it weren't for the tops of trees—hit the river three hundred feet below. The road is a winding ribbon cut into the side of the canyon, with no shoulder.

"Holy eagle shit," he said. He scooted over my way on the seat. "You know what's over there!?"

"The river."

A loaded blue Kenworth bore down on us. Jesse jammed his left foot to the floorboard, where a brake wasn't, and threw up his arms to cover his eyes. The truck whooshed past and our pickup shuddered in its wake. Jesse went pale.

"Is this a kidnap?" he said. "You'll get money. I got money coming. Whatever you want."

Another log truck passed, like condensed February.

"Go back," he said.

But of course you can't just turn around on the river road. From his position near the floor of the cab, Jesse recovered the two golf balls he'd dropped.

"I get it," he said. "It's about that waitress, isn't it? You've decided to kill me."

"These guys are good drivers," I said. I figure if they manage to miss each other, they have plenty of room to miss a pickup. They always do. You just have to get used to loaded log trucks and how they take a turn.

On the left turns, Jesse could see oncoming trucks a split

second before I could from the driver's side. His body went rigid each time. I glanced at him.

"Watch the road!" he screamed.

After a time Jesse began to adjust to the trucks, although he still flinched. Without dropping elevation, the road regained the level of river, which now tumbled green and frothy white on our right. A yellow road-warning sign showed black rocks falling off a black cliff. Jesse leaned forward and checked the steep bank to our left.

He'd calmed down a little by the time we passed Memaloose Bridge. "You know what memaloose means?" I asked him. Which I probably shouldn't have asked—memaloose is Indian for burial grounds, or dead Indian, I think.

"It's Chinook," he said, eyeing me warily, "for screw you."

In his right hand he was worrying those two golf balls.

"I want you to stop at the next store," he said, "so I can get me some lunch. You don't have anything to drink, either," he said. Which was true. I forgot to get something in town.

"No store out here. We left the next store back in Calamus."

"Austin Hot Springs doesn't have a store!?"

This information shook Jesse to the roots. "Why are we doing this?" he said. "I thought Austin Hot Springs was one of those resorts. For fat white people. Eat fry bread and sit on hot rocks."

"It's just a campground," I said. "Steam in the river."

Despairing, Jesse noticed his radio had gone dead. He spun the dial a couple times. With the volume up, he got a faint signal and a lot of static. Which only confirmed to him that he was off the world.

In silence, he watched the river for a while.

"If you want," Jesse offered, "I'll split that orange with you."

One of my favorite parts about an orange is peeling it. I like to get it all in one peel, working around and around so you can put it back together, hollow, in its same orange shape.

This huge navel orange had the potential for a new personal record, I thought, for size of continuous peel. But Jesse was already hacking away at it with his thumbnail and flipping scraps of peel out his window. He made a mess of it. The smell of orange juice filled the cab.

He handed me a dripping section.

I pulled off the road at Big Eddy campground. If I was going to salvage a fair share of my own lunch, I'd better have both hands free.

"Who's Big Eddy?" Jesse said. "I'll bet it was Big Eddy who got me in a head lock at the barbershop," he said. "If I ever catch that cock sucker alone, Big Eddy will be taking his meals through a straw."

I cranked the emergency brake, and Jesse shadowboxed his way out of the cab. The campground was deserted. I'd parked within view of the road, but we walked to a picnic table close to the river. We sat on the table and Jesse opened my lunch.

"Tell you what I'll do," he said. "I'll trade you the baloney sandwich and the cheese sandwich, *both*, for this tiny slice of pie, here, which doesn't look all that good."

"No deal. That's huckleberry pie."

"Huckleberry! Huckleberry is Indian food," he said. He slapped his forehead. "Huckleberry is traditional. Salmon, roots, and huckleberries. If an Indian doesn't get his huckleberry pie, he breaks out in a rash."

I put the container of huckleberry pie on the other side of me, away from Jesse, where I could feel it on my hip. We ate on the sandwiches, which shut him up for a while, and watched the river swirl into the wide green eddy like it was eager to get on with things. But there was no hurry, if the river only knew. This water would get collected at Calamus, at the dam, soon enough.

When it was time, I carefully—maybe too dramatically— moved the pie from its container onto a piece of wax paper. With my pocketknife I sliced the wedge lengthwise in two. Jesse watched as if this were brain surgery.

I offered him his choice of which wedge to take.

"This is excellent pie," he said, with his mouth full.

"My mother."

"May Coyote guide her to many more berries."

When there was nothing left to eat, Jesse stripped off his clothes—all of them—and dove from a rock into the greenest part of the pool. He shot up quick and planed out of the water. He yipped and splashed back to the bank, shaking his hair like a Labrador. He gave me an accusing look.

The Calamus is cold, all right. Not like your Willamette or the Columbia, big wide rivers that roll flat and slow to warm up. This stuff tumbles straight off snowmelt and mountain springs. I'd never gone skinny dipping in broad daylight, but that seemed to be the way to do it here, with nobody around. I stripped and waded up to my nuts, took a deep breath and pushed into the water. I made it a point to stay in longer than Jesse had before I got out.

We sat on flat rocks to dry out.

"So I saw your mother downtown," I said. "Is your dad around somewhere?"

"Any fish in here?" he said. It was something I would get used to. A question could ricochet off him like sunlight off the river. And things just came to Jesse, out of nowhere.

"Rainbows," I said. "Cutthroat. Salmon don't get up this far. They can't get past the dam. The dam at Calamus. So where's your dad then?"

"Dam," he said.

Or maybe, "Damn," he said.

We sat in silence for a while. But then Jesse tends to get back to you.

"There was this old man," Jesse said. "He who died."

He tossed a stick into the river and watched it swirl into the eddy.

"I'm sorry to hear that," I said. "What was his name?"

"He-Who-Died."

I thought about that for a minute.

"I mean before he died."

"You're not supposed to say his name," Jesse explained. "Or it will mess him up."

I guess I looked a little confused.

"He-Who-Died was the last of the Dreamers, I think," Jesse said. "Him and Lawrence White Fish. Momma kind of looked after him. Mashed his food. No teeth. He dreamed the big lake over Celilo Falls before the dam went up. And he said it. When the dam went up, people saw what a great Dreamer he was. So he didn't work. He just had to grow his hair. Was all he did."

"So this He-Who-Died, what did he die of?"

"The dam. Old age."

"Was he, like your grandfather?"

"No. He-Who-Died was a Dreamer."

Across the river this big mean crow hopped from limb to limb on an alder and scolded us for using his campground. It seemed like, you know, I mean if you were an Indian . . . You might be kind of worried about a big black bird like that, so upset. Jesse didn't pay it any mind.

SINCE Jesse had come out of the river before I did, he was about dry. Except his hair still dripped. The drops beaded with rainbow colors on his dark shoulder. The discouraging thing was I'd thought I had a pretty good tan myself.

"What are you staring at?" Jesse said. "Are you one of them homos?"

He stalked away to get dressed.

So I put on my clothes and gathered up our lunch papers and felt stupid for a while. Jesse found a dry stick of fir limb and broke it off about three feet long. He brought it back to the table. With a sharp rock he knocked the bark off and rubbed a smooth grip on it. He'd made himself a bat.

"Old Indian trick," he said.

By the time I laced up my boots, Jesse had retrieved the two golf balls from the pickup. He said we each get one swing, one ball apiece, for distance. Actually I beat him—he got under his, popped it into an alder across the stream. But then the golf balls were gone. Which seemed to surprise him. That was another odd thing about Jesse. Like he had these sudden ideas, with no thought to consequences. *Let's hit these golf balls. Now the golf balls are gone.* He could think loops and curly-Q's, but he had trouble thinking a straight line.

So we hit rocks with the fir bat.

Then we began pitching to each other, with flat rocks to swoop a banana curve. It turned into a whole nine-inning game. I called what was a base hit, what was just a long out. Jesse accepted all my calls. Then he got two runners on, two outs in the ninth. Jesse hit a screamer that would've won it for him, but I said the shortstop made a sensational play on it to end the game.

I thought he would argue.

"You're right," he said. "Hell of a play. You never know about baseball."

I'd forgot all about the fuel pump, which is not like me at all. When we pulled out of Big Eddy campground it was well past noon. By the time we got to Austin Hot Springs, Bill Norton, leaning against his fender and whittling a cedar branch, was p.o.'d. Where had we been?

Me, I'm no good at excuses.

Jesse explained how the fuel pump wasn't ready when we went to get it, and then we stopped to help an old lady with a flat—an unbelievable thing on the river road—but Norton seemed to buy it. He wanted to buy it. Which was another thing about Jesse. He was so different and so sure of himself he could fog you into thinking, *Well, yeah, that ball must be square.*

Trouble is—we didn't know—Norton had flagged down a log truck to look for us on the way down. Within an hour the whole Mount Hood National Forest except Norton knew our pickup was at Big Eddy, which is not a NWG campground. Me getting paid by the hour. Which is something a logger loves to discuss, how Northwest General, the electric company people, don't work.

FOUR

~~~~~~~

DUNCAN MET MY MOTHER when he was in the Navy, Back East. He brought her to Calamus, with me, and then they had three girls.

Mother watches Calamus like it's a movie she's not in. She seems to like the movie, but she's nervous about how it will turn out. Maybe she'd be nervous even if she'd stayed Back East. What she brought to Calamus was some fine old family silver and crystal for special occasions. And a close attention to manners. Which makes her seem more East than West. Mother doesn't talk about what she left behind, and she's not a sad person. Just jumpy. Surprise her in the kitchen, maybe she's cooking up breakfast, and she'll go, "Eeeeep," like Jack the Ripper walked in on her.

Mother is big on Oregon history. Books and maps. She likes to pack up the family and take us to McLoughlin House, say, at Oregon City. Or to the Astor Column or the Barlow Trail. She knows all that pioneer stuff from her reading.

Up in the attic is her painting room. The best of her pictures are about old barns or a dented milk can, that sort of thing. She never shows anybody except me. And now Lorna. Her buildings are excellent and she can paint people at a distance, but she can't seem to get fir trees right.

One time Lorna and I went up to her attic, quiet, so as not to wake the baby. The door was open, and Mother was painting. Brown hair hung straight to her shoulders. Her slender hand worked smooth and steady, not a bit nervous like her hands usually are.

"Hello," I said.

When she recovered, she said, "Lorna, Wade, come look at this. Did I get this right?"

Mother and I had discussed this fir tree problem before. I studied the painting. "The dock looks terrific," I told her. "And the water is really good. But these trees are maybe a little blurry," I said. "You might want to touch that up."

She breathed a deep sigh and fixed her brown eyes on Lorna, for help. "They are *supposed* to be blurry," she said. Mother bites her lip a lot. "Fir trees *are* blurry."

And then there was nothing much to say.

I PICKED up Lorna when she got off work at the barbershop. She stepped into the passenger side of Link's pickup. I latched her door shut with the chin strap and walked around. To start it you touch a pair of wires beneath the steering column. The motor coughed to life and held. Link hardly uses this old brown and tan International, so it's pretty much mine. The floor-mounted gearshift can be rude to a passenger if she's not expecting third gear, but Lorna's used to it. I drove through town and over the narrow lake bridge toward Day Hill, up the gravel road. Past our spot, I turned around in the Dubrowskis' driveway and drove back. Always get the pickup pointed downhill before parking.

Lorna had heard about Jesse and me goofing off at Big Eddy.

"That's just what I loathe about Calamus," she said. "Gad. You can't pick your nose without everybody knowing what color it was and telling the neighbors."

Lights of town spread below us. The mill, working graveyard, was the biggest splotch of light. Streetlights traced only two streets. Main Street. Broadway.

"You shouldn't pick your nose," I said.

"Don't get smart with me," Lorna said. She was steamed. "I'm talking about the quality of news in this grimy fishbowl. All they do is cut people down. The bunk I have to listen to. Who's dyeing her hair, who's off the wagon, who's switched to the Holy Rollers . . . Counting you and me," she said, "there's about enough functioning gray matter in this town to make up three whole brains."

When Lorna gets in a black mood you have to wait it out, like poison oak. Don't scratch, or it will spread. It might spread anyway.

"When there's real news going on." She poofed a wayward strand of hair. "Like this U-2 incident," she said. "And Castro. The Russians and their satellites." I could imagine her tongue working her chipped tooth, although it was too dark in the cab to see. "They'll blow the world up before I get out of Calamus. I'm stuck here. *Calamus* is stuck."

I pictured a blue and green-brown globe spinning, with Calamus stuck. Muddy Calamus left a smudge mark through Boise, Boston, Glasgow, Vladivostok, Seaside, and back to Calamus again. No, it would go the other way. Through Seaside, across the Pacific . . .

Lorna wouldn't let me touch her.

"It's a hideous accident I was born here," she said. "I, will, never, ever, come, back, to, Calamus."

If she could just leave. I'd heard all this before. Sometimes I think reading, for Lorna, has left her waiting for things to happen. All those murder mysteries. Lorna was waiting for life to happen. It's just my theory. Not the sort of thing I would mention to her—she's so smart.

She stayed at the far end of the seat.

"If we had a big enough bulldozer," she said, "we could shove Day Hill over the town. Cover it up. Fill it in. Would anyone notice?"

"We'd have to save some folks," I said. "Of course people would notice."

"Right. The *Oregonian* would have an article on page

five," she said. " 'Mill Relocated, Calamus Missing.' Zellerbach and the boys would saw their logs someplace else. Maybe a fisherman from Portland would wander through and have a vague feeling something had changed. But he'd go on up the river," she said. "Sure, it would be noticed. But it wouldn't *matter*."

I do think it's those books she reads. That damn cripple at Notre Dame. *On the Beach* set us both back. But like I tell her, you have to just forget it. I mean she's right, but you can worry too much about the world and miss Calamus. Like here, parking, I wanted to tell her—if I could get her to listen—what I'd found out about Jesse and Celilo. Jesse was news, something happening, but I couldn't get a word in edgewise.

She yammered on some more.

"Listen," I said. "You're all wrought up. Let me tell you a story."

"A story," she said.

Lorna loves a story. My other moves she can resist, but not a story. I maneuvered her into story position, which is with my back to the driver-side door and her on my lap, both of us facing the other window and the lights of Calamus. I wrapped my arms around her. She was stiff as lumber.

"Once upon a time it was seven or eight years ago," I said. "Mother brought out her maps and red crayon. That day it was going to be Celilo Falls, she said."

"True story?" Lorna said.

True stories, as a rule, are not Lorna's favorites. But she leaned her head back on my shoulder. I smelled her hair and cupped her left breast, like weighing a cool fruit in my right hand.

"True story," I said. "But listen. We left after breakfast, the whole family, except Martha wasn't born. Five of us in the old green Chev. We picked up the Columbia River at Troutdale, and Mother aimed Duncan onto the old gorge highway. We stopped at falls crashing silver off the green cliffs. Bridal Veil Falls. Multnomah Falls. Horsetail Falls."

I was only what—ten? But the memory of that trip to Celilo was fresh as yesterday . . .

IT WAS late afternoon when we passed Hood River, where the land changes. We left the green country and entered the brown country like driving over a Rand McNally road map with different colored states. But we were still in Oregon, still following the Columbia upstream, east. Tall cliffs squinched down into tired round hills. Douglas firs and lush undergrowth gave way to rusty-barked lonesome pines, then to stunted junipers, and finally to gray, dusty sage. We reached the shimmering heat of The Dalles, a city asleep in bald, brick-orange hills.

Mother said we were getting close.

I wondered where the falls would leap from in this strange rolling country. We came around a bend and Mother pointed. Celilo Falls. Not at all like Multnomah Falls and those others cascading off side cliffs, these falls were in the main river. The blue Columbia narrowed into rocky chutes and broken islands, tumbling over crooked flat steps. Water boiled white at the bottom of each step, throwing spray high as a church.

Next to the falls were rough board shacks of the Indian village. Duncan parked and we walked down toward the village and the river. Scruffy dogs and naked kids had the run of the place, scratching themselves. The stench about knocked me over. Most of the smell, but not all, came from salmon racks and smokehouses. The dwellings might have been thrown together from anything the Indians found lying around—metal scraps, tar paper, plywood, tin roofing. Some had glass windows but many were cellophane, or open. One house seemed to be made entirely of license plates and hub caps.

Mother took pictures with the Brownie.

"They can't help it," she said. "That's just the way they live."

Car parts littered the village. Of the cars that looked complete, many were Cadillacs. Chryslers. They weren't all relics, either, although everything in the village was caked with a fine orange dust. Duncan counted TV antennas. Almost every shack had one. This was before we had TV at our house.

The smell was less powerful when we reached the river, and I forgot it as soon as I saw what was happening. I was amazed. These Indians, fishing.

Rickety wooden platforms extended from the bank over each step of falls. Indian men—barefoot, bare-chested—stood on these platforms. Glistening from spray, the men were roped at the waist. The wood surface they stood on was slick with spray and fish slime. With hoop nets on long wooden poles, the Indians dipped for salmon. Sometimes they needed two men on the handle to support the weight of a fish.

The best of the salmon leapers moved quickly and got through. Catches were in the pools or on the rebound, where a salmon didn't quite make it onto the next highest ledge. He'd jump up and then slip backward, the force of water canceling his leap. The fish ended up tail first in the waiting net, thrashing and flailing as the net swung it toward the bank.

A woman, waiting on the bank, thunked the fish on the head with a club. She dumped it from the net and passed it to a row of other women, who sliced and gutted it on the rocks. Gulls and crows squawked and squabbled over the remains.

Steps of the falls looked taller up close than they had from the road. It seemed impossible that any fish could leap that high. But they did. Working through ten- to twelve-foot vertical jumps, one big salmon took each step on his first try. He stayed far enough from the bank that the nets couldn't reach him. His body was darker than the Chinook we get with Link at the mouth of the Columbia, but I could tell from his hook nose and his size and just the *attitude*. This was Chinook, all right, getting closer to home. Sea lice were still on him.

I guess the platforms were reserved for men. Below, along the bank, were kids. Some held what looked like javelins—harpoon-tipped spears with a cord at the nonsticking end.

From the bank, one kid threw a spear. Another hauled it back. I thought they were just fooling around. But on one throw they stuck a salmon square behind the gill. It took them both, struggling, to drag the fish onto the bank. After clubbing it to death, they carried it to where the netted fish were dropped. There were no special congratulations from older Indians. Everybody had his job.

Mother and Duncan were ready to leave, but I was not.

Duncan explained how only Indians could fish like this. It was against the law for anyone else to net salmon upriver. Treaty rights. I was ready to cash in my citizenship, whatever it took. I'd never seen anything like this. We stayed until the Indians quit the river. The sun dropped behind the hills, and dusk turned to dark.

"AND THAT was Celilo Falls," I told Lorna. "It could have been Jesse, one of those Indian kids I saw."

"It's all gone now?" she said.

"History," I said. "Nobody will ever see that again. I'll take you over there sometime, but there's nothing to see. It's just a lake behind The Dalles Dam. They built a little green park with a boat launch, where you can waterski. And a plaque. A historical marker," I said. "The Indians got moved across the road, on the other side of the tracks, Jesse told me," I said. "He lived there for a while. Then he moved to the reservation at Warm Springs, but it wasn't any good, is what Jesse said."

Lorna reminded me, with her body movement, that I held her left breast in my hand. She'd warmed up considerably in the course of the story. She seemed to get it.

Lorna and I did our usual business there in the front seat for a while, which you probably wouldn't be interested in. It wasn't much. What Lorna and I had was this understanding, this pact. In the event of atomic bomb—at the first flash—we were to meet under the grandstand, in the drama room, and really go at it until the fallout hit. Or until the grandstand burned down on us. Die in each other's arms. In the meantime, there were limits. That's what I mean about Lorna having definite ideas, how far you can go. Actually, since she made up this pact it had taken an odd twist, as if our not doing it might *prevent* the end of the world. Not that I'm complaining. Lorna and I can steam up the windows pretty good. The best of it is Lorna's broken tooth. Just kissing her is a lot.

When that was done, Lorna sat up and straightened her white uniform.

"So this Jesse," she said. "They say he got a lot of money. The government paid the Indians off."

"Not yet," I said. "Not all of it. The lawyers are still on it, Jesse told me. He hopes they'll settle it by the time he turns eighteen, which is April, he said. He wouldn't get his big money until then anyway."

"How much?"

"He didn't know. A lot."

Lorna thought about that for a while.

"I don't see how money would do it," she said.

Which is correct, but saying it sucked the air right out of the pickup cab. You try to think what would do it, and there isn't anything. Once the falls are gone, they're gone. It's not an easy thing to think about.

Now I'd gone and got Lorna in a funk again. But at least she had something other than her own troubles to think about. I'd forgot to tell her the part that most qualified as news, even on her scale.

"Jesse told me he was going to move in with Link."

"With Link!" she said. It threw her, all right. "Why Link?"

"I don't know," I said. "Jesse didn't know. I guess Reno Howl and Link know each other from way back. It's all worked out. Jesse will stay at the bunkhouse with Link. His mother went back to the reservation."

"Well!" she said.

That's what I was thinking, too. Why my grandfather?

But thinking is not what we go to Day Hill for.

I wrestled her back down on the seat. Like I said, there's something about Lorna's chipped tooth that just about drives me crazy when she gets it going. It makes you wonder how life could be so good and we hadn't even got our clothes off, for Chrissake. We never had. Saving it.

After which the pickup windows were completely fogged. Which was just as well, not being able to see out. The window on Lorna's side had a faint glow, as if Calamus were reminding us it was out there. The light didn't penetrate the cab but stuck there, fuzzy, on the damp glass.

She said, softly, "Tell me again what we're going to do."

It was time to head home. Lorna and I always finish parking with a story. "We're going to get a lookout tower," I said. "Way up in the . . ."

"No," she said. "The one about the raft."

"Right," I said.

Who knows how our raft story ever got started? Long ago. Now it was more like the pledge of allegiance. Just the sound of the words make you feel good, and you don't even think anymore about what the words mean. Lorna didn't sit up in story position, but she twisted on the seat so her back was to my front. I held her tight and whispered it straight to her hot ear.

"We're going to build a raft, a great big one, out of cedar that will float high in the water," I said. "We'll build a cabin on it, big enough for a king-size bed with goose-down pillows and big enough for a garden and rabbits and a rock fireplace. And a sail, maybe, but maybe not because we'll have a rudder, which will be enough. We'll launch it where the water starts blue below the dam and just follow the current, let the current take us, wherever it will."

"Yes," she said. "That's it."

FIVE

~~~~~~

ONE TIME, YEARS AGO, I went to cut down a little Douglas fir
back of Link's place. For a Christmas tree. It was bushy and
well formed, about five feet tall. Link said I couldn't have it.
He told me to go out in the woods somewhere and get one.
"This *is* the woods," I said. He wouldn't miss this one little
tree. I kept badgering him. Finally Link relented, or I tired
him out.

He said all right, I could have it. "If you dig 'er up," he
said. "Don't cut 'er down. All the roots or nothin', the whole
entire tree."

We shook on it.

So I went to digging, and it was easy going at first. Careful not to damage them, I bared the main roots and followed
them out into tougher soil. The wider and deeper I dug, the
roots kept going, every which way, with no sign of stop.
They crawled under the thick root system of a full-grown
Douglas fir. They wrapped around cedar and yew, and into
underground tangles of dogwood.

I dug and scraped through one full day and again the
next. From Link's shed I got the pick. Then the crowbar, to
loosen soil and rock. The worst part after that was whenever
Link came out to watch.

Christmas came and went. I never did get to the end of that little Douglas fir.

MY GRANDFATHER Lincoln Curren's place is a massive shoebox of river rock and mortar, the only place around Calamus that will stand forever. It used to be the bunkhouse for Link's lumber camp. Or actually his father-in-law's camp, but Link married the boss's best daughter and took over the mill. Gustav Schwarz, my great-grandfather, had the first logging claim in these parts. Big Creek Logging. Gus Schwarz brought his horses up from Tillamook, knocked down trees, built a sawmill, started a town. Calamus.

The way I picture it, the great west-surging wave of pioneers must have broken right over this spot, missing it. The wave hit the coast range, washed back into the Willamette Valley, and finally lapped and filled as far back as this. Gus Schwarz came east, from Tillamook, to get here. Not your textbook example of how the West was won. In the old days they used horses and oxen to drag logs to the river and float them downstream. On Saturday nights, loggers rode logs down the river to town.

Link's bunkhouse is the only thing left of the old lumber camp. Everything else was drowned when Northwest General Electric built the dam and made the lake.

"Flood control," Link says. "They tossed up this here dam for electricity and flood control. Best thing coulda happened," he says. "Camp ain't been bothered by flood now for years and years. Was a *drought*, though, back in forty-nine. Lake dipped so low you could make out the sawmill roof. If it'd kept up, I might of had to go back to work, a creaky old fart like me."

Calamus grew up on the other side of the skinny lake from him, the new mill on higher ground.

Link's bunkhouse sits right across the lake from our house, hidden by trees. Because the road on his side of the lake is impassable nine months of the year—and the bridge is a mile upstream—the way to get to Link's is by boat. The pickup stays at our house. Link does have electricity, which was part of his agreement with NWG when those paper-serving slicksters from Portland couldn't budge him off his land, he says.

"I kept pointin' out—with my thirty-ought-six, here—that old Gus Schwarz and Link Curren was in place long before NWG or the county. Them fellers finally saw the justice of it."

Link's blue eyes spark as if he's just daring you not to believe him. They call him Red, but now Link's hair is white and bird-nesty, self-cut. His bushy eyebrows and a full mustache remind you of Sam Clemens, except Link doesn't smoke a pipe. He rolls his own.

Link and some of his sons—he had six—ran a gyppo logging outfit after his mill went under. But they bumped into the depression, I guess. Bad times. When Duncan, Link's youngest, came back from the Navy with his fancy eastern bride and went to college on the G.I. Bill, that was about the end of Big Creek Logging. Of Link's sons, only Duncan stayed in Calamus. And he works in Portland. For Northwest General Electric.

"Stuff the good old days," Link says. "Let them other dunderheads go knock down trees. Never get 'em all cut down anyways."

These days, Link sharpens saws and sews leather. Deerskin slippers and mukluks are his big items, but he also does vests and purses if he's in the mood. Above the bunkhouse is a large neon sign in red script. It says: LEATHER. The woods are so thick over there you can't see the sign from town. Even from our house it just spreads a red glow in the night branches.

So anyway, within a week of Jesse's arrival Jesse struck up with Link over at the bunkhouse, and about a week after that Reno Howl was gone. As if she had just come to Calamus to deliver him, that was all. She split. Jesse staying at the bunkhouse was a natural enough setup, once I got used to it, just an extension of Link's habit of welcoming stray dogs and other unattached life-forms. Link attracts deer like other people raise cattle. Plus he has the best television around. He'd topped a tall fir with an antenna that pulled in both channels just about perfect, far better than at our house.

LORNA and I had been out the night before, and I awoke with that start you get when you think you're late for work. But it was a Saturday. Time for the Game of the Week over at Link's. Jesse would be there, I figured.

I got down the steep path to the lake before I noticed that both boats—the green rowboat and the white Birchcraft—were over at Link's dock. I was wearing cut-offs anyway, so I put my wallet and shirt and shoes behind some ferns and swam it. Transportation would be a problem now, with Jesse here. Like one of those brainteasers: Three missionaries and three cannibals have to cross the crocodile-infested river in two canoes, or however it goes. We needed a different scheme for the boats. Or another boat, I thought, as I swam across.

At Link's dock I hoisted myself from the lake and walked barefoot up his path, mindful of slugs. I heard the neon buzzing of Link's sign before I saw it, still on. The bunkhouse door, with planks as thick as railroad ties, was open a crack. I shouldered it wide enough to step inside. The two of them were watching TV in the far corner by the fireplace. Jesse, draped over a lumpy gray lounge chair, pointed his foot at me.

"Ho," he said.

"Well, look what come out of the river," Link called. "Come on in. Siddown. Snag yourself a blanket offa the bunk," he said. "We got Channel Six, here, clear as a boogerin' bell this morning, look at this here pitcher."

The bunkhouse, with its wood stove in one corner and fireplace popping by the TV set, was plenty warm. But I did grab a blanket and wrapped it around me to dry off. The musky odor of blanket mixed with the smell of leather and burning wood. The bunkhouse has a low ceiling with whole-log beams. Its small high windows don't admit much light, so it took a while for sight to catch up with smell. The easy chair with the red cover was positioned and waiting for me.

"How come your sign is on?" I said.

"Quiet now. This . . . Oh, I plumb forgot 'er. Switch 'er off there, Wade, before you get too comfortable," Link said. "It ain't business hours. A man's got to set back and relax every now and again."

I walked back to the door and switched off the sign.

A commercial was on. The man on the screen pushed a jar of Ovaltine toward us.

"Good idea!" Link said. He slapped his canvas pants. "A little hot chocolate would hit the spot right now, that's right. Wade, as long as you're up, why doncha fetch us some hot chocolate? Up in the cupboard there," he said. "I ain't got Ovaltine. I don't know why old Wilkins can't get Ovaltine in. But that Nes-Quik there on the shelf, over some, top shelf, by the mustard. There you go."

I poured milk into a pan and put it on the stove to warm. The wood fire glowed orange through cracks of the smooth black stove top. Link had the volume up, and I sat on the wood box and waited.

When the Gillette commercial for the ball game came on, Link stood up and overcalled the goofy parrot. *"Look sharp! Feel sharp! BE sharp!!!"* He slapped his canvas pants and fell back into his chair. His laughter boomed off the warm rock walls, and the back of Link's chair rocked in time with it.

I smelled the milk and grabbed it off the stove in time.

Link threw a hunk of alder on the fire, and sparks flew onto the smooth stones on the floor around the fireplace. He kicked embers back toward the fire, which turned from quiet red to a lapping yellow around the new log.

They showed Wrigley Field, and the infield was covered with a tarp. The brick wall behind home plate reflected off standing puddles, and rain was pelting down. Dizzy Dean's voice came on. "Howdy, podners . . ." But all Dizzy had for us today was bad news. No game. Rain in Chicago.

"Hell, I should of known it," Link said. "Had that rain here two days ago, like a cow pissin' on a flat rock."

He clicked off the set. The picture squeezed itself into a bright silver dot that faded slowly on the gray screen.

As if the rainout were his fault, Link went to the stove and began frying up venison steak. Thick cuts, in the cast-iron frying pan. Since there are no rooms at the bunkhouse—the kitchen is just where the stove and sink squat along one wall—the smell of venison spread to the whole space. Which can make you real hungry. I went over to see what I could do, and Link put me to feeding bread into the toaster. The meat sizzled, snapping liquid sparks. He wore a chewed-up logging glove to get the fork in there and flip the steaks. Link doesn't mess around with potatoes and vegetables, but he made milk gravy from what was left in the skillet.

We sat on benches at the food-stained end of a chunky, thick-grained wood table. Link had salvaged it from the old cookhouse, said he was worried it might float up and wipe out a town or two below the dam if it ever got away. The table could have seated twenty people, easily. Link bunched us together at one end as if he expected the other seventeen to drop in any minute.

Not even Link bothered to talk as we started eating.

Jesse's thin arms and hands operated quickly on the meat. The mystery to me was how he could throw a baseball so hard. Usually you associate big bones and muscles with strength, but Jesse's arms were no thicker than my own. Around his elbow, as he cut on the meat, muscles and tendons were fast flicks. I could see right through his skin, like bronze cellophane, how an arm works.

He was eating right-handed.

"How did you learn to throw left-handed?" I asked. "Or which-handed are you, actually, left or right?"

"Both," Jesse said. He kept eating.

"No. You know what I mean," I said. "Are you right-handed or left-handed? I mean really."

Link wiped his face with a forearm, missing juice at one corner of his mouth, and broke in: "He means which one you hold your dong with, when you're taking a piss."

"Thanks," I said.

" 's all right." Link belched. He sawed off another piece of venison.

Jesse put his knife and fork down and brushed hair from his eyes with one hand. His right hand.

"I don't know," he confessed. "Over in Celilo, see, you do better if you're right-handed. That is, if you live on the Oregon side. If you live on the Washington side, it's better to be left-handed. And Momma, she . . . We lived on both sides of the river. Sometimes on one side and sometimes on the other."

Link's flinty blue eyes were skeptical. "You puttin' us on, boy?"

"I don't get it," I said.

"Well, over at Celilo, the falls in the river . . . It all had to do with the angles," Jesse said. "First of all, only men could use nets from the scaffolds. Us kids would go along the bank and under the scaffolds with spears."

Jesse explained what I had already seen, years ago, about spearing salmon as they take the falls.

"Couldn't you just fish for them?" I asked.

"They don't bite. Salmon aren't hungry by the time they get that far. All they got left is to find home. That's all they think about."

"That's right," Link confirmed. He stopped eating and listened closely.

"So it all depends on the angles," Jesse said. "Figure it out. Your best spear flingers on the Washington side are left-handers, see, because you stand in there on the bank, below a ledge, close to the up-and-down wall. And the best way— the only way, really—to spear a salmon is when he goes up. When he hangs in the air for you. If he's strong enough to make it over, you don't get him. Sometimes you can spear them in pools before they jump," he said, "but they see you moving. They stay out of range until they jump."

Jesse paused and grinned. He took another bite of venison. I still didn't see what was so important about the left or right hand.

Link didn't have it straight, either. "I guess they only got left-handed spears in Washington, and right-handed spears—"

"No," said Jesse, chuckling and shaking his head. "No, the spear's the same. It's the angles, like I told you. See, you don't want the spear to hit the wall if you miss. Because the rock wall busts the tip. Or dulls them up. You want to throw out there straight, you know . . ."

"Parallel," I said.

"That's it. Parallel to the wall. So if you miss, the spear drops into the pool, and you just haul it back. You want to fling that spear from smack in next to the wall. Oh, you can do it with the other hand," he said. "Some people do. Not everybody's left-handed on the Washington bank. But the best spear throwers are."

Forgetting he was seated on a bench, Jesse leaned back as if in a chair. His legs caught the underside of the table, and he righted himself.

"Easy there, son," Link said.

Suspicion had vanished from Link's eyes. He either accepted Jesse's story or decided it was pure bull. He leaned across the table toward Jesse: "Now let me get this. If a salmon makes it over the falls, you don't take a shot at him?"

Link had a white-knuckle grip on his steak knife, as if to stab that little part of Jesse's story.

"Oh, we might take a fling at him," Jesse said. "If things are slow. But you never get one if he's that strong. Moving too fast."

"That's right!" said Link. He swabbed at a puddle of gravy with a crust of toast and his forefinger. "Yessir, the best of them salmon get through."

"The best of them all," Jesse said, nodding, "stay out in the strong current. Too far from the bank. Nobody gets *those*."

It finally dawned on me what Link was so excited about.

The notion hit me like the updraft on a hawk. It lifted me out of the bunkhouse, over the treetops and up the big river to Celilo Falls for a view of the whole scheme, now defunct, of people-before-dams.The way it was set up—for as long as there were Indians on the river—the strongest of the salmon made it back upriver to spawn, yet the most skillful of the people caught the most fish. It was a dizzying kind of glimpse at a more perfect world. It fit with a lot of other things I had picked up from Link and the salmon.

The thought of dams and reservations brought me back into the bunkhouse and across the table from this Jesse Howl and my own grandfather, who share that same excited what'll-we-think-of-next quality of how the eyes work. Jesse's eyes are dark, of course, almost black, and Link's eyes are Crater Lake blue. But that's just color. If you could peel the years off Link, like the rind off an orange, I'll bet you'd find the same juice.

I wondered who Jesse's father might have been. Somebody from Calamus, most likely.

Jesse finished eating.

Link took out his red Prince Albert can and his papers. He rolled a cigarette and licked the paper taut. I hoped for some clue from Link, if he had any idea what had occurred to me. He took the first drag on his cigarette and exhaled a fine blue stream of smoke that I could tell from his eyes was full of Chinook salmon.

"Come Labor Day," he said to Jesse, "the three of us we'll go salmon fishin'."

SIX

~~~~~~~~~

BUBBLES WOBBLE UP from the bed of the lake. In shallow water you can see bubbles wiggle up from tiny craters—round lips of mud. Further out, a white pancake of air might come ghosting to the surface and go *glurp* beside the boat. If you don't see it coming, that glurp can spook you.

One cloudy time Lorna and I were out rowing when this young family—mommy and daddy and a baby, probably from Portland—got out of a clean car at the point. They took their picnic gear and a blue blanket toward the shore. From under the cover of fir trees, daddy studied the lake. It must have looked to him as if drops of rain were plinking the surface. But it was just those bubbles. Daddy pointed to the lake and spoke to mommy. She got this disappointed look, like just our luck. They packed up their picnic gear and drove off.

They didn't get it.

SUMMER was winding down, the days growing shorter. Alder leaves appeared on the lake. Baseball was finished. I had my job at the dam, but Jesse didn't have much of anything to do. He was supposed to replace the rotten planks on Link's dock, but so far he'd done more talking about it than doing it. He got in the habit of meeting me over at the house for breakfast, where he was a big hit with my sisters, and even with my mother.

He rowed me down to the dam each morning, just for something to do. Then he'd come back and pick me up after work, usually with the .22, sometimes with fishing gear, or both. We messed around on the lake.

Jesse wanted to know all about the dam and my job. There was nothing much to it, really, just a summer job. Better than setting choker or haying, which most people did. That summer I painted a lot. And cleaned turbine number 3, which was down for annual maintenance. Crawl right up inside it and polish the red plastic on the coils, which is real interesting for about twenty minutes or so but gets to be the most boring thing in the world. If I got lucky, they might put me out on a brush crew under the power lines. It paid $2.35 an hour, good wages, which I was socking away for college.

So Jesse kept grilling me about my job. When he picked me up after work one day I said, "You want to come in? I'll show you the dam."

Jesse stiffened, like a dog scenting a snake.

"Oh, I couldn't do that." He shivered. He fidgeted with the oarlock like it was broke. Then he looked up and said, "Sure. Could you do that?"

Inside the control room, at the gauges, Betts and George Sayers were taking their first coffee of the night shift.

"This barefoot Indian brave you see here is Jesse Howl," I told them, "descendent of the great Chief Tommy Thompson himself, soon to be Grand Poobah of the Amalgamated Indian Tribes of the Great River Oregon and All of Its Tributaries and Customary Fishing Holes."

I had to kind of shout. Older dam workers tend to be hard of hearing.

"Do not be deceived by his humble appearance," I added.

Jesse drew himself up straight and gave the men a silent and serious nod.

"I intend," I said, "to give this visiting dignitary the grand tour of our facility."

Well, of course the men knew Jesse. Everybody in town knew Jesse already. About me, they don't know what to think.

"Fuckin' kids these days," George said to Betts.

I picked up the key ring and grabbed a hard hat for Jesse. Also some earplugs they keep there for the kind of visiting dignitaries who call the dam a facility.

I showed Jesse how to fix his earplugs, and I put in my own, from my pocket. Shouldering open the door to the powerhouse, what you feel is this great rumbling vibration of the water rushing through the two working turbines. Each the size of a small house. Air inside the powerhouse is about ten degrees warmer than outside. They keep the windows open so it creates a wind, whether it's blowing outside or not. Although the air inside is warmer, the cement floor is cold. Jesse's toes curled under, and he seemed to be shivering again. There wasn't much I could tell him, earplugged, but I crawled into turbine number 3 and waved him on in. Jesse's eyes were big, and he shook his head no.

He was spooked.

Perhaps it was a mistake, bringing him in here.

He took a couple of steps back, but I signaled there was more to see. The powerhouse blocks only about one-third of the width of the lake. The other two-thirds is spillway. We entered a concrete envelope, walking a high erector-set catwalk suspended about halfway up. Below lay rocks of former riverbed. On our left rose the concave wall that held back the lake. Above us, thick black timbers crossed in support of the dam. Water dripped everywhere, making it clammy and dank. The light wasn't good.

I got partway across the catwalk and turned to Jesse, who was not there. He wasn't following me. Back at the start of the catwalk, he hugged an iron rail.

"Hey," I hollered at him. Even through earplugs, the sound was like inside a huge drum. And then the idea of sending up vibrations got me scared, too. I returned to where Jesse was frozen.

His lips moved, but I couldn't make out what he said. I took out my earplugs.

"What's holding it up?" he said. He stared the length of the concrete envelope, studying the latticework of black timbers. He might have been inspecting the tomb of his ancestors. It was definitely a mistake, bringing him in here. And it *was* scary, to know you're maybe fifty feet below the lake, pushing the other side of that wall.

"It'll hold," I said. "Why would it give way right now?" I said, thinking, *Because we're down here thinking about it, that's why. Questioning it. It could go any minute.* "It's been here forty years," I said. "Something must be holding it up."

I was ready to leave, but Jesse's curiosity got the better of his fear. We walked the length of the catwalk. At the end you could see how the concrete footed into the rock wall of canyon, underneath the dam.

"I wonder how thick that is?" he said. "That cement."

"Plenty thick," I guessed. But I doubt if he heard me. Jesse can go into a kind of trance, where his black eyes turn inward. It was my fault for taking him in there. What a dumb idea.

JESSE let me row back up the lake. He sat on the bow. I had my back to him as we left the dam. When we got around a bend and out of sight of the dam, he took pot shots at floating alder leaves with the .22, missing badly. He blamed it on my unsteady stroke at the oars. But Jesse was rattled, I could tell by his voice.

After a time he stopped shooting. I glanced over my shoulder to see how he was doing. He was very intent, watching the water.

"What's all these bubbles?" he shouted.

"Take those earplugs out," I said.

I eased up on the rowing and let us glide between strokes. We watched bubbles plink the surface of the lake.

"Reverse rain," I told him.

Reverse rain is Lorna's theory, but I offered it here as my own. According to Lorna, this crude country is so wet that evaporation doesn't apply, or can't keep up. And it's true, springs burst from the ground in the unlikeliest places. The canyon sides drip water even in August. Then we get all that rain, in winter. The lake has to compensate for all that, Lorna says.

"These bubbles are the opposite of rain," I explained. "It's an exchange the lake makes with the sky. The lake gives back some air. The sky comes out ahead in summer, and rain feeds the lake in winter. Keeps things in balance. Scientists come from all over the world and Corvallis," I said, "to study this lake. It's rare. The only one of its kind in the free world."

Jesse may have believed me. I couldn't see his face because I was rowing, lightly, with my back to him. "I never heard of that," he said.

"That's only one theory," I told him.

Actually I have no idea where those bubbles come from. Nobody seems to know. Maybe it's because the lake, formerly a river, doesn't have a proper bed. Decomposing trees and brush. Or maybe the bubbles come from the old lumber camp and mill that the lake covered up. But that makes little more sense than Lorna's theory, and it's not nearly so symmetrical. The dam was built forty years ago, and the bubbles keep coming.

"My own theory," I said, "is those bubbles are spirits."

Which sounded good, so I told him: "It's the wandering, homeless spirits of all those Indians the pioneers buried. Legend has it this whole place was a memaloose," I said. "The Great Calamus Massacre, you probably heard about it. Measles and smallpox got the rest."

Then I remembered that Jesse, behind me, had the gun. I wasn't really thinking he might do something careless with the gun. It was more like an instinctive thing—a little twinge of wonder. There was a lot I didn't know about Jesse. Rumor had it that he had avoided Wasco County juvenile court by agreeing to take his act elsewhere, and that was why he'd come to Calamus. But that was just talk. You can't put much stock in barbershop talk. I hadn't even bothered to ask Jesse about it. What if it was true? If he got in some trouble. I mean so what? Didn't he deserve a fresh start? Although Jesse was unpredictable, I hadn't seen anything to think he might be dangerous.

It also occurred to me, however, that Jesse had come unhinged once today, at the dam. When I glanced over my shoulder, he had a big old jackass grin on his face.

"Shoot, I don't know," I said. "What do *you* think those bubbles are?"

"Reverse rain," Jesse said.

Although plenty of daylight remained, the sun was off the lake. Guarding the steep slopes were black-green firs. A hatch of caddis fly swarmed in low clouds above the surface. Birds swooped, but only an occasional trout rose to feed.

"What was it, again, you told those guys at the dam? About me," Jesse said. "That was pretty good."

"You liked that. Well don't get a big head," I said. "I probably couldn't say it again."

Which was true. Sometimes the words just come out. If you try to say them again the words are gone, like white stones into deep water.

"I forget," I said.

"The Grand Poobah."

"The Grand Poobah," I said, "of the Obliterated Indian Tribes of the Great River Oregon and All Its Tributaries and Customary Fishing Spots."

"Fishing Holes," he said.

"Fishing Holes."

"Say it again."

I said it again.

Jesse repeated his title, with great emphasis.

"I thought it had Tommy Thompson in it," he said.
"Maybe it did."

I don't know why it was such a big deal. It was just a bunch of words that came out. But I was dealing here with the slow part of Jesse's brain. Sometimes it was like he had overdrive but was missing second gear.

A FLY-FISHERMAN at the point hurled wide lazy esses across the water. Which looked like an interesting way to do it. You get these fly-fishermen from Portland, from somewhere. It isn't something a Calamus person would do. Like fly-fishing is dainty. You would as soon hear classical music at the barbershop as see a Calamus person with a whippy fly-rod and one of those Bing Crosby hats with flies hooked on it.

This guy on the point wasn't having any luck.

I kept rowing, and soon he was out of sight.

"Quiet," Jesse whispered, although I hadn't said anything. He cocked the .22. I glanced over my shoulder, and he pointed at a spot ahead of the boat, on the town side of shore.

"Something moved in there," he said.

I couldn't see anything.

He pointed to a thin cigar of mud beach, overhung by alders and maidenhead fern. I rowed us closer to the bank. Sure enough, something was in there. A big old bird. It was gray, standing, just resting on the shore and watching our approach. It wasn't a heron. Looked more like a goose. It was partly obscured by branches, and I couldn't tell.

After each pull on the oars I brought the blades back flat along the water.

Jesse kneeled in the front of the boat and rested the rifle barrel on the bow. For him to get a good shot, I would have to move us closer. The only shells we had were .22 shorts. I gave the oars one more silent pull, which glided us within twenty yards or so of the bank. Then I held the oars close to the boat and watched, holding my breath.

Jesse shot and missed.

Or maybe his shot penetrated no more than feathers.

Whoosh, that bird came whapping and splashing out from the bank, bleating and trailing yellow-brown poop. It flew right at the boat, so close he could've swung the gun and knocked it down. And then veered on up the lake. By the time he cranked another round into the .22, it was too late for another shot.

This was an enormous bird. White on the underside, gray on the back. It was some kind of goose, all right, and Jesse had blown that shot.

"Way to be." I laughed. "You scared the shit out of that goose."

It didn't leave the canyon but flapped on up the lake, parallel to shore and beyond a rock promontory, out of sight.

"Goose, huh?"

"Canadian honker," I said. But what did I know? You never see those Canadian honkers. You only hear them, flying high over Calamus. Or if it's clear and you do see them, they're so far away they are only specks in a ragged V, honking. I'd never known a honker to stop at the lake.

"Hell of a big bird," said Jesse, recovering. "I think I winged it."

Maybe he had. That bird didn't fly right. It flew low, more like sprinting across the water. Its wing tips touched the surface on each down-flap. Or why had the bird let us get that close? That, too, should have tipped me off.

Jesse said, "I bet I can get another shot."

I was thinking how good it would be to walk in on Link at about dinnertime with a Canadian honker, shot with a .22. This wasn't the sort of thing that comes up every day.

The goose had veered behind a rock promontory just ahead us.

"I bet *I* can get another shot," I said. "The Grand Poobah had his chance."

"Aw," Jesse said. But he'd screwed it up.

I stood up to trade places with him, and Jesse gave up the gun. He took over at the oars.

"Head in close to that rock," I said.

Just beyond it lay a stretch of flat mud beach. If the goose was still there, I might get a clear shot. Dusk was settling on the lake, but I figured we had time. I maneuvered to get comfortable and rest the gun on the bow. Jesse rowed us silently forward. I was ready. There wasn't a sound in the world. As we slid forward, more and more flat beach revealed itself, like the curtain drawing back on an empty brown stage.

Then I saw the goose.

He stood on the beach with his head cocked high, watching me with a wary eye. The goose didn't move. I steadied the sights on where his heart must be. I wondered if the shell would penetrate all those feathers. A .22 isn't much gun for an animal this size. So I raised the barrel slowly, following his gray neck up to the head and his eye. The goose looked composed, resigned, as if he recognized me and knew his time had come.

Actually this is my weakness as a hunter. I tend to see things from the point of view of the hunted. Yet it would be unthinkable not to pull the trigger. That wouldn't be fair, to the goose or to anybody.

Jesse, behind me, exhaled very slowly: "Sshhoooot."

I squeezed through the trigger. The goose's head snapped back like a rock on a loose rope. The shot knocked him sideways, off his feet. I cocked the rifle for a second shot, but it was over. The bird's orange feet twitched and webbed the air, and then he quit.

"Good," Jesse said.

I blew some imaginary smoke off the tip of the gun barrel.

Jesse turned the boat straight into the beach. He needed one more stroke on the oars and we landed. On shore, we took turns lifting the goose. With the life shot out of it, the carcass was a heavy pile of laundry, warm through the gray feathers. Jesse tried to spread its wings, but they were too long for him. I grasped one wing and he took the other. We opened it up. Jesse fingered the down for evidence that he, too, had shot it.

Then I saw our mistake.

The goose's wings had been clipped. Feathers were shorn beneath each wing and all along their span. That's why this goose hadn't flown away from the lake. I'd shot somebody's tame goose!

"Hey, what's wrong?" said Jesse, looking at me.

I pointed at the clipped feathers. "This is a tame goose," I said. "It's been clipped. See?"

Mrs. Gilbertson has geese, raises geese. This one must have got out and stumbled down to the lake.

"A pet goose!" Jesse laughed.

"Not a pet goose. A *tame* goose," I said. "A farm animal."

He inspected the wings, but he didn't grasp the problem. "Does this make it poaching?"

"More like rustling." I groaned. "But that's not the point."

Jesse tried to cheer me up. According to him, if the goose had escaped and made its way to the lake, it was fair game. After all, he pointed out, I didn't know it was a pet when I shot it. So we ought to take it back and cook it up.

"You shot at it, too," I reminded him, but that wasn't the point either.

The point, and it just made me sick, was we had just stalked and killed a farm-fat and defenseless cripple. I knew what Link would have to say about that. What the world had come to. The point, which I never could have explained to Jesse, had more to do with a vague sense I carry with me, here confirmed, of having arrived on the planet too late. Or at least in Calamus too late. Call it the Link factor.

SEVEN

TWO RIVERS. The blue one and the green one.

"How come this river's green?" Jesse said.

Jesse grew up on the big blue one, the Columbia. We were out messing around on the lake, and I guess here on the Calamus it was like he was seeing pink grass. Or reverse rain. I didn't get it, when he asked. I thought it was another dumb Indian question. Smart me, I told him why. How water color was all reflections, whether the river was picking up woods or sky. Green or blue. A scientific explanation.

"See, the water itself," I said, cupping a handful of lake, "is a colorless liquid. No color at all."

Which was correct but the wrong answer. I watched the focus drain from Jesse's eyes.

ONE THING I always wanted to do, but never had, was drift the lower Calamus. From below the dam. I'd floated parts of it by inner tube. One time Duncan and I did another part, but that was steelhead fishing. We never just let the boat go. August water would be too low for a drift boat, but I figured we could borrow Emery Walsh's rubber raft. Emery has a small yellow raft he packs into the high lakes for trout fishing.

Jesse thought it was a good idea.

"How far does this river go?" he said.

I told him how the Calamus flows into the Willamette at Oregon City, and the Willamette joins the Columbia at Portland. There were no dams after Calamus, and you could go all the way to Astoria. Honolulu. Which we didn't have time for, I said. But in a day, easy, we could get to Oregon City.

I got the raft and a pump from Emery, a wiry bachelor logger with a kennel of Dobermans. The hard part was explaining it to Lorna. What we needed was her to drive to Oregon City and meet us, bring us back. The difficulty, of course, was Lorna's and my raft story, even though that was just fantasy. Now that Jesse was kind of in on it, she was a little testy.

"It's just a two-man raft," I told her. "If it's good, we'll do it ourselves."

"Well that's just great," she said, poofing her bangs with an upward blast. "Gad. What fun. Maybe I could devil up some eggs? Meet you men with the picnic basket?"

What it took, finally, was I had to more or less grovel at her feet. It was a thoughtless, selfish thing, inviting Jesse instead of her. Not thinking clearly. But now the trip was arranged. I'd already asked him, and I couldn't back out.

"How am I supposed to get to Oregon City?" she asked. It got her leaning in the right direction.

"Take Link's pickup," I said. "Take it all day. Drive into Portland, why don't you?" Lorna's a good driver and she loves to go to Portland, although most of her money goes to her folks, who are hard up. "You could go to Lloyd Center, get your school clothes. Meet us at Oregon City."

She made a sucking sound with her tongue over her chipped front tooth.

"We'll go to Lani Louie's afterward," I offered. This was the clincher. Lani Louie's is a Chinese restaurant on Mc-Loughlin Boulevard. Deep-fat-fried prawns. Lorna and I had been there before, after the prom. "We'll make a full day of it."

So the evening before, Jesse and I pumped up Emery's

raft, which inflated in three sections. We tossed it in the pickup bed, roped it down and drove uptown to pick up Lorna. The three of us went to the show and then drove up Main Street and back down Broadway a few laps. Which is what you do on a Friday night. Lorna was in a surprisingly good mood. Naturally we had to explain, to everyone who asked, what was up with the raft. You'd have thought we were Lewis and Clark with Sacajawea, on our way to Fort Clatsop.

THE WAY I had it figured, if we drifted at five or six miles an hour we could leave Calamus at daybreak, below the dam, and reach Oregon City by early afternoon. Lorna was to meet us with dry clothes at two o'clock.

Jesse and I were still getting used to our equipment—a pair of aluminum paddles—and experimenting how to sit in the raft to make it go. We'd barely drifted beyond sight of the dam when we heard rapids ahead. The smooth green river narrowed to a V. At our low angle, we couldn't see what the river was doing.

We paddled hard to the right bank before the V took us in.

From the bank, the rapids didn't look bad. Ahead lay fifty yards or so of fast water past rounded boulders. Jesse found a slab of cedar bark. He tossed it upstream, to see where it wanted to go. He decided we could make it through if we stayed to the right of that head boulder, as the bark slab had, and shot the chute.

To be safe, I figured, we could carry the raft around and launch it again downstream. But the whole idea, after all, had been to drift the river, not to hike down it.

"You're right," I agreed. "We can make it."

And we did.

We hit the head of the rapid just right, where Jesse said we should. The raft spun a couple of times, and our lunch sack sailed past my right ear. We came out backward but upright, the last jolt bouncing Jesse high enough that I saw space between him and the yellow raft. He came down laughing, inside the raft, and we swept into a small foaming eddy.

We paddled ashore, looking for the lunch sack. But lunch was nowhere in sight.

"Good thing." Jesse laughed. "You got to feed the river spirit, and then it will be good to you."

I was still looking.

"What did we feed it?" he asked.

"Baloney and cheese sandwiches. Carrots. Cinnamon rolls."

"I don't know about carrots," Jesse said. But he seemed to think we had made our peace with the river.

When we lifted the raft to dump the water out of it, it bent sadly in the middle. At first I thought we might've punctured it. But all three sections were limp about the same. The problem was, we had inflated the raft with warm air. As soon as the rubber hit cold water, the raft went limp. I should have known. The raft wasn't disabled or anything, but we should've finished inflating it on the water, this morning.

The only thing close to real rapids on the whole lower river was right there at the start, less than a mile below the dam. The river from there dropped gradually in a series of slow pools and quick rushes, most of them shallow and gentle over rounded river rock or bone-white limestone. In the deep green slow parts we had to paddle, to keep going, until current picked up again and sped us toward the next set of riffles. Cottonwoods and alders lined the riverbank and leaned out over it.

Not a house or a road or anything but river and trees were visible in the first couple of hours of our drift. Morning fog hung on the shore where sun hadn't found it.

The raft pancaked more by the time we got to Jack Knife, a sharp bend with modern homes on a low ledge.

We paddled to shore next to the Kiplers' place, to see if they had a pump. Jo Ann wasn't home, but her little brother was. Richard found the hand pump in their garage, and we got the raft pumped up. Jesse grilled him about what they had to eat. The kid brought us apples and raw wieners and root beer. By the time we pushed onto the river again it was ten-thirty. I'd figured to pass Jack Knife a lot earlier than that, maybe nine o'clock.

What I'd forgotten was a river doesn't exactly take aim at things. It winds through a lot more country than a road does. A river ricochets down the valley, deflecting and echoing what it wants to say. Maybe it'll get you thinking about the salmon and all that, but the river won't take you straight there, either. The river will bounce you off a tall cutbank and slide you through the next riffle, saying, Look at this: a fat beaver scurrying up a side creek for cover. Or, Look at this: a blue heron lifting its great slow wings and folding slender legs into flight.

If Jesse hadn't pointed them out, I would have missed a doe and her fawn at streamside. They watched us pass.

Anyway, after we pumped it up at Jack Knife, the raft rode higher on the water and was easier to handle. The sun, too, rose higher. Colors got sharper, and the river was very beautiful and quiet. At the lazy spots we paddled steadily to make up time. The slightest breeze turned cottonwood trees from green to silver. In clear deep water, the shadow of our raft sent trout scudding from our river path.

I peeled the cut-offs from over my swimsuit and took off my T-shirt. More streams joined the river—Eagle Creek, Deep Creek, others I knew no names for. We no longer brushed bottom through the riffles. Wide spots in the river became more blue than green.

"If this river were a song," I said, "who would sing it?"

You could pull stuff like that with Jesse. You could throw him the change-up, and he'd pick right up on it.

"Jimmy Jones," he said.

"No," I said. "Harry Belafonte."

"That's right." He laughed. "That's about right."

At one straight deep stretch in the river I happened to look behind us, where Mount Hood was a massive white-capped sentry that I hadn't known was watching. Jesse, with his back to me, was paddling in the front of the raft.

"So this He-Who-Died," I said. "The old man at Celilo. He taught you a lot?"

Jesse hitched in the dip of his oar. We slid through a set of riffles and came to another wide slow spot before he answered.

"Tried to," Jesse said. "He knew a lot. But I wasn't very good at it."

The Calamus took us into a wide bend where the road came close. A log truck shifted into the corner, riding its air brakes, and growled away to the right. The river pushed us left and carried us slowly away from the sounds.

"There was this main thing you're supposed to do," Jesse said. "And I never got it right."

He stopped paddling to dip his hand over the side of the raft. Which zippered open the glassy surface. A lone fisherman on the bank dipped his spinning rod in salute, as we passed, and Jesse waited for him to be gone.

"When He-Who-Died died," Jesse said, "it was Lawrence White Fish who sent me on my search. You're supposed to find your special power. Your guardian spirit. Like it might come in a dream. You go alone in the hills, and you can have a fire, or sleep." He was real serious about this. "But nothing to eat," he said. "You find your spot and wait for a voice from a bird or an animal. Something. Maybe the wind."

"What do you mean, find your spot?"

"A special place. You go out alone, maybe four, five days. Lawrence White Fish said I would hear a song, or the spirit would speak to me. A certain place. 'You'll know it when you see it,' is what Lawrence White Fish said."

A mallard hen scolded her brood away from the raft. She eyed us past.

"So you went?" I said. "You did this search?"

"Yeah. But I never found it. I went up in the hills back of Celilo, there. A lot of places looked pretty good. All kinds of places. I followed deer trails and came to a spring. Another place had a good view."

I was doing all the paddling. Jesse, in front, sieved river water with his fingers, as if to find words.

"I think the trouble," he said, "was I had my radio. I shouldn't have took the radio. Air waves messed me up."

"Could have," I said. "Interfered."

"No doubt. Plus also I got hungry," Jesse confessed. "The second day I dropped into Dufur for a Look and a Big Hunk," he said. "What's better, a Big Hunk or a Look?"

"Big Hunk," I said, guessing.

"That's right," he said. "So anyway I got back to Celilo and the trouble is," he said, "you're not supposed to say anything about what you found. No one could tell what their spirit was. What they'd found. So Lawrence White Fish . . ."

"You couldn't tell him."

"Worse," Jesse said. "I acted like I'd *found* my spirit. I mean the way you walk. I just didn't want to let him down. Make him sad. Such an old man, with bad teeth."

It sounded like Jesse had goofed it up, all right. I felt bad for him.

"Maybe you could still find it," I said. "This spirit."

Jesse seemed to think that was pretty strange.

Anyway it snapped him out of his story. He whapped his paddle on the water and drenched me, which I guess I deserved. How could I understand any of this? It was just a story, I guess. Part of a make-believe world. Still, I liked it. It was interesting to think about. And I felt good that Jesse would tell me all this. Maybe I was encouraged, also, that Jesse had failed at his search. I wasn't used to him failing at anything.

"So . . ." I said. "I mean you don't really believe in that stuff about the guardian spirit. Do you?"

"Naw," said Jesse, too quick.

I mean he answered too quick. I had asked the question wrong. There's only one way he could answer a question like that, and I was sorry as soon as I'd said it. With his bare back to me, Jesse shrugged his shoulders.

"It used to might have happened," he said. "Not anymore."

To Jesse it was probably like heaven or something. Like you say your prayers every once in a while, just in case. I mean it's not something you can actually believe in, but apparently a lot of people do. And what if they're right? How would you know until you're dead, is what gets me. Myself, I always felt like a fraud when I did remember to check in with God. Like if He really does know everything, He would know what I think about it, that I'm just kind of hoping He's not paying too close attention. But then why *would* He? To one single person. With all the things He has to worry about. If it's true.

I wished I had asked Jesse that question differently.

Jesse got bored paddling. He rolled over the side of the raft and into the river. Something about Jesse's color, he seemed to belong just fine in the emerald pool. He dove for a silver dollar somebody had dropped on the bottom, but it was just the top of a Rainier beer can, catching sun. After coming up for air he went back down again, and when he got deeper he got narrower. Jesse's black hair bushed and caught up with him whenever he took a frog kick. Then it streamed back straight with each narrow surge forward.

When Jesse launched himself back into the raft, I went for a swim myself. The water was warmer than I expected. Just about perfect, as a matter of fact. *Certain places are better than others*, is what I was thinking. *You'll know it when you see it.* The river was so beautiful and sad and quiet. I wondered if you could find a special place if you weren't looking for it, if you weren't on a search. Or whether that spot could be continuous, like this. A river.

Which wasn't getting us any faster down the river, however. I struggled back up onto the raft, a little clumsier than I would have liked, with Jesse watching. I told him to get the lead out. We had to make some time. Which we did, for a while, beating the slow current, and the muscles crawled in rhythm up Jesse's brown back.

From three monster towers on each bank, power lines

swooped the river and crackled overhead. Made my nose hairs buzz. Jesse raised his paddle toward the power lines as we floated beneath them. "I'm getting Channel Six, here." He laughed, blinking rapidly. "Clear as a boogerin' bell."

So ANYWAY I was about satisfied with our expedition, thinking we had the world by the tail, when the river reached up and grabbed us by the short hairs. Never—ever—get satisfied on a river. What got us was a single, bald, easy-to-miss boulder in midstream. I saw it coming. Jesse, in front, reached back for an apple and I said watch out for that rock.

I paddled to take us to the right of it. Jesse sat up and paddled to take us to the left of it.

Our raft hit the rock belly-on.

Although we weren't moving fast, the collision was forceful. My first hope was we might bounce over the rock. Instead, the raft whapped right around it and became a fat yellow sweet roll with a rock core. I found myself standing on the rock, watching Jesse and both paddles, one of which was still in his left fist, rushing downstream. I hollered to him to catch the other paddle. Either he couldn't hear me or he couldn't see the free paddle.

Jesse splashed to shore and crawled from the river. I tried to free the raft. But the river had it right where it wanted it. The raft, still inflated but with its middle catching water, was about half-submerged, pressed by current against the rock. I couldn't budge it. I might as well have tried to lift the boulder while standing on it.

Jesse worked his way through the brush and back upstream. He stood on the bank and we surveyed the situation. The paddle he held wouldn't be a strong enough lever. Jesse found a thick driftwood limb on the upstream bank and rode it down to me and the wreck.

"It was those carrots," Jesse said. "The river spirit didn't like your lunch."

It took everything we had to begin prying the raft, a bit

at a time, from where the current held it. Then the limb snapped. It ruptured the soft belly of the raft, which gave a sickening underwater gasp as large bubbles glurped out.

We'd punctured the middle section, the floor of the raft.

When we finally got going again, the raft was an elongated inner tube with a flat rubber floor. We sat one on each side and took turns paddling with our single remaining oar. In this position, riding one side of the raft, I noticed another— even more sickening—lack of pressure beneath my butt. My wallet was gone. That is, my cut-offs, with the wallet in them, were gone. The river had taken my wallet.

EIGHT

≈≈≈≈≈≈

THE THING ABOUT THE TOWN of Calamus, it's not very old. The place, though, is old. Before roads, before the first sawmill, Calamus Indians used the river as their route up to the mountains to get berries. They were fisherman Indians. Their base was down at Willamette Falls, what became Oregon City. They used to troop up the Calamus valley on their way to High Rocks, Squaw Mountain, toward the slopes of Mount Hood. To gather huckleberries.

The Calamus Indians have vanished, but Link tells what old Gus Schwarz told him. The Indians used to stop at the Schwarz place on their way back from berry-picking.

"Couldn't speak English *or* German," Link says, "these squaws. Come a scorcher in August they moved in on Hilde's kitchen. They shooed her out, her and the kids. Helped themselves to flour.

"They cooked their berry pastries, sang Indian songs. Nobody could go in there. The Indians slept in the woods and came back the next day, baked some more. Then they cleaned up the kitchen slicker 'n a whistle, left Hilde three, four gallons of huckleberries," Link tells it.

"Picked up their baskets next summer, on their way through."

OUR RAFT limped into Cliffs, where there's a bridge and a boat ramp, the Rock Creek Tavern, and a little corner grocery. It was quarter to two. Lorna would be waiting at the mouth of the river, and we were only halfway there. We counted out the money Jesse had on him: a single soggy dollar bill and sixty-three cents. I thought of aborting our trip, but only for a fleeting moment. Not as long as the raft would still float. Also there was no way to get word to Lorna. I took Jesse's dimes to the phonebooth outside the tavern, while he went into the grocery store.

The pay phone ate the two dimes without a blink or a buzz. So I went inside the tavern to use their phone. Which was awkward, as I was undressed and dripping. Silence fell. Ball caps turned to stare and listen.

"If Lorna calls," I told Sarah Ellen, who answered the phone at home, "tell her Jesse and I are OK but we're running a little late."

"Where are you?" said Sarah Ellen. My sister the eighth-grader has a way of going straight to the core of things. Sarah Ellen is a Lorna-worshipper. The wonder of her life is that Lorna would have anything to do with me, her own brother.

I told her we were at Cliffs.

She asked where Lorna was.

"Listen," I said. "All you have to do is tell Lorna we're running late, but we'll get there. If she calls. She might get worried."

"How late?" Sarah Ellen said.

There was no getting around Sarah Ellen. Lorna might not call at all, so we couldn't wait here at Cliffs for her. What else could we do?

"About six hours late," I said. "We'll get there before dark."

On the other end of the telephone line I heard this awful silence, Sarah Ellen's brain working. "Whew," she said, like a whistling sound.

After hanging up, to mild applause from the bar, I left

the tavern and looked around for Jesse. He was down at the raft, waving me to hurry. So I got down there and we pushed off. He had Snickers bars and two large bottles of 7UP. Which really hit the spot. Something about a river, it can make you awful hungry. I polished off my candy bar and wished we had more. We took turns paddling, around a bend and out of sight of the Cliffs bridge.

Jesse, whose turn it was, stopped paddling. He lifted his shirt from where it lay beside him in the raft. Beneath it were more Snickers, a packet of Cheez-Its and some Almond Joys and Mounds.

"How'd you get all that?" I said.

Jesse reached in his swimsuit pocket and pulled out the dollar bill. He had a proud grin on his face. It took me a moment to put all this together.

"You stole that stuff!"

I couldn't believe it.

Jesse looked surprised, I guess at my reaction. The grin on his face froze and cracked.

"That's . . . that's *thievery,*" I said. I didn't even know what to say.

"Well, it's for both of us," he said. He was hurt. He couldn't seem to figure out why I was so pissed about it. Like how could I not appreciate this?

"I was going to share," he said.

"Oh, great," I said. "So we're both crooks. For crying out loud, Jesse, you can't just steal things."

We argued it out, but Jesse didn't get it. "Aw, man, they had plenty," he said. "Don't take it so hard. I just sort of took some. No more than we need."

The trouble is, you can't go backward when you're drifting a river. Which is what I would have done. I really would have. I would have returned the goods. At first I wouldn't even eat the stolen food.

But I was hungry.

After a while I ate an Almond Joy. Later some Cheez-Its.

WE MADE it to the mouth of the river by dark, but barely. Lorna sat on the running board of the pickup at Calamette Park, where the Calamus and the Willamette come together. At the park they have picnic tables and restrooms and a boat ramp, all supervised by mallard ducks. Lorna set aside her paperback and walked down, barefoot, to meet us at the shore. She helped carry the raft to the pickup. She had called the house, all right, and got the message. Also there was more canoe and raft traffic on this lower river, and news of our slow progress from Cliffs reached Lorna before we did.

Cheerfully, she inspected the slash in the floor of our raft. She wore a light blue denim skirt with a madras belt, and a fresh white blouse with short sleeves. She'd been shopping.

We tied the raft into the bed of the pickup.

"I went and drove to the Canby Ferry and rode it across the Willamette," she reported. "Have you ever done that?"

"No," I said. "I've never done that." I was willing to concede as many points as Lorna needed. I expected a much chillier greeting than she was serving up.

"I'll take you there sometime," she said, with slow emphasis. "You would like it."

Jesse had no idea what was going on here.

"Wade lost his wallet," he said, "to a band of pirates. You got money?"

Jesse and I took the dry clothes we'd stashed in the pickup and headed for the bushes to change. When we came back, Lorna realized it was true about my losing my wallet. She brightened even more. My losing the wallet, and driver's license, meant she would get to drive. And she would pay for dinner, too. Was there no limit to her good fortune?

"You adventurers must be famished," she said.

"Naw," said Jesse. "We're just getting started. Could use something to eat, though."

When she pulled onto the blacktop, Lorna popped the

clutch in second gear and laid rubber. Actually, it's not that difficult, laying a patch with the pickup. But still. Jesse looked back through the gun rack to verify the marks on the highway. McLoughlin Boulevard. We were on our way, toward Portland. Traffic was heavy, and the lights of the city were taking over from faded daylight. Mostly it was car lots, with strings of lights, flags, balloons. The air was much warmer than on the river, and everything smelled like restaurant food.

The warm breeze from Lorna's open window billowed her new sleeveless blouse.

"Don't stare," said Jesse, leaning across me to get a better look at the start of Lorna's white bra.

"Isn't that pretty?" I said.

Lorna dropped her right hand to the lower part of the steering wheel, and pretended to concentrate on city traffic. Her light brown hair, lighter with summer, blew loose and free, and she wore her driving grin. I may have mentioned before that Lorna is not what you'd call a beauty. But sometimes she is, too, when she's on.

At Lani Louie's, a please-wait-to-be-seated kind of place with cloth napkins, the waitress didn't appear to be enthusiastic about our bringing our business to town. She gave us the once-over, top to shoes, before leading us to a semicircular booth. Red leather seats with high backs.

Jesse had nabbed a toothpick at the cash register and was working it over in his mouth as we studied the menu. When the waitress came back to take our order, he gazed up at her.

"We'll have six Lucky Lagers to start with," he said.

"Knock it off, Buster," the waitress said.

She was a hefty one, no spring chicken, with a platinum beehive and thick ankles.

We ordered the fried prawns all around. When she stumped off, her step vibrated the floor. Even Lorna, who reminded us that waitresses have to put up with all kinds of guff, and maybe this one was just having a bad day, had to admit she was rude. Jesse hadn't started it, either. She'd given us the evil eye since we walked in the door.

"Maybe . . ." Jesse whispered, in a strange-but-possibly-true tone of voice. "Maybe she doesn't know who we are."

"More likely," said Lorna, "she does know who we are."

This was an opening for one of Lorna's favorite theories. I'd heard this one before, but Jesse hadn't. We were Calamus, Lorna explained, a form of lowlife that no amount of suave or clothes could hide. The Calamus in us, like an unsettling odor, would seep through at Lani Louie's no matter what we did. It wasn't our fault, being Calamus. Nor was it their fault for noticing it in town. Calamus was not, however, a lifelong condition. According to Lorna's theory, we could hope to overcome it by leaving Calamus permanently. It was this hope, which I had heard over and over again, that sustained Lorna. To Jesse, however, it was fresh news.

"Ho!" he said.

Whether he agreed with her or was just surprised, I couldn't tell. But now Jesse studied Lorna as if she were the boss raven.

The prawns, when they came, were terrific. And salad on a separate plate. Little vats of soft butter and sour cream with chives for your baked potato. The meal was enough to capture my full attention after our long day on the river. Jesse, who could talk and eat at the same time, gave Lorna a selected version of our Calamus River adventures and the stupid mistakes I'd made to slow us down. The waitress, meanwhile, lurked in a dim corner near the kitchen when not waiting on other tables. She hadn't taken her eyes off us.

Before Lorna had quite finished her meal—and while Jesse and I were divvying up the last of her French fries—the waitress marched over and gave me the bill.

When she stomped away again, Jesse brushed a shock of hair from his eyes. He said, not kidding: "It's because I'm an Indian. If you guys were alone, you wouldn't get this shit."

In fact, that idea had occurred to me. Not because Jesse was an Indian but because he was Jesse. He didn't exactly blend in. On the other hand, it was beyond me how he could focus on such a thing, so soon after having stolen groceries at Cliffs. Which he hadn't bothered to tell Lorna about, and I didn't either. I was beginning to get the idea that Jesse's world was a little more complicated—or a lot less complicated—than my own.

Lorna left a whole dollar tip. Which seemed excessive to me, but I guess waitresses stick up for each other no matter what. At the cash register Jesse stuffed his pockets with after-dinner mints. He smiled sweetly at the waitress, who took Lorna's money and followed the three of us with her BB-brown eyes until we pushed out the door into the hot night.

We piled into the cab of the pickup. Lorna crossed the ignition wires. The motor coughed and held, vibrating the cab.

"Whew, that was great," Jesse said, apparently meaning it. "What's next?"

Lorna and I could think of no pressing reason to head straight back to Calamus. The store at Cliffs, I thought, would be closed now anyway. I could straighten that out with Jesse later. We ought to call home, I said, just to report that we were safely off the river, but I didn't want to go back into Lani Louie's to do it. We could find a pay phone somewhere.

So Lorna laid rubber out onto McLoughlin Boulevard again.

Jesse wanted to try The Speck, a drive-in chicken place which is mainly a showcase for custom cars. I had my doubts. Lorna and I had driven Duncan's car in there once, and mostly what you feel is foolish. And now we were going to go to The Speck in a battered tan and brown fifteen-year-old pickup, with the gun rack? With Lorna driving?

I guess my confidence level was low, after Lani Louie's. "We would queer the joint," I said.

Which fired Jesse's interest even more.

WHEN we got to The Speck, the parking lot was throbbing with custom cars, all buffed and dechromed and lowered and mean. We were so out of place it was actually no problem. Jesse struck up conversations with perfect strangers, who came over to joke about what we had under the hood. Jesse even tried to pick up the waitress. It was as if we actually knew what we were doing, having Jesse there. I guess you can be so uncool that you become acceptable, which had never occurred to me before. Lorna seemed to catch on sooner than I did, which is often the case.

She ordered us a round of lime phosphates.

Jesse began asking around about a place called And the Horse You Rode In On. He said he had a friend who worked there. One guy knew where it was, out on Division, in the general direction of Calamus.

And from then on, it was more or less Jesse calling the shots. I kept waiting for Lorna to object. Perhaps she was waiting for me to object. Anyway it was like we got outvoted, one to two abstentions. With Jesse, it just seemed to be all right. The lights of the city, the sounds and smell of driving in real traffic . . . The night seemed full, waiting to happen.

At And the Horse You Rode In On, Jesse directed Lorna to pull in behind the tavern. Which is what it was, a beer joint. The parking lot was filled with mostly pickups. And I guess Jesse really did have a friend working there. He came out lugging a case of Olympia.

Stubbies.

We stayed in the pickup, in shadows thrown by the streetlight. Jesse seemed to know how you do it. Lorna and I had no experience at all drinking beer. We sipped it. Beer didn't taste all that great, to tell you the truth, but we remarked to each other how good it was. Cold. You bet. Refreshing. Jesse guzzled three bottles before we finished our first, which seemed to be all right with him. My second beer went down better than the first one had, and after that I began to get the idea why people like beer.

"It's the water," Jesse said. Which is the Olympia slogan. He excused himself to the back of the pickup to give Lorna and me a little privacy. That was good of him, but he was back in no time, pounding at the door. He challenged me to a pissing-for-distance contest, which we did into a set of rhododendron bushes. Jesse won, as he put it, "hands down."

"Hands up, you might have won," he said.

I'd had a little trouble and delay, getting my whanger out and trying to relax.

Jesse and I sat on the running board and opened another couple of beers while Lorna took her turn at the rhododendron bushes.

"What a shame," said Jesse, "to have to squat to pee."

When she returned, all three of us sat on the running board and listened to the night traffic on Division. Jesse had found or bought some Lucky Strikes somewhere, and he lit up. Which smelled good enough to try, but I didn't. Neon signs in the tavern window flashed orange and blue, RAINIER . . . and yellow bubbles rose in the OLYMPIA circle . . . and red and black MABEL, BLACK LABEL . . . HAMMS, in THE LAND OF THE SKY BLUE WATER, with a moving waterfall. Folks coming to and from the tavern, if they noticed us at all, were really friendly. Everything seemed just about right, to tell you the truth.

Lorna and I were in the cab and Jesse, standing in back on the yellow raft, was singing Grand Poobah to the tune of "Teen Angel" when we drew attention from inside the tavern. A large man in a cowboy hat—not Jesse's friend, apparently—came out and encouraged us to move on. He was real nice about it. He talked first to Lorna, then to me, but I couldn't stop laughing, I don't remember why. It seemed to be a serious occasion. This cowboy was real serious.

Lorna drove home. She kept it in second gear all the way, as the cowboy had instructed her. Jesse slept on the raft in the back of the pickup, not even waking when the pickup backfired all the way down Ammersaegger Hill. I kept talking to Lorna, hoping she could see a steadier road than I could, and telling her how much I loved her and how I should have taken her instead of Jesse down the river, she was right.

NINE

～～～～

YOU'D NEVER CATCH LINK in the Methodist church, where our family goes. The one thing that rings Link's bell in a religious kind of way is the annual run of fall Chinook. Every year, ever since I was old enough, Link and I have gone out to meet the fish off the Columbia River bar. Salmon gather there at the end of summer, waiting for whatever mysterious signal sends them surging up the river and home.

"Old Man Chinook," Link calls them.

The really amazing part is how salmon know where to go. Some kind of homing instinct—imprinting, they call it— guides a salmon to the very same mountain stream where it hatched and awoke to fishdom. Something in the water calls home, to a salmon. He can find his way back to Eagle Creek, say, rather than to some place in Idaho he might just as well swim to. You'd think finding the mouth of the Columbia again, after three years in the Pacific Ocean, would be miracle enough. But they come back. They come back to spawn in the same shallow freshwater riffles where the whole thing began. At each branch of river, something in their tiny fish brains and wiring tells them which fork to take. And when.

Imprinting they call it. As if that explains it.

• • •

THE FIRST time Link took me to the mouth of the Columbia it was more like a kidnapping than a fishing trip.

It was still dark out my bedroom window, years ago, when I awoke to the sound of voices—loud and angry voices—downstairs.

Grandpa's baritone boomed through a jumble of downstairs noise, Duncan shouting and Mother crying. "Gonna take the boy with me," Link bellowed. His voice carried the strange and powerful animal smells of Grandpa's bunkhouse across the lake. On his voice I could picture Link himself, too large and disorganized to be loose in our house.

"He's big enough now."

I was just a little guy, maybe seven or eight. The stairwell light came on, and Grandpa came galumping up the stairs in his hip boots. His white head, lit from behind, rose into view and glowed in the semidark. By then I was up, standing dumb and waiting beside the bed. Link stomped past me and began tossing things from the chest. Long johns and parka, wool socks and sweat shirts, scarf and a stocking cap. I put on layer after layer until he grabbed me by one stiff arm and bounced me down the stairs.

Link marched me straight past Mother and Duncan to the laundry room, where we picked up rain gear and my boots.

I felt incredibly important, not knowing why or exactly what we were up to. We left through the back door, screen door banging, and I climbed into Grandpa's pickup.

The pickup dodged potholes up the lake road. Calamus was dark, deserted, except for the Silvertip Tavern still working on yesterday. Link headed up Main Street and past ghostly schools and the sawmill onto the road toward Portland. He grappled the wheel with both hands, his chin just above it. Against us, heading woodsward, orange- and yellow-lit log trucks roared through the Cliffs curves.

Past Cliffs the road straightened, and so did Link. Ahead was the red night sky over Portland. He fiddled with the radio dial and began singing, drowning the signal that faded in and out as power lines crossed the road. *"Mule train,"* he sang, his gnarled hands slapping time on the steering wheel. *". . . clippity clop, clippity clop."* Whenever the radio came back after a fadeout, he was right on time with the music, never missed. *". . .* clippity clop, MULE TRAIN!"

The road widened. We passed a shopping center in its lake of empty asphalt under cold blue-white lights. Link aimed us onto a bridge that made the tires sing as we crossed the Willamette and into downtown Portland. On a sidewalk, black-coated lumps of men huddled against a brick building that said ALL YOU CAN EAT 69¢ and SALVATION ARMY JESUS SAVES. Link honked, and two or three heads snapped up like on puppet strings.

Up into the Portland hills we drove. Then the road stretched ahead straight, as far as I could see. Morning light spread pink in the sky. In the confusion of leaving home, our destination—our purpose—had not been explained.

"Where we going, Link?"

He looked over at me in surprise.

"Well, now," he said. "Just where would a coupla Curren men be goin' in the week before Labor Day? We're going to see!"

To see what? I thought. But I didn't ask. Around Grandpa it was often smarter not to ask. He checked over his shoulder, out the back window.

"Yessir," he said. "We're goin' to see, that's what."

Perhaps this was some sort of riddle. I loosened my scarf and looked through the rear window, like Link had.

"Hey!" I started to warn him. A boat was bearing down on us, right on our tail. But it was Link's boat, of course. It rode up behind the pickup on his trailer.

"You brought the boat," I told him.

"Well, I'll be a bat's ass!" he said. He whacked the dashboard, then slapped his forehead. "If that don't beat all. How did you think we was goin' to see without a boat? Salmon are a-runnin', boy. We're going to *sea!*"

The pickup charged from the valley floor into this new set of mountains. Other rigs passed us, many trailing boats. It was a good long haul. We stopped at Elsie to let the radiator settle down. And then down off the mountains we rode, bending through lush sweeping trees that were different from home. Going to sea, I thought, and I liked the sound of it. The boat pushed us deeper and lower into rain forest. Undergrowth thickened. We followed a small stream and then coasted onto green spongelike land dotted with slow, black-white cows.

From Seaside we followed a trough between mountains on the right and sand dunes on the left. Trees on the dunes twisted inland like scrawny boxers, frozen in midfall against a wind that didn't seem to be blowing. Link wheeled us into Warrenton, a boom town, where we ordered pigs-in-a-blanket and eggs sunny-side up at a loud restaurant.

We were just in time, Grandpa said, to catch the outgoing tide. "Old Man Chinook's gonna jump right into the *boat* today. Yessir, be bitin' at the gaff."

On the river we joined a gathering parade of boats, all heading the same way in a mix of salt smells and gas fumes. Link called out where they were coming from: from Hammond and Astoria on our side of the river, and from Ilwaco and Chinook on the Washington side. All the boats were bigger than Link's open fourteen-footer. One had double 35-horse Mercurys. Others had no visible motor at all but sounded smooth and powerful next to our 12-horse Johnson. They whipped past as if we were dead in the water, but the Astor Column grew smaller and smaller behind the boat.

The river widened. And got rougher.

Fishermen in other boats wore life jackets, which added to my growing sense of being different, not so comfortable a feeling out here at all.

I sat in the wide seat facing Link, who whooped and slapped his thigh with the hand that wasn't on the outboard motor arm. "This old river's just a-waitin' for you and me!" he said. "Gonna suck us right on out there. Look out, Old Man Chinook," he shouted. "Yessireee Bob!"

If the river was sucking us on out there, how were we going to get back? Link never bothers to explain the most important things. I hung on tight to the edge of the seat and felt waves chop at the bottom of the boat.

"There's North Head off there, son, see 'er?"

It was just a mountain, apparently, that had quit late and now jutted into the river on the Washington side. A clean white lighthouse stood on the point.

"And Cape Disappointment," he said, happily.

He shouted that we would be crossing the bar pretty soon. I turned to look, but I couldn't see a bar out there anywhere. Were we going to float over the bar or duck under it?

Waves rose higher than before, and many had whitewater crests. Sometimes our propeller lifted clear of the water and made a whining sound, churning air.

"Tell ya what, boy," Link shouted. "We need more weight on the bow. Hop right up there, give us a little ballast in this here tub."

He pointed toward the bow, where the front four feet or so of the boat is decked. "Just crawl on out there," he said. "We'll cut right through this here chop."

Terrified, I turned in the pitching boat and edged forward on hands and knees. It dawned on me that Link had brought me out here to drown me, like the runt of a litter. Because I would never be good enough. I knew it would be better to die bravely, without protest. He would never see me cry. I crawled forward onto the triangle bow. With my toes hanging back over the open middle of the boat, I clamped a death grip over the edges. My chin jutted past the point of the boat.

Waves pounded the wood deck into my stomach. White cold spray hit my face in short bursts. The next big wave might sweep me overboard, I imagined, and they would hold a big funeral back at the Methodist church. Everybody sobbing. Link would be sorry for this.

Waves rose higher now, the troughs deeper, but they no longer had whitewater crests. Huge rounded swells pushed us back and pitched us forward. When we were down, a solid wall of water faced the boat. When the boat corked up, I saw a long line of boulders on the right shore.

"North Jetty!" Link shouted.

We were moving fast. We pitched down into the next trough, and spray broke all the way over me, into the boat, where Link was laughing. There was nothing I could do. We were out of control. Terror got swallowed by hopelessness. I shut my eyes for a while, and that seemed to make the swells lower and smoother.

"We crossed the bar, boy!"

When? I wondered. Where? I hadn't even felt it.

"Whee!" Link laughed. "She's gonna be smooth as a lake out here."

The swells got flatter and bluer as the river pushed us out to sea. The tip of North Jetty was well behind us when Link cut the motor. The boat settled easily, comfortably in the water. Like waking from a nightmare into a calm warm bed. Sun sparkled off dappled water, and the horizon out front was the most perfect line, unbroken blue over blue.

I licked salt from my lips and slid back into the boat. As I turned to face Link, he was running double hooks and leader through the first herring. He glanced up at me with one eye shut and his head aslant, as if he were taking a sight, or measuring something.

"Wipe that goosey grin off your face, boy!" Grandpa said. "We got to catch us that Old Man Chinook."

NOTHING much changed about those annual trips out to sea. Over the years Link came up with a more reliable trailer, and he traded the 12-horse Johnson for an 18-horse Johnson. But it was the same boat, white with red trim. And the same old International pickup to get us over the Coast Range to Warrenton.

Link's one concession to family was when he bought us a pair of Popsicle-orange life vests. But he always "forgot" them when we went over the bar. Link's idea was that life jackets would only get in the way of a strong swimmer in August. His rules of ocean safety were two. First, never wear boots in the boat. Second, if the boat breaks, find the biggest part and hang on.

What did change, a lot, was my own idea of the trip.

Terror, after that first time, was no longer a factor. But the pleasure of getting out there never dropped a notch. Never, in all those years, did I see a smaller or lower-horsepowered boat cross the bar. We were different, all right. We were also more correct. Although boats around us got bigger and more powerful each year, the river and the bar never changed. We crossed the bar on the same terms Link had settled with it, long before. Link's terms. In that fourteen-foot open boat the two of us were good enough. Which maybe, now that I think about it, is a source of the Link factor and what it does to you.

Link could read the tides and rips like scanning the morning *Oregonian*, and he had a sixth sense about danger.

One time we headed out on the river and things looked normal to me, but he didn't like the looks of it. Of what?— the color of the water, the feel of the air, the cloud patterns? Something. He couldn't say. Other boats pressed on. We headed back to Warrenton, pitched the tent and played double solitaire. On the radio we listened to Coast Guard reports of trouble on the bar, and it was bad. Link had known.

Another time, over the bar, we hadn't limited out but the bite was on. I hooked a nice silver and began playing him. Link pulled the watch on a leather fob from his pocket.

"You got twelve minutes," he said. "Lose this fish or boat him."

So I tightened the drag. I got him nearly up to the boat before the fish took another dive. Link reached over and sliced my line with his jackknife. The pole whapped up and conked me. It was time to head back, he said. We had to catch the incoming tide just right.

Link tried to explain it to me, lots of times, but it wasn't just a matter of tide book and pocket watch. It also had to do with weather and the angle of buoys and the chop. I thought I was figuring it out, but one time Link headed us in early because no sea gulls were cruising.

"Just a feeling you get," he said.

It was a feeling I never got.

The feeling I did get was that Link was in touch with larger forces in a way that I, with all the books of a lifetime, could never match. He was checking his own pulse— every year, once a year—against the river and Old Man Chinook.

I was along for the ride. It was a good ride.

To tell you the truth, salmon fishing was less interesting to me than getting there. Being there. I mean I liked catching salmon all right, but not the way he did. Link was Chinook fishing, not just salmon fishing. Chinook require more patience, because Chinook salmon are outnumbered about three to one by silver salmon. Silvers run smaller than Chinook.

As a rule—not always—Chinook stay deeper than silvers when the two breeds are swarming off the bar. Link rigged his line with more weight than I did, which meant I landed more fish, mostly silvers. When things got hot, Link's challenge was to sink his bait quickly enough to not get hung up on silvers.

"It ain't that there's more of 'em," Link says. "Just they're stupider. Snappin' at anything that wiggles. Dad-burn inferior breed."

Another rule—Link's rule—was that the last fish we caught must be a Chinook. When the limit was three salmon apiece and we could bring in six, I would maybe get four of the first five fish. Then I'd have to put more weight on the line and fish deeper, for Chinook, like Link.

Often we didn't get a Last Fish.

If the sixth fish was a silver, we released it.

• • •

A THIRD person changed the way the boat took the water, but not much. Although it wasn't really necessary for ballast, I took my usual spot on the bow, with my head leading the way. Link handled the motor, and Jesse sat in the middle seat.

High wispy clouds laced the blue sky, and the breeze was from the north, a good sign. The bar was milder than usual, which I shouldn't have been sad to see. I'd done little to fill Jesse in. He could discover it the first time like I had. I couldn't see him from my position at the bow, but Link was calling out the sights to Jesse, as he had to me years ago.

"We crossed the bar, boys!" he bellowed.

He cut the motor, which is the best part, and I slid back into the boat to see how Jesse was taking this.

I'd always thought it was just a figure of speech, how they say somebody turns green when they're sick? Jesse was green. Sour olive green. His face bloated before he leaned over the left gunwale. "Gabraaaaacck," he said, vomiting a terrible thick stream of bacon bits and egg fragments into the blue ocean. His barf lay suspended below the surface. Even the all-accepting ocean wouldn't take this gift.

"Gabraaaacck," Jesse said again. His chest heaved and his shoulders trembled. He bent over the side of the boat, gasping for breath.

It was awful. He spat and hacked until he had nothing left, and then he did it some more. Woozily, he sat up in the boat. His dull brown eyes didn't recognize us.

"Some fisherman Indian you are," Link said. "A little finicky about water, is all."

I threaded a double hook through a herring and got it cinched and bent just so. Jesse looked over at the herring in my hands and lurched toward the side for another series of dry heaves.

Link and I dropped our lines in the water. After he got his own outfit where he wanted it, Link rigged up a four-ounce weight and a double-hooked herring on the pole he'd brought for Jesse. Link let the line out for him, set the drag and stuffed the pole into Jesse's stone hands.

"Let's go back," Jesse said.

But you can't just go back. It would be four hours, maybe five, before the tide began to change. After Link explained this to him, Jesse looked longingly to shore, a dim outline. Maybe he was thinking about swimming it.

Link broke out the Oreos and poured half a cup of cold milk from the steel thermos. Jesse eyed the Oreos as if they were horse turds. He leaned over the side of the boat again.

"Don't watch the water," Link said. "Keep your eye on that there ship, yonder."

A tanker was approaching the bar.

I got a fish on, which helped lift me off Jesse's problems. Maybe it helped him, too. The fish, a medium-size silver, broke water about twenty yards from the boat and spit out the hook, neat as you please. Which was disappointing, but a pretty thing to see. By then, Jesse was regaining his normal color. He stood up, unsteadily, and ground his teeth as if he had a mouth full of sand. Link got him to choke down a couple of Oreos, and Jesse took a swallow of cold milk.

He kept it down.

What cured Jesse, finally, was feeling that first nibble on his line. He yanked on the pole, which is exactly what you don't want to do.

"Criminy," Link said. "Pulled the dang dinner off his plate. Just leave it there. Let him take it."

Jesse relaxed the pole, but his blood was running. He let the line out a couple of pulls, like Link told him.

"He'll come back and grab it," Link said.

The fish, following Link's instructions, did just that. Jesse's pole bent to the pull of the fish. He reeled, but the drag was still letting line out. The way he shouted and fought that fish, he must have thought he'd hooked the king of the ocean, the derby winner. After Jesse, laughing, got the fish turned around and was gaining on him, the fish leaped off the water and danced a furious few steps on its tail, trying to shake the hook. It was a midsize silver again. This might have been the twin to the fish I'd just lost, or maybe even the same fish. Silvers are not too bright. Not too smart, I mean. They're very bright in color, and terrific leapers.

Jesse got him up next to the boat. The fish sounded once more and surfaced on the opposite side of the boat. Link spun around, kicked the steel thermos against the gas can and teetered sideways before he caught his balance. "Don't panic, boys!" he shouted. He lifted the prop so Jesse's line wouldn't shear. By the time Jesse got his pole on the same side of the boat as his salmon, the fish was about tuckered out.

So was Jesse.

"You got yourself an eighteen-pound silver, there," Link said, when he had a good look at it in the water. Link can eyeball a fish and weigh it to the nearest pound. I'd have said sixteen pounds, but I didn't. Link is always right.

"Twenty-eight pounds!" said Jesse. "Feed a family of six for two days."

From under the seat Link pulled out the gaff, a sawed-off bat with a fist-size steel hook on its business end.

"No!" said Jesse, when he saw the gaff.

He thrust his loaded pole at me.

"I'll get it," Jesse said. He reached over the side and, after a couple false stabs, slipped his left hand into the gill. He held the salmon underwater while he worked the hooks out, which was no easy deal. It had one hook in the upper jaw and another in the roof of its mouth. I thought Jesse might release the fish. Instead, he lifted it into the boat and hugged the damn thing against his shirt. Jesse stood there embracing the fish, which flapped its tail and whapped seawater and slime all over the boat. He put his cheek right against this fish. I thought he might actually kiss it, but he didn't.

Then Jesse laid her—it was a she, a female plump with eggs—back in the water.

She lay on her side in the water, stunned. Her black button eye gazed up as if she, too, were thinking, *This is not the way you do it.* Her gills flared a couple of times. Then she rolled silver and flashed down, out of sight and away.

"Well," Link said. "Whatever blows your skirt up, as we used to say at the mill."

Jesse was in no mood for Link. He was far, far away. Although he was enormously pleased with himself, the way it came out was not in words but with a welling of tears in his eyes before he looked away.

This was not, I figured, a time for words.

Link and I rigged up again and went back to fishing.

Pretty soon Jesse did, too.

When Jesse hooked the next fish as well, and fought it to the boat, Link looked like he didn't know whether to grab the gaff or say grace. It was the strangest thing, Link not knowing what to do.

"Do we free this here beauty too?" he asked.

"Are you nuts?" Jesse said.

So Link gaffed the fish and hoisted it aboard, where he conked it dead with the fish bat and pronounced it a sixteen-pounder. He looked up at Jesse, who owed us an explanation.

"That other one," Jesse said, "was the First Fish." The way he said it, I knew the words were supposed to be capitalized. "The First Fish," Jesse explained, "is the one that goes back and tells all its brothers and sisters it's all right to come into the river."

Jesse looked at Link, then at me. I guess he thought it was OK to continue.

"You always put the First Fish back," Jesse said. "Ever since Coyote put the salmon in. If the people set the first one free, the salmon will run another year. If you don't," he said, "the earth breathes fire. Mountains blow up. The ocean comes up over the trees."

He looked over at me.

"Well, maybe not," he said. "I don't really believe this," he apologized. "But maybe so. It's happened. The old people say. Over at Celilo," he said, "the First Fish was the biggest potlatch of the year. People came from all over. Big feast at the longhouse. Dancing. Presents. The First Fish was bigger than Christmas."

Jesse said the Indian elders still did the ceremony after Celilo Falls was gone, but he hadn't attended for a long time. In fact he wasn't sure they did it anymore.

"A lot of things have changed," he said. "But you always put back the First Fish."

TEN

~~~~~~~~

WITHIN WALKING DISTANCE of Calamus, out behind Link's place, you get about an hour up Ripple Creek and it's easy to imagine nobody's ever been here before. Up where they haven't logged, you can place your foot on a piece of the planet where no other human foot has stepped. Chances are. Is the way I used to think about it. Lie in the cool moss and look up through the branches. Plunk a tree with a fir cone. In the history of the entire earth, nobody has ever plunked that tree with a fir cone.

I don't know. Just the idea of it.

THEN again. One time I walked way up Ripple Creek and came to an outcropping of rock above a hillside spring. It wasn't quite a cave, but an overhang. The rock, at its base, was obsidian. I went poking around and found arrowheads. There was no mistaking what they were—hand-chipped black arrowheads, transparent at the edges. They were imperfect. Each had a wing missing or a tip snapped off, or something else wrong. They were rejects. Seconds. I had stumbled upon the arrowhead factory.

. . .

BEFORE Jesse arrived in Calamus, I used to practice throwing the football through a swinging tire. Back of the house I'd rigged up a tire about chest high on a rope, which hung from the limb of a yew tree. Set the tire swinging back and forth, and then fire the football through a moving target. You have to lead it just right. I got the idea from a *Sports Illustrated* article on Norm Van Brocklin.

Jesse came over and tried it. He had never played football, except messing around. But of course he could sail them through the tire right away, using either hand. He got bored with that in no time. Jesse's idea, then, was to swing the tire not just back and forth but also spinning. He twisted the rope before he let it go. Then it was far more difficult to drill the football through the hole.

Naturally, Jesse could do it.

"What kind of practice is that, anyway?" I told him, when I had trouble with it. "How many times will you have to hit your receiver while he's *spinning* out for a pass?"

I figured Jesse would make a better receiver than a passer. That, too, he picked up right away. Inside him, just waiting to get out, were all these skills I'd spent years trying to get right. He made all the feints and cuts, and he had terrific hands. The football loved Jesse's hands.

I made up this drill called "Impossible Catches." I sent him out on patterns and then fired the football at his ankles. Or behind him, or just out of reach. Outrageous contortions and near catastrophes were worth points in Impossible Catches. Say, if he caught one while hurdling the end of the wood pile. It was a teamwork deal, not me against him. If I failed to throw the ball in a bad spot, he might pull it in one-handed, or tip the ball from one hand to the other, and still get points.

One evening we took our act up to the school grounds, where we would have more room to practice bombs. The deep stuff. His stride was so deceptive I had to try to overthrow him. He always seemed to get to the ball. Jesse angled out for one of my passes, nearing the limit of my range, and I cut loose with a good spiral. As the ball dropped toward him, it was slightly underthrown. Jesse looked up late—as you must in Impossible Catches. Without breaking stride, he put his arms behind his back. The football settled softly to rest, like an egg in the nest of Jesse's open hands, behind his back.

Earl and Larry Wirtz had dropped by and were walking toward us, watching.

Jesse turned and casually lobbed a perfect left-handed spiral back to me from about ten yards beyond where he'd caught it, at the edge of my range.

He must have thrown that ball fifty yards.

"Nice pass," he said to me, jogging back. "Ho, guys. What's up?"

Well, the word gets around. Calamus holds few secrets, and there already was speculation about Jesse and football. Even without Jesse, we had talent. Now folks had us winning the league before we even put on pads. One topic was how Jesse could throw the ball. A quarterback with his speed who could roll out and throw with either hand . . . Which was true enough, but I did nothing to encourage this talk. I was the passer. I was the quarterback, a two-year starter.

Jesse should be the receiver.

The way Rolph Gullickson put it, as he and a clutch of loggers gathered around coffee mugs at the barbershop, was not quite the way I would've put it. But I was glad to hear it.

"Because you couldn't," Rolph pointed out, "have an Indian calling signals."

"Ah," someone else said.

"That's right," said another. As if this were as fundamental a truth as the law of gravity.

WHEN Coach Garth and Palermo lined us up for the two-mile run, Jesse took off like a startled crane. He had his thigh pads upside down, and his shoulder pads didn't fit. Still, Jesse

could run. And he did, quickly pulling ahead of the pack.
What Jesse didn't understand about daily doubles, though,
is you have to pace yourself. The two-mile run is just a lim-
bering up exercise.

In the calisthenics that followed, Jesse and I were next to
each other in the middle row.

"Where did all these big guys come from?" he asked me.
We held our arms out parallel to the earth, drawing little circles in the sweltering air. There wasn't a breath of wind over
the field. Limbs of fir trees hung limp and dusty over the
bank at the baseball diamond.

"These big guys are your friends," I whispered. "These
studs are going to protect us, if we are kind to them."

"OK," Jesse said.

His arms drifted lower and lower until Palermo came up
behind him and swatted them back up. His helmet didn't fit
him, either. And with his hair sticking out the back, he looked
very little like a football player.

"Why are we doing this?" he asked me, when Palermo
had passed. "When do we get to the football part?"

We sweated through jumping jacks, sprints, and the terrible grass drill that coaches love. My helmet trapped rising
heat, and the only decent view all morning was of the grass
receding at arm's length on that last push-up.

Coach Garth blew the whistle. We paired off for sit-ups.
Jesse held my feet to the scorched grass as I did my sit-ups.

"Suffering," I explained, "is the key . . . to building . . .
character."

"I see," said Jesse, nodding gravely.

"Knees down," Palermo bellowed. "Suck it up, you
pussies."

Morning practice ended with the duckwalk. We began to
waddle, knees bent, around the perimeter of the fields between the grade school and the high school. It must be half
a mile, a much bigger lap than around the track. Not only is
the duckwalk tough, in full football gear, but it's also pretty
stupid-looking. You're not supposed to put your hands on

your thighs, either, so the duckwalk—when you're pooped—
becomes a balance problem.

When we were about a third of the way around, Jesse
got the giggles. "Quack," he said.

"Quack," I answered.

"Quack, quack, quack."

Others picked it up.

Pretty soon the whole team was quacking, raising quite
a racket. The trouble is, in a duckwalk, it's hard to breathe.
With quacking, and now laughing, my chest was about to
burst. And I couldn't stand up, or I'd have to do another lap.

Others were in trouble, too.

Clement Lars, the left tackle, was the first to topple over.
Gasping and quacking, Clement went face down. He was toward the lead, so we quacked and waddled around his body.
Then Bobby Schrenck staggered sideways and fell to the hard
brown earth. Jesse quacked up before I did. Pretty soon the
whole team was sprawled out in a line, as if strafe bombed.

From across the field I heard the shrill whistle, like a
toothache. But the coaches might have been in Uruguay. The
whistle did remind me, briefly, of my own leadership duties.
But it was too wonderful just lying there among dead ducks.
Free of suffering, free of building character, I lay on my back
and watched a silver dot of jet draw a white vapor trail across
blue sky.

My muscles wouldn't move.

Finally Schrenck, who could speak Donald Duck, got us
up and moving again. We finished the lap in a duckwalk,
although no coaches were left on the field to witness it.

When we got to the locker room, Coach Garth stood at
the open green door of the coaches' room. He watched us file
in, cleats clacking on the concrete floor, heads down to avoid
his eyes. When I passed, he called me aside.

"Wade," he said. "I'd like a word with you."

Coach Garth is a decent man, not a hard ass at all. He
also is the high school principal, although he isn't an old guy.
His kids are in grade school. He was a punter at Washington

State, and he really knows his football. You'll get no argument about that. Unlike Palermo, who is new, Coach Garth has proven himself and is highly respected around town. Because his hair is thinning, he wears a baseball cap wherever he can, even inside the coaching office. In his office, now, his nostrils flared.

"Have a seat, Wade," he said.

Which I did, in a straight-back chair. The coaches' room is a small cubicle with a shower stall. Palermo must be in there. Coach Garth went behind his desk.

"I'm sorry, Coach," I said. "We just sort of lost control. I should have—"

"I expect you to be a leader out there," he said. "A coach on the field."

"Thank you, Coach," I said.

I couldn't think of anything to say. Truth is, I didn't think it was that serious a deal. I mean it wasn't mutiny, which he seemed to think. He discussed the need for team discipline and example-setting on my part.

Steam from the shower filled the room. On the wall was a blackboard, where he had drawn a depth chart. In the position slots I could see no surprises except he'd chalked in Schrenck at center instead of guard. Off to one side, he'd written Howl. The name was circled, with a question mark by it.

"Are you getting my drift?"

"Yes, sir," I said. "Discipline. Self-control. I lost it out there today, Coach. Things just collapsed."

He looked me in the eye, man to man. I returned his stare with what I hoped was a disciplined, self-controlled look.

"You know, Wade," he said, shifting in his chair and shuffling papers on his desk. "People have high expectations. But I'm really concerned about this year's team."

Coach Garth is a well-known worrier. Although his teams win year after year, he's a predictor of doom.

"We're loaded, Coach." I tried to cheer him up.

"That's just the sort of attitude I'm concerned about," he said. "I just don't know if we have it *here*," he said, thumping his chest. "Heart. You have to want it, Wade. You have to want it so bad you can taste it."

Which is true, I guess.

"Now about this Jesse Howl . . ." he said.

My attention ratcheted up.

The door to the shower stall opened and Palermo, swabbing his hairy torso with a light green towel, dripped toward us in a cloud of steam. "Wade," he said.

"Coach."

He puddled to the vacant chair and sat down.

"Coach Palermo here has informed me about Jesse," Coach Garth said, "and I think there's little doubt Jesse could help this football team."

"No doubt," I said. "He's good. Great hands."

"What concerns me," Coach said, "is Jesse's influence. One bad apple can spoil the barrel. Football, you know, is ten percent skill and eighty percent desire. Attitude. I just don't know if he's the kind of kid who will put his nose to the grindstone and give us a hundred and ten percent."

While I was reviewing his math and preparing Jesse's defense, Coach Garth continued. "As principal—wearing my other hat—I am aware of certain difficulties Jesse had at Madras High School."

"Difficulties?"

"He's a screw-up," said Palermo, looking at me.

"The record, of course, is confidential," Coach Garth said, ominously. "And what you don't know won't hurt you. But where there's smoke there's fire."

"They *arrested* him," Palermo said. "Took his driver's license and kicked him out of school."

Which about knocked me out of my chair, I don't mind telling you. I'd heard rumors, all right, but I hadn't put any stock in them. Just barbershop talk.

"Wait a minute," I said. "I know this guy. Jesse's a good man. Just give him a chance, Coach," I said. "You'll see."

"Now don't get your dander up," Coach Garth said. "You got a head on your shoulders, Wade. I understand you and Jesse are friends. Just keep your eyes peeled, is all. As far as I'm concerned, Jesse Howl comes to Calamus with a clean slate."

He and Palermo nodded. Coach Garth stood up.

Our meeting was finished.

I left the room, undressed, and took a hot shower in coach-think. They had him pegged. They were going to give Jesse just enough rope to hang himself.

AT THE barbershop, I caught up with Jesse. He and a bunch of the guys were on their second round of sodas at a corner booth. They made room for me and wanted to know what Coach Garth had had to say. I told them about the discipline and wanting-it part. We had a chance to really do something this year in football. Which was true, and I meant it. As soon as I could, I hustled Jesse out of there. We walked the lake road.

"OK," I said, as soon as we were out of town. "Give it to me straight. What did you do at Madras High School?"

"What?" said Jesse, puzzled.

"I mean to get in trouble. What was that all about? Coach Garth knows about it, but he wouldn't tell me."

"What does he know about?"

"Jesus," I said. "How would I know? I just told you he wouldn't tell me. What did you do?"

"Nothing," Jesse said. "Or almost nothing."

I kicked at an egg-shaped stone, and it scooted ahead of us on the road.

"I got booted out of school," he said. "For not going."

When we caught up to the stone, Jesse absently kicked it.

"Hey, look," I told him.

I quit walking and he had to stop. I don't think he was trying to be evasive. I just couldn't get him to focus.

"That can't be it," I said. "How come you lost your driver's license? Or got arrested. It's on your record."

"Oh, that," he said.

We started walking again. Jesse walked easily, like some people can swim, with a loose-limbed, pigeon-toed glide. He kicked the stone ahead—*tock*—without even looking down. He could do the simplest things with such easy rightness, effortlessness. He was hooked up to a different system.

Was he even hearing me?

"I borrowed this guy's car," he said, "and didn't get it back in time."

"You borrowed this guy's car."

"That's right. Actually he didn't know I borrowed it."

"Friend of yours?"

"Not exactly."

"You *stole* this car."

I punted the stone, and it caromed in front of us for Jesse.

"Actually it was the game warden's car," he said. "A state car. That was the trouble. No sense of humor, those guys."

I took a deep breath. I'm not sure what I expected the trouble to be, but this sounded pretty serious.

"Drinking beer, were you?"

"Not much," he said. "We'd been drinking a little beer, yes. How'd you know? Actually that's what we were doing. We were out drinking beer, a bunch of us, out by the Crooked River. The warden thought we were night fishing," he said. "But we weren't. We weren't doing anything. This jerk of a game warden, they all have a hard-on for Indians. The game warden; we knew him. Shoop. Shoop had us staked out. He was going to surprise us, right? Night fishing. But you can't sneak up on Indians."

"You took his car when he was out there?"

Tock. He kicked the stone again, and it scuttled up the road like a stuck crab.

"I wasn't the only one," he said.

"You and this group, then, you took his car. Why don't you just tell me what happened?"

"I am!" he said. "What are you, Perry Mason?"

A car passed us. When its dust settled, our stone was still on the road.

"We left him out there, yes. It's not like it sounds," Jesse said. "It was just something to do. More like a joke."

"This Shoop guy didn't get it, I suppose."

"Shoop was a young guy. Pressed his uniform and thought he was cool. Sunglasses. A toothpick. He'd come up to town and shoot the bull. Lean against the car door and buddy you."

"The jerk," I said.

"A real snake in the grass. You're right."

Jesse scuffed the top of the stone with his right foot, missing it. But he quick did a little stutter step, without looking down, and flicked the stone ahead of him with his trailing left foot. That's what I mean about Jesse, right there. It was a terrific move. A Jesse move. I doubt if he even knew he did it.

"So what did they do?" I asked him. "I mean they expelled you from school. What else?"

"Naw, I told you," Jesse said. "I got kicked out of school later, for not going. The stuff about wrecking the game warden's car was the summer before."

"You *wrecked* it?"

"I was trying to get the spotlight to work. The car caught some loose gravel and dove into the ditch," he said. "They said it was totalled. But I don't think it was. They were out to get us."

"They had it in for you."

"That's right," he said. "I got probation. Lost my license for a whole year. Which is about up now," he said, brightening, but only momentarily. "Everybody I knew lost their license, one way or another. Pretty soon we had to take the school bus."

"Sounds like you got off easy," I said.

The thing was, this was no big deal to Jesse. He was telling me this like it was a "Captain Midnight" episode he was trying to remember.

"So how come you got kicked out of school?"

"When I quit going to school, that's when I got kicked out. Momma was fed up with the reservation anyway. A dove among vultures, was what Momma said. I was a dove among vultures, and I better go learn about vultures."

"Oh, come on," I said. What bullshit.

"It was her idea, leaving Warm Springs," he said. "I didn't have to leave. I would've gone to school if I could've drove. I always liked school."

"Does Link know all this?"

"Sure," said Jesse. "I mean I guess he does. I know him and Reno talked. But Link doesn't ask all these nosey questions. Not like you."

ELEVEN

WHEN A LOGGER GOES in for a haircut, he's got that indentation around his head from wearing a hard hat. The mark won't go away. Even after a haircut, a logger has that inch-wide strip over his ears and a red horizontal dent above his eyebrows.

"Pinched minds," says Lorna.

I don't know. It reminded me of Chinook Indian tribes, how they used to strap newborn babies to a headboard? Made their forehead slope back to the top. The mark of the high-born.

Loggers are the high-born in Calamus. The ugliest name you can call a logger or his son is a farmer. You farmer. Nobody gets any respect for growing things. The greater challenge is to keep things *from* growing. Loggers bare the land around their houses and cut lawns to the white root stalks. Hunting poison oak with DDT is what a logger likes to do around the yard.

CALAMUS Union High School is two stories of red brick facing Main Street, up on the flat. A wide, close-clipped lawn stretches between the school and the road. The flagpole rises from the green lawn. The school is larger than you'd expect, drawing students not just from in town. They bus them in from strawberry-field and holly-farm country, and from up in the hills, where who knows what people do. The Calamus Lumberjacks. Which is too bad. Only somebody from Portland, or from Back East, would call a logger a lumberjack.

Jesse rowed over early on that first day of school. He wore his jeans and Converse lowcuts. Which is not really the way you do it. You want to dress a little for school. Me, I wore white cords and cordovan loafers. It was a little warm yet for a Pendleton shirt. And my green letterman's jacket with the white leather sleeves. Which Jesse didn't have, of course.

What Jesse did have was a necklace he'd made of salmon vertebrae on a rawhide thong. From the fish at the Columbia bar. In fact he made me one, too. But I mean a necklace? I couldn't wear it. On Jesse it looked pretty good.

Sarah Ellen and my other school-age sister, carrot-head Carol Ann, piled in the back of the pickup after breakfast, and we drove up to the trailer court to pick up Lorna. She was waiting at the mailboxes, because she doesn't like people to see the trailer she lives in. It's pathetic, all right, but she can't help it. Lorna's dad got laid up from the woods with a bum back, and what can you do? Her mother works at the hardware store. They say her old man has a drinking problem, but not that I've seen. Whenever I've been there, he just lies around with a crossword puzzle and you can't get much out of him.

Lorna's eyes were amber lights when we picked her up. School is vacation for Lorna. No more long hours at the barbershop. Jesse stepped out to let her in, and she hefted an armload of paperbacks into the pickup.

"What's this?" Jesse said. "Taking books to school?"

"Got to have something to read."

She wore a poofy skirt that pretty much filled the cab between Jesse and me.

"Don't they give you books?"

"Not good ones." She punched down her skirt.

I drove through town, down Broadway.

"You ought to read the books they give you," I said.

"Gad. Let's not start that."

But it's true. The trouble with Lorna is she could be a good student if she just paid attention. School goes way too slow for her. She and her murder mysteries, reading in class. Drives teachers nuts. If she concentrated, she could have skipped a grade. Which would make her a senior now, like Jesse and me, instead of a junior.

"Wade, here," she explained to Jesse, "is a fraud. He just does what they say, and they think he's smart. That's disgusting, don't you think?"

Jesse said he thought so. He wasn't quite sure what to make of Lorna.

"School and I are just the right speed," I said.

"Exactly. Exactly my point," Lorna said.

On our second or third lap through town, down Broadway and back up Main Street, yellow school buses started arriving. I stopped at the grade school to let off the girls.

There are rules, unwritten but clear, about how you pull into the school parking lot. And who parks where. The Show Row runs along the tennis court fence, at a right angle to Main Street. Cars in the Show Row back in and face outward, ready to peel out. Spaces fill up in descending order of sharpness, from Main Street. In this year's place of honor was Olin Burt's '57 Chevy with a candied metallic paint job, midnight blue. Seats tucked and pleated in white leather. His Chevy was chopped, and chrome pipes passed along the side of the car. Glasspack mufflers gave it a good husky growl. Fuzzy dice on the rearview mirror.

Some cars other than Olin's might have taken the place of honor this season, but what would I know? The car crowd, the greasers, are a mystery. They and the jocks, my crowd, might be Mexicans and Swedes for all we mix.

I parked the pickup well away from the Show Row.

Inside the school we paced the hardwood upstairs hallway, back and forth, smelling the varnish and looking for
who was paired with whom after the summer. Things can
change.

Jesse and Lorna and I were a threesome.

"Did you ever get the feeling you were invisible?" Lorna
whispered to me.

She was right. All eyes were on Jesse. We'd had a couple
of foster-home Indians at Calamus before, but they were
sad, beaten-down characters. And a family of Negroes, once,
but they hadn't stayed.

Jesse licked two fingers and slicked his eyebrows. With
that easy gait of his, sometimes walking backward, he trolled
the hallway.

THE MORNING was taken up with issuing lockers and books,
getting registered. I straightened out Jesse's schedule. They
had him down for shop and ag, and special English. Bone-
head English. Jesse wasn't sure they'd made a mistake, but I
switched him. "If you can read a stop sign," I told him, "you
don't belong in special English." So we got English and government together. And health/P.E. Jesse was behind in math,
and he had to take general science.

After lunch at the cafeteria we went outside to the senior
steps. Lorna, a junior, could join us because she was with
me. Lorna is a special case anyway. Nobody would tell Lorna
where she could or couldn't sit. But the senior steps are for
seniors only, of course. So we were out there comparing
schedules and watching the log trucks go by and basking in
our new status when this poor baffled kid with zits and a bad
haircut came wandering across the lawn.

He was headed for the senior steps.

"Hey, kid," John Buzhardt said. Buzhardt stood up and
cut him off at the lowest step.

This kid must have been a freshman. From some stump
farm up in the hills. I'd never seen him before. Buzhardt

pushed the sleeves of his letterman's jacket up his forearms. He stood with his arms crossed, blocking this kid's path.

"You got your papers?" Buzhardt asked him.

Buzhardt has a face like an anvil, and he wore a fresh flattop for the start of school.

"Let's see your papers," he said.

Fat Bill Froman and a couple of others stood up with Buzhardt.

The kid fished through his pockets and produced his schedule card. He uncrumpled a white slip of paper with his locker combination on it.

"Not those," Buzhardt said. "Let's see your masturbation papers."

The kid didn't know about those.

But he knew he was in trouble. Like a chipmunk looking for the nearest tree, he glanced right, left, then turned on his heels to leave. Froman grabbed his skinny shoulder blade and spun him around.

"You got to get those papers," Buzhardt told him.

"Where?" the kid asked. He was terrified.

"At the office," Buzhardt said. "Right up these steps. Tell Mrs. Dubrowski you don't have your masturbation papers."

Lorna dug her elbow into my side, like I was supposed to do something.

It was cruel, all right. But I was kind of curious, to tell you the truth. Also I wasn't anxious to cross big John Buzhardt, the right tackle. Not that I was afraid of him or anything, but sometimes it's easier just to go along. So I was observing this scene like it was a bad orange I had already peeled and might as well eat, when Jesse, sitting to my right, bolted up.

"Hold it!" he said, bounding down the steps.

Jesse was hot. The mad rippled off him like heat waves. He stepped between Buzhardt and the kid, facing the much larger Buzhardt, and his eyes shot dark flames. "This is horse shit," he shouted.

He pushed Buzhardt backward.

Buzhardt was so surprised he just sat there on the third step, where he'd landed.

When he moved to get up, Jesse shoved him back again.

"Fucking wagonburner," said Buzhardt, rising again.

Fat Bill Froman grabbed Jesse's left arm. Which was a mistake. Jesse caught him flush upside the head with a lightning right. Froman spun across the sidewalk and onto the green lawn, where he lay blinking and feeling his jaw. The greasers streamed over in a wave from the parking lot, but by then it was over. Jesse stood facing the senior steps with his brown fists clenched and his arm muscles tensed and twitching.

Nobody moved against him. Even Buzhardt thought better of it.

Miss Drees was the new English teacher, fresh out of Monmouth. She was so young, or so young-looking, that Jesse mistook her for a student.

We were doing a run-through of classes that afternoon—not full periods but twenty minutes or so in each room. The bells were haywire. People didn't know where they were supposed to be. So we got to fifth period, English, and the room was only about half full. While we were waiting, Jesse zeroed in on the prettiest girl in the room. She was leaning against the radiator by the windows.

Jesse went right up to her. I guess there's nothing like winning a one-punch fight to get your juices up. Not that Jesse lacked confidence anyway.

"Hello, I'm new here," he said. "My name is Jesse and I think you're very beautiful."

He stuck out his hand and gave her his woman-getter grin.

"Why thank you, Jesse," she managed. Miss Drees wore a matching lavender skirt and sweater with white shoes. She was skittery. She shook his hand.

"I, too, am new here," she said.

"Is that right!?" Jesse exhaled. He still held her hand. Now he inspected it as if he were holding solid gold. "Then you must be real lonesome."

"*Really* lonesome," she corrected him.

"Me too." He shook his head, hardly able to believe his good fortune. "Well! I do know some people here," he said. "That's Wade Curren over there."

I nodded.

"Wade has a girlfriend, but I don't," he assured her.

She tried to interrupt him, but Jesse was on a roll, introducing everybody whose name he knew. When Jesse gets going it's hard to stop him. Not that I was trying to. This was very interesting to me, as I'm sure it was to others. We—the rest of us in the room—had figured out she was the teacher, of course, because we'd never seen her before. To Jesse, everybody was new.

What Jesse was right about was that Miss Drees was beautiful. I thought at first she was blushing, but she wasn't. Her face was always flushed peach like that, with light freckles around a small nose and pouty lips. Her auburn curls weren't well organized and it was easy to imagine she had just awakened, soft and kind of needing help.

"Since you and I are new here," Jesse was telling her, "we ought to get together. We could go to the show."

"Jesse, please, I . . ."

Miss Drees rescued her hand from Jesse's grip. She tried a scowl. But she got it only about half right, the brow part. The rest stuck on her lips. She wasn't mad, just flustered.

The bell rang.

Jesse went into a boxer's crouch and came bobbing and weaving away from the radiator like Joltin' Jesse Howl, the Brown Bomber. He shuffled toward the desk nearest mine and slid into its chair.

"Did you see those knockers?"

"Shut up," I hissed at him.

"What's her name?"

"I think we're about to find out," I said.

I nodded toward the teacher's desk, where she positioned herself to address the class. Jesse did a double take. His hair flopped.

"Ho!" he said. "You're the teacher?"

She smiled weakly but otherwise ignored him.

"My name is Miss Drees," she introduced herself. "I'll be teaching senior English."

She wrote her name on the blackboard in fat curly script. When she moved her head, her hair bobbed. Some of those long curls wanted to fall frontward, over her shoulder. She pushed them back. Then she made a dumb joke about how her name, Miss Drees, was not to be confused with Missderies. You know, Mysteries.

I guess I was the only one who got it. There was this awful silence in the classroom.

Then Jesse got it. He cackled and slapped his hand on his desk top. Which I'm sure was meant to rescue her from embarrassment, but it didn't.

Miss Drees fixed her brown eyes on Jesse like *Don't push it, Buster.* In her hand she held a long stick of white chalk. Looking straight at Jesse—and with a crooked smile on her tight lips—she put her other hand up to the chalk stick and snapped it in two. It was a simple little move. You see that move all the time in a classroom, breaking a fresh stick of chalk. But Miss Drees put a chilling kind of authority into it that actually made me squirm in my seat. Maybe she wasn't such a helpless babe-in-the-woods after all.

When I glanced over at Jesse, his eyes were still wide with wonder. He was in a trance. His elbows rested on the desk, and he cupped his chin in his hands, admiring Miss Drees.

She sat on the front of her desk and told us how fortunate she was to be in Calamus for her first teaching assignment. She was really looking forward to it. Then she launched into what sounded like a prepared speech about literature and life. Which was true, I guess, but I was having trouble concentrating. Between the two soft mounds on her lavender sweater hung a locket on a gold chain. The locket was just heavy enough to depress the sweater where you might put your ear to check her heartbeat.

I was so worked up I didn't hear her question. The words flew right out the window before I could catch them. Only the rising inflection, of a question having been asked, was left to expand in the silent room.

"Well?" she said. "Anybody?"

She pointed. "Jesse."

He hadn't heard the question either. He pivoted his head from side to side in the swivel base of his hands. He was signaling bewilderment. Or surrender.

"I love you very much," he said.

TWELVE

≈≈≈≈≈≈

LINK SAYS AN OCCASIONAL SALMON will take the fish ladder at the dam. Maybe he's right, but I've never seen it.

Something is wrong with the fish ladder.

Maybe what's wrong is the ladder lacks pools where a salmon can rest. Each step is the same height, about a foot, and then a salmon doesn't get much more than the length of its body before the next step in the ladder. There are 126 of these steps, in a series of sharp switchbacks. Not that a salmon couldn't climb the fish ladder if it took a mind to. Salmon—even battered from the ocean and their trip back—can muster amazing strength. But the ladder isn't what a fish might find in nature.

The other problem—more likely the real problem—is the water feeding the ladder. It's lake water. The dam holds up the Calamus River and makes the water stale. Warmer. Probably the smell, too, is different. It's just the wrong water.

For a while they planted hatchery salmon above the dam, in the upper Calamus. Some of the fingerlings made it downstream and out to the ocean. But when they got back as adults, years later, they wouldn't take the ladder past the dam.

One time at a deep green pool below the dam I saw a big old humpback male take a running swim at the concrete base of the dam. He smacked right into it, head on. *Whump,* he hit it. I could hear the silent impact in my own stomach. The fish dropped back dazed. Then he took another run at the base of the dam. *Whump,* again, he butted the concrete with his snout.

It was too terrible to watch. I left.

ONE THING about school is it frees your mind from things that are too big to think about. A routine settles in. You hit a familiar kind of groove, with bells ringing, people moving, assignments due. Days get their edges rounded, their middles polished, and pretty soon it all falls into place. Not that I was bored—I've never been bored with school—but things happen that you expect to happen, and there is comfort in that.

Jesse put some odd dents in the everyday shape of school, but he got along just fine. In fact he was a big hit among other students, mainly because he did whatever he felt like doing, and trouble couldn't catch him. I guess Palermo was right that Jesse was a screw-up, but he was a natural screw-up, not calculating or malicious.

At the barbershop and around, Jesse was the hot topic mainly because of football, but there was a strong undercurrent of let's-wait-and-see about it. You'd see a shine in their eyes but hear an echo in the voices. "Uppity" was a word you heard a lot. But you couldn't really dislike Jesse, and people didn't. It wasn't that. It's just that he was so different, I guess.

Women seemed to get it better than men.

Jesse, of course, was oblivious to all this. What did he care—or even notice—what people thought?

At the school cafeteria, three hefty women who dish up food at the serving line giggled and nudged one another when it was Jesse's turn in line. Pink-faced, fleshy-armed, these ladies wore identical white smocks and white hairnets. Jesse lit them up. When he complimented them on how good the food looked, they just melted back there behind the steaming counter. They vied to see who could pile more food on Jesse's plate. They watched him eat, too, while serving others or after the line dwindled. Their eyes said, *Look at that boy eat.* As if Jesse were their own, or what their own sons should have been.

And here comes Jesse back for seconds: *My land, you put all that away already? Gracious, yes. Take a thigh, here, two of them. You want some more gravy?*

One day Jesse, ahead of me in the serving line, lost control of his loaded tray. He grabbed for the tray but it rose, as if of its own power, high above his head. Jesse snatched at it, but it eluded him. The tray toppled and crashed to the floor as if it had been thrown there.

The crash jolted the whole cafeteria.

Shattering glass echoed over the tables and off the walls. On the polished cement floor, splotches of brown gravy and green spinach and orange soup overlapped in a central pile of glop. Milk splayed out. Mashed potatoes and gravy were sprinkled with slivers and jagged edges of broken glass.

The crash was followed by a freakish silence. Those who hadn't seen it looked up to find the source. Mild at first, the clapping built to a crescendo of applause that included whistles and foot-stomping.

Jesse was extremely apologetic.

One of the pink-and-white serving ladies brought out the mop. Jesse grabbed it himself and began cleaning up his mess. I held the scooper on the floor so he could sweep the grossest piles into it. When I looked up, expecting a smirk or a wink from Jesse, he gave me no sign.

A couple days later, the same thing happened.

If anything, the crash looked even more like an accident this time. The tray rose up again, magically getting away from Jesse as he fought to get a grip on it. Food and glass crashed to the floor, followed by the cheers.

Coach Garth, in his role as principal, lumbered over from the teachers' table to set things straight. He gave Jesse a spirited little lecture, but Jesse's black eyes were so innocent, so pure, that Coach had to back off. Another factor here was that Coach Garth had, by this time, seen what Jesse could do in football. Anyway, his lecture lost its steam and became mostly for the benefit of other students.

Jesse shrugged his shoulders and tossed his head, as if truly baffled. "Bad hands, I guess."

He grabbed the mop to help clean up.

And the third time, a few days later, the sound of that crashing tray was even better than before, if that's possible. The pleasure it brought to so many people—me included, I have to admit—was something probably not even Jesse could appreciate, although he knew how to do it. When others began dropping loaded food trays, which became the thing to do for a while there, it was a cheap imitation of the real thing. It wasn't the same at all. Not the way Jesse could do it.

JESSE never understood, however, about English.

We were reading Henry David Thoreau, who lived on a pond and wrote it up. Big fucking deal, was what Jesse thought. "Nothing happened!" he said. "I read twenty-six whole pages of it. Tiny little print and no pictures." Which was not the point, I tried to tell him. With literature you got metaphors, I said. Symbols. Not what happens. Building that cabin on the pond was like self-reliance, making your own way on nature's terms. Actually I didn't think it was that good a book, but I figured that was my fault, not Thoreau's. Jesse thought we'd do better taking Miss Drees for a row on the lake than reading *Walden*.

Which she declined, however.

Or in class one time we were chopping up this poem, trying to figure out why Richard Cory put a bullet through his head. We chewed that poem until the juice was about out of it. Finally Jesse couldn't stand it any longer. "He just did it, that's all," Jesse said. "He shot himself." Which is not what English is about at all. It just sucked the air right out of the classroom. I felt sorry for Miss Drees, trying to teach poetry to somebody like Jesse.

On the other hand, there were times I didn't think Jesse was getting a fair shake. Like we had this section on myths. Greek and Latin gods and stuff, and what they did. Jesse had a good feel for it, because of the myths he had.

"A long time ago when the animals were people . . ." Jesse began. There was never any problem getting Jesse to speak up. "A long time ago when the animals were people," he said, "they had this monster Beaver. Wishroosh, was his name, and he had big waters. He had a whole ocean, on the other side of the mountains."

Jesse paused. Nobody said anything.

He glanced at me, and I gave him a nod. Go for it.

"This Wishroosh was a bad one," Jesse said. "He kept all the fish to himself. Bear and Eagle and everybody were scared to do anything about it. So Coyote said he'd take care of it," Jesse said. "He'd kill Wishroosh. Coyote didn't really have a plan. But now he had to do it."

Something in Jesse had risen, and he with it. His black eyes were glazed as he stood and put both hands to the sides of his head.

"So Coyote asked his huckleberries," Jesse said. "He kept these huckleberries in his stomach. How am I going to kill Wishroosh? They told him to make a big spear with an elkhorn tip. Ho, said Coyote. That was my idea all the time."

Jesse paced the aisle between desks. He was kind of acting this out. Nobody knew whether to laugh or what.

"Huckleberry told Coyote to tie a thong to the spear, so he could haul Wishroosh in. Ho, said Coyote. That's what I was going to do. That was my idea all the time."

Miss Drees looked at the wall clock. The big hand jumped a minute forward.

Jesse finished his story, which was long, about how Coyote speared Wishroosh but didn't kill him. The huckleberries had tricked Coyote with that thong-on-the-spear bit. The thong tied Coyote to Wishroosh and they had this terrific struggle. Tore through the mountains and made the Columbia River Gorge. Let the fish come up where everybody could get them.

Jesse was about out of breath when his eyes came back on. He seemed a little startled.

"Are you finished?" Miss Drees said.

This was not in her lesson plan.

"Plus also," Jesse said, "Coyote was so mad at his huckleberries he put them way up high in the mountains. Where they are now."

"Thank you, Jesse," Miss Drees said. She said it in such a way that people thought it was OK to laugh. Which is what I meant about Jesse not getting a fair shake. Anyway you could see a quick cloud cross his face, which is about all you'd ever get that Jesse was set back, or fazed.

THE NEXT time Jesse told a story it was different. Like it was all a big joke, a way to buy time and throw Miss Drees off her feed.

"A long time ago when the mountains were people . . ."

"Jesse, I'd like to finish this thought," Miss Drees said. "I don't think this is applicable."

"I think it is," I said.

Which is not like me at all. It threw her just enough that Jesse seized the opening. He started telling how Coyote put the stars in. But Miss Drees was determined. She wouldn't let him finish.

Jesse and I never talked about this on our own, of course. It wasn't something you could talk about. But I think he knew. He knew that I knew, that he wasn't pure goofy. But you think about it and it just makes a cold wet knot in your stomach, the things nobody gets.

I took one last shot at it.

For this paper that was due—Jesse was having trouble figuring out papers—we worked up a thing about Coyote.

How Coyote was basically a braggard and a joker but he had these powers and was trying to help. "Miss Drees doesn't hear you because she thinks it's a joke," I told Jesse. "If we write it down, maybe, that's what a paper can do."

"That's not why," Jesse said. Which was right, but I didn't know it yet.

We were down at the house, at the dining room table. Jesse was more interested in the aroma of fried chicken coming from the kitchen, and whether or not Mother would ask him to stay for dinner. Which she usually did, but she hadn't, yet. At the stove, she had her back to us. But she was listening. She's always listening.

"Mother hopes you will stay for dinner," I told Jesse.

"Ho!" he said. "I think I will."

"So anyway," I said, moving papers around. It's hard to keep Jesse's attention. "What is it about Coyote? He's like a man, right?"

"The animals *were* the people."

"Right. This was before Indians?"

"Things weren't ready," he said. "The earth wasn't fixed."

Sarah Ellen brought the cutting board and some tomatoes from the drainboard to our table. She took a seat and started slicing them. Sarah Ellen would do just about anything to be in the same room with Jesse. She was all ears. Don't mind me. But actually she was OK, because Jesse likes an audience. He told some Coyote stories.

I wrote notes. *A woman chaser*, I wrote. *Greedy. Not bright. Gets killed over and over.*

Sarah Ellen, mooning up at Jesse, sliced her left index finger with the paring knife. Drew a little blood, but it was mostly tomato juice. Her yelp brought Mother over from the stove. Sarah Ellen didn't want to leave the table, so she stuck the damaged finger in her mouth. Mother, too, seemed more concerned about having interrupted Jesse than about Sarah Ellen. Mother was real interested in this stuff, but she acted like if she said anything he wouldn't talk.

"So then what," I told him, and he got going again.

Shared his fur coat. Likes to look in the mirror. Likes tricks, which backfire . . .

By the time Duncan drove up and Mother told Sarah Ellen to set the table, I figured we had about enough for this paper. Jesse's paper.

"Who was The Changer?" I asked him. He had mentioned once or twice The Changer.

A lot of this stuff didn't make sense at all.

"The Supreme Being," Mother said. She bit her lip and wiped her hands on her apron, as if to erase her words.

Duncan came in the back door, which brought Carol Ann down the stairs and set the baby to crying in her playpen. Dinnertime. I cleared papers off the table for Sarah Ellen, who hovered over us clutching silverware like an eagle claw full of arrows and exercising her lipstick.

"Maybe you could write about The Changer," Jesse said. He was into it, now.

"It's your paper. I'm just trying to help. Let's stick with Coyote."

"Whatever you say, Kemo Sabe."

Which struck Carol Ann as about the funniest thing she had heard, ever, in her whole life. Duncan went to comfort the baby, patting her on the back and trying to figure out what everybody was so happy about.

So anyway we did it. Jesse wrote up this paper, and he kept saying, "Aw, this is no good." But it was. We got it in Jesse's words and punctuation, and it was really a good paper. I still believe that.

When Miss Drees handed it back, however, it was bleeding red ink. She'd corrected it with an axe. I mean he got a C on it, which Jesse thought was great, and I said, "Yeah, see? You can write." But it really got me. If *I* had handed in that paper, it wouldn't have got that treatment. She'd written a big red WHAT'S THE POINT on it. THESIS???

Well, the point—and I didn't push it after that—was that Jesse's stuff didn't really apply. That was the thesis.

THIRTEEN

BY TROLLING THE LAKE you learn, over the years, where bottom is. Where the snags are.

Which is what made it so surprising when I hooked something solid, nowhere near bottom. I was out in Link's boat before school one morning, to catch some trout for breakfast. Rowing, I had the pole in the pole holder. Not much line out, maybe fifty feet, trolling a nightcrawler behind Ford fenders. The pole bent real gradual. Not like a bite—where they hit it and scramble. I pulled in the oars, grabbed the pole, and the tip kept turning down. I let out line while the boat lost its forward momentum. And then this whatever-it-was *kept going*. Not fast, just a steady slow pull. Down and away. When I tried to stop it, the leader snapped.

The short hairs rose on the back of my neck.

There were no witnesses.

What I'd hooked wasn't a snag, because it definitely moved. And this was the deep part of the lake. A lunker salmon? It didn't act like a fish on the line, and salmon won't take a worm. Even if you could find a salmon in the lake. I guess it's one of those things I will never know. Like the Link factor, it's enough to make you believe in ghosts.

• • •

WE WERE having a terrific early football season.

Which is a big deal in Calamus. Football brings them crawling out of the woodwork and scrambling from the hills. The Broadway Theater closes down for home football dates. Calamus—pop. 988—has a football stadium that seats over 1,200, under cover. And then you get folks on the sidelines, too, for a big game. The grandstand gapes like an enormous shark with rows of bleacher teeth, and lights are mounted on topped fir trees around the field. A tall laurel hedge surrounds the field on the three sides not protected by grandstand.

This year we creamed Hood River and won our next two games while hardly breaking a sweat. It wasn't just Jesse. We would've had a good team without him.

But Jesse was sensational.

All I had to do was get him the ball in the open field. Once he got a step on somebody, they couldn't catch him. And if he didn't yet have that step, Jesse would figure something out. As for getting the ball to him, the only question was whether or not I would have time to throw, which I usually did. Maybe it was from Impossible Catches, but I knew when and where he was going to cut. As if we were wired. I just knew what he was going to do.

He never got around to learning the plays. When it was time, I'd call "Jesse" in the huddle. The only signal we had, except the snap count, was when Jesse decided to buttonhook. On his way out, he would slap his butt. My job was to throw the ball to where he'd slapped his butt. Jesse flew on down the field for another ten yards or so, screeched to a halt while his defender kept going, and came back to where I'd thrown the ball.

You'd think somebody else would notice and figure it out, but they never did.

Our fourth football game was against Reynolds. Reynolds was this brand-new high school over by the big aluminum plant on the Columbia River. Although Reynolds wasn't actually in Portland, it was a much bigger school than Calamus and it was a city school. Which made this a big game. The grandstand was packed, even for warm-ups. Palermo was so fired up when we hit the locker room for pregame that he went in the john and threw up. He came out pale, clenching his fist. I, too, was cranked. After Coach Garth gave the pep talk, I stood at the urinal and pissed about a teaspoonful.

We clattered up the ramp and out onto the field.

The night was crisp and clear under a three-quarters moon, and the band blared "On Wisconsin." Popcorn smells wafted over the field, clipped green and lined into a perfect grid under the lights. The cheerleaders worked everybody into a frenzy. After the coin toss, which I called right, and the anthem, we lined up to receive. I'd called a reverse for the opening kickoff. If Ray got the ball, he was supposed to head to his right and hand off to Jesse, up the left sideline.

The referee's whistle split the cool night air.

The Reynolds kicker approached the football and darn near missed it. He squibbed the ball, which bounced like a headless chicken for fifteen yards or so, and one of our linemen fell on it.

Which was a disappointment, but not much else went wrong.

Jesse was open all night. The first three times we got the ball, he scored twice on passes and once on an end around. It was the kind of thing that happens every once in a while in sports, but seldom in real life. You're in complete control and can make things happen any way you want.

At one point I switched Jesse to right end, from his usual left end spot. I gave him the ball on what was supposed to look like another reverse. I guess it did. The Reynolds guys followed Jesse like iron fillings to a magnet. I slipped out of the backfield and down the right sideline. Jesse pulled up, winged the ball left-handed and hit me right on the numbers for our fourth touchdown of the first half.

It was my first touchdown ever, in fact. I'm not what you'd call fleet.

Jesse said it looked like I was carrying a piano on my back, but he did award me, after the game, an FGW for that play. Jesse wasn't much for stats, but he gave out FGWs. Mostly to himself. FGW comes from baseball, when I'd tried to explain to him about RBIs and ERA. FGW was a statistic Jesse made up. It stood for Fans Go Wild.

AFTER the game, others were in a hurry to get to the dance. I took a long hot shower. I rubbed analgesic balm on my left thigh, more to smell it than to soothe a minor ding. Leftover steam hung over the lockers and benches and clung to the mirror as I combed my hair.

Times like this, it would be nice if Lorna understood a little something about football. To Lorna, football is mayhem, safer than war but just as pointless. What really gets a burr up her shorts is the crowds we draw, and how nobody shows up for school plays. And she couldn't get the school to pay for costumes. Drama people had to do a car wash and a bake sale, while football got new uniforms. Which is the way it should be, I tell her, because sports are more interesting. In drama you know how it's going to turn out. There's no opposition. Just learn your lines.

But Lorna has a closed mind on this subject.

I'm not sure she even went to the Reynolds game, but I was to meet her for the dance.

I came out of the locker room and headed down the empty hallway with my letterman's jacket slung over one shoulder. Dance music caromed off metal lockers and came down the hall amplified but muddled. Everly Brothers, "Cathy's Clown." A couple of bulky desks blocked the hall and marked the entrance to the cafeteria.

Lorna was at the entrance, chatting with chaperones. On duty were Mrs. Farnham, the Home Ec teacher, and her husband, Les, the electrician.

"Nice game, Wade," he said. Les's brown mustache wiggles more when he's thinking of something to say than when he actually speaks. "Sure enjoyed that one."

I thanked him.

"I hear you killed 'em," Lorna said.

Les wanted to talk about the game, so we discussed it for a while. Until Lorna squeezed my hand. Time to move on. Cindy Mueller, a plump junior, took my four quarters, dropped them in a cigar box and stamped our hands with a red triangle inside a circle.

Lorna wore her pleated skirt, plaid, with light blues and greens and yellows. And a yellow sweater. The way to wear a sweater is the way Lorna does, soft and loose. Some of these tight sweaters, you get the front sharp and pointy like lemon strainers. It's much better the way Lorna does it, kind of understated. Also she wears no makeup.

They had a slow number on, "To Know Him Is to Love Him," and we started dancing right away. Might as well. Can't see anything until you've been in the room a while. Tonight it was the red light bulbs. Which gave off more color than light. But I guess I was comforted, in blindness, by the fact that others could see Lorna and me even if we couldn't see them.

Lorna's face was cool against my cheek, and her body felt stiff. Sometimes it takes Lorna a while to find the mood. My eyes adapted and things began to reveal themselves. Volleyball nets draped the walls, and they had cardboard cutouts of sea shells, fish, an octopus, a seahorse.

"The Red Sea," I told Lorna.

She groaned, but I thought it was pretty good.

When a fast one came on, we found a pair of chairs free. The main thing to watch was Jesse, who had already worked up a bigger sweat at the dance than in the football game. In his jeans and a black T-shirt, with his white Chinook-bone necklace, Jesse danced everything. Sometimes with a partner. He just let himself go, as if the music came from his spinal cord. He hadn't cut his hair since he arrived in Calamus. It fell in sweaty streaks across his forehead and flopped loose in back. Every song he danced differently, except he kept returning to a kind of stand-in-place twisting routine he'd picked up on "American Bandstand."

Spotting us, he glided over.

"Should have brought my feathers and rattles," he said.

When "Runaway" came on, he nabbed Lorna and they danced it. When it was over, they came back.

Jesse said, "You see who's sniffing Miss Drees?"

I hadn't. I'd been busy watching Jesse and Lorna.

Over in one corner, where Jesse indicated, were Miss Drees and Palermo. This was another fast number, and Miss Drees wasn't a bad dancer, not bad at all. Without moving her feet, or not much, she just raised up on her toes and swiveled her hips. Her skirt wrapped first one way and then the other. She got a few up and down movements in there as well.

Palermo did little to help her out. Dangling her hand off his stiff arm, he arched his back and pinned his shoulders back as if he were in awful pain. He twisted his head from side to side, maybe trying to avoid looking at her.

The dance floor cleared around them, and people began to clap, on the downbeat instead of the upbeat. "Gad," Lorna said. "You'd think they could get *that* part right."

The dance returned to normal, and Lorna and I did our share of dancing. She was in a funk, though. The room was hot and sticky, all right. At the next break, she said, "Let's go outside. Get some fresh air."

We passed the Farnhams and walked the hallway. Just outside the door, near the bushes, stood a group of boys. Guys with their blue and yellow FFA jackets with merit badges. Ag Club awards.

"Good game, Wade," said Norman Burgess, shuffling feet. Others nodded and mumbled things.

When we were out of earshot, Lorna said, "Why do they hang around out here? When the cowgirls are in there sweating it up with each other. Future Farm Wives of America."

"What's eating you?" I said. "There's all kinds of folks. They're not bothering anybody."

But when Lorna gets in a black mood . . . We passed in silence around the side of the building, where cars lined the tennis court fence. At night the lights are straight above cars in the Show Row, so they get a good reflection off the wax jobs. Also the light—blocked by car roofs—can't penetrate directly inside. An orange cigarette tip glowed, then faded.

Lorna and I made our way to the front lawn and sat down, facing Main Street.

"So what's wrong? What's the trouble?"

"I don't know," she said.

I put my arm around her shoulder, but that wasn't comfortable in a sitting position. I withdrew my arm. The air was cool, not quite chilly. We could still hear the music. I offered Lorna my letterman's jacket, but she didn't want it. So I spread the jacket on the lawn behind me and lay down on it. Lorna remained sitting, with her arms around her shins. Her chin rested on her drawn-up knees.

"Everything is so *predictable*," she said. With her tongue, she worked her chipped tooth. "They box people up in tight little packages," she said. "Your cheerleaders, your farmers, your hoods, your jocks."

"Nothing wrong with that."

I guess I didn't get it.

To me, predictability was a comfort, as I may have mentioned. You sort of have a role to play, like in her beloved drama. Try to play it well. Which I knew better than to mention to Lorna, however. I guess I just didn't understand why she hates Calamus so much. Calamus seemed like a pretty rich place to me.

Around the three-quarters moon, high above the school lawn, was a fuzzy white halo. It would rain tomorrow.

"So what?" I said. "If things are predictable?"

"You have no idea," she said, turning to look at me. She poofed the bangs from her eyes. "You have no idea what Calamus is doing to you."

"To me!?"

"Calamus is a factory," she said. "They box you in a tight little package. They only have a few sizes. And even fewer labels," she said. "I saw you swagger down the hall tonight. The hero. The quarterback. The guy in the white shorts. They've got you right where they want you."

"I don't swagger."

"You swagger," Lorna said. "You swagger even sitting in a chair. You're dipped and soaked in swagger. The way you treated those FFA boys. The trouble with you," she said, "is you *want* to be packaged. You love it. You lap it up."

"*You* bad-mouthed the FFA," I said. "Not me."

"You really have no idea."

In the blue-white glow of streetlight circled moths, gnats, mosquitoes, dragonflies, all kinds of things. They orbited and swarmed, jockeying for position around the light.

"Well the trouble with you," I said, although I don't think as fast as Lorna, "is you think everything about Calamus is negative. You don't even try to fit in."

"The trouble with you," she said, "is you fit too well."

"Well what do *you* care, then?" I said. I'd had about enough of this. Lorna can be a pain in the butt. "At least they don't have a box for you."

"Ah, but they do." She sighed. "It's a very small box. I am Wade Curren's girl."

Well. What was I supposed to say to that? You poor thing? What a horrible fate?

What I should have said—it always occurs to me later what I should have said—is we could easily spring her from that box if it was so damn tight. But she was all lathered up. The trouble is, I hate scenes. I couldn't think of anything to say that wouldn't make it worse.

It was as if, so to speak, she had me boxed in.

Up at the streetlight, one big dragonfly left his orbit and dove, head on, into the bulb. *Ping.* He dropped, stunned, down and out of the halo of light. Soon he was back up there and went into orbit with the other bugs. Then he did it again—*ping*—and dropped. I guess he wasn't heavy enough to hurt himself, or maybe he couldn't get up enough speed. Again he dove toward the light.

"Well what about Jesse?" I said. "Nobody's got a box for him."

"Sure they do," she said. "He's not in it yet, but they'll get him."

As if on cue, Jesse—barefoot, carrying his shoes—appeared from the shadows. He ambled toward us, still dancing.

"Why are you lurking out here?" Lorna said.

"Lurk, lurk," he said. "I'm the private eye." He winked a big private eye. "Detective work." He leaned toward Lorna and said: "Wade Curren's mother will pay well to know what's going on out here. Nothing escapes the private eye."

"See what I mean?" She nudged me.

I snagged Jesse by the ankles and jerked his dancing feet from under him.

"*Almost* nothing escapes the private eye," he decided, from the ground. "That's your first tackle tonight, isn't it?"

Perhaps I should broaden my circle of friends. In the span of a couple of hours, Lorna had completely smashed that feeling, during the game, that I had total control and could make things happen any way I wanted. But I was thinking about Jesse, too, and Lorna's theory of the boxes.

Dance music stopped.

People wandered from the school in pairs, groups. Car engines growled to life. Headlights blinked on. Now there would be a gathering parade of cars, like slow fish, through Calamus. You could count on it.

WHEN the parking lot cleared, we went to the pickup. I crossed the ignition wires, but the pickup just gave a groan. Then nothing. Dead battery. I'd left the radio on, and now the motor wouldn't turn over. Jesse hailed D.K. Barr, who had jumper cables and knew how to work them, and we got it going. I drove Lorna straight home, which was rude, and Jesse and I headed down toward the barbershop.

Jesse was full of plans. Now that his one-year suspension was up, he was going to get his driver's license. He was going to hit up his mother for advance money to buy a car. He was going to take us to Las Vegas. He needed a girlfriend. What about Judith Horton?

At the barbershop, a lively post-dance crowd had gathered and the jukebox was going good. Cheerleaders were there, still in their green and white uniforms. I headed Jesse into a vacant booth, and he began knobbing the jukebox selector, flipping the cards. He found "Good Timin'," and put his nickel in.

When Mrs. Swenson came over, he ordered us plain Cokes and hamburgers. As a waitress, Mrs. Swenson is much slower than Lorna, can get rattled. Keep the order simple.

"Look," I told him, when Mrs. Swenson left. "I have a problem with Lorna."

"Who's better?" he said. "Jimmy Jones or Elvis?"

"Jimmy Jones," I said. When Jesse gives you an obvious choice, you want to pick the other one.

"Right again."

"Listen," I said, "Lorna and I are in a slump."

But Jesse listens like a hummingbird feeds. He was looking around for Judith Horton, who wasn't there.

"Pay attention, would you? I'm talking to you. We had an argument tonight," I said. "I mean not a fight, but she was real crabby about . . ."

"What is it, anyway, about Lorna?" Jesse said. "Do you guys screw?"

He leaned forward with his elbows on the table top.

"No, hey, listen. No, that's not what I . . . It's like I can't even talk to her lately without getting into The-Trouble-With-You-Is . . ."

"Well, do you feel her up?"

"That's not what I'm talking about. You got a one-track . . ."

"Well, do you?" he said.

"Not so loud," I said, glancing around. "That's not what the trouble is," I said. "But if you want the truth, no, I don't feel her up. Lorna isn't that kind of girl."

Jesse studied me over the rim of his Coke glass. He took a deep draw on the straw, and the level of his Coke slipped down about a third of the way.

"Well what do you do?"

"Look, this is private. But no, we don't do anything. We make out. That's about it."

"That's retarded," Jesse said. "You got to work those tits. That's part of making out."

"It is? I thought that was feeling her up."

"No, that's just making out. Feeling her up is when you get to the hot wet part. Pussy. You really are retarded. You've never done that?"

"Nothing below the waist," I admitted.

Mrs. Swenson came over with our hamburgers. Feeling a little feverish, I used the napkin to wipe my brow. I guess it's true Lorna and I are slow about these things. We'd known each other so long, maybe we got behind and didn't realize it. But retarded? I mean you want to treat someone decently, too, and how do you know?

Jesse's black eyes were dancing, and I felt like a perfect fool.

"Well," he said, like a belch.

"I've never been out with anyone else," I said. A drop of Coke lay on the red Formica table top, and I spread it around with my finger until it got thin and evaporated, leaving a filmy arrow on the table. "And it just doesn't seem like Lorna would like that stuff."

"They all like it," he said, shaking his head. "You just got to show some leadership," he said. "That Lorna, she's stacked."

"Keep your voice down, would you?"

"Lorna ever give you a hickey?"

"OK, that's enough. I've had enough of this."

We ate on our hamburgers for a while. Jesse, when his was finished, tapped time with his straw to "Stupid Cupid" on the rim of his empty Coke glass.

"They like it a lot," he said. "You could ask Rhonda Rheinbeck if you don't believe me." He nodded toward Rhonda, in a booth by the jukebox with two other cheerleaders. "Rhonda likes it a lot."

"Come on," I said.

"No, she does."

"How would you know?"

"Ask her," Jesse said, laughing. "I'll ask her for you."

When he scooted out of the booth, I grabbed his shoulder and got him out of there, out of the barbershop. Some people you just can't talk to.

The pickup started up OK, and I drove down the lake road toward home. The headlight beams skimmed potholes and made them blacker and deeper, like craters.

"Aw, cheer up, man," he said. He reached across the seat and clapped me on the shoulder. "I was just kidding. Take it easy. You take things so serious," he said. "Always thinking about things. Have some fun."

I pulled in behind the house and parked the pickup. The back light was on. I turned it off, meaning—to anybody who might be awake and listening—that I was home. Jesse and I walked to the edge of the bank, overlooking the lake. We sat on a log at the top of the bank. The moon topped the crest of fir trees across the way, splashing a silver reflection on black lake. Link's sign glowed red in the woods across the lake.

"I have fun," I said. "That's not fair."

The thing about Lorna is we'd grown up together. From as early as I can remember, we'd hung out. Mainly it was a matter of keeping up with her—reading, swimming, diving from the rock at the point. She'd done all those things first. Maybe that's what bugged her now about sports, come to think of it. Lorna just isn't in sync with the way things are organized. I don't know. There was no sense explaining this to Jesse.

Anyway Jesse had shifted gears. Something in the puddle of moon on lake had grabbed him. Or maybe it was the call of an owl on the opposite bank. He hopped down off the log and took a couple steps toward the path. Then he came back to lean against the log. Maybe it was something I'd said.

"When I was little," he said, "I got killed."

"You got killed." Had I heard this right?

He stared at the dark lake.

"Run over with a pickup." he said. "I was out by the fish racks. Over at Celilo, and this pickup backed over me."

Which was a difference between Jesse and me. The type of thing we worry about, or don't. I mean I worry about a game coming up, or whether I got an assignment all correct, or what Lorna might think. And as far as I'd been able to tell, Jesse didn't have a thing in the world to worry about.

"How old were you?" I said.

"A crawler."

He grabbed a lemon-size rock and lofted it over the alders. It plunked in the lake below.

"You remember it?"

"No," he said. "I didn't see it. What I remember is the wailing and moaning. People coming out. He-Who-Died was crying, how he didn't see it. Didn't see me. It was his pickup, him driving. He felt real bad about it."

The ripples from his rock toss spread to where moonlight puddled the lake. Ripples scrambled the moon, made it dance and wobble.

"Hurt you bad?"

"Killed me," he said. "Dead. It didn't hurt at all. It was just one of those things. An accident."

FOURTEEN

≈≈≈≈≈

TOM CREEK SNEAKS OUT of the woods behind the school like
a wiggle of gum-wrapper tinfoil. Yellow and brown rocks
make a ripple here and there, and the edges of the creek are
lined with watercress. Crawdads and brown frogs hang out
in Tom Creek, which runs so low in summer you can hop
across it on stones and not get your feet wet. Beyond the
highway, a small spillway backs up Tom Creek to form the
millpond, where log trucks dump their loads.

I used to fish Tom Creek and the millpond. I caught some
good-size trout in there, some of the bigger ones maybe sixteen inches. I *thought* they were trout. Then the clues began
to mount up. For one thing, these fish in Tom Creek were
poor fighters. When I hooked one he'd give a little tug, to
see if it was true, and then just lie on his side and let himself
be hauled in. These fish didn't have the spirit of a real trout.
For another thing their meat was pinkish, not the ivory meat
you get with trout.

What they were was landlocked salmon.

They must have been trapped upstream when the millpond went in. Now they didn't reach the Calamus and go
out to sea. They survived, they multiplied, but they didn't
develop.

"Not exactly landlocked," Link says. "They can get out. Come spring freshet, they can shoot over the spillway, and some make it past the dam. They can go outbound," he says, "but they can't get back."

The fish in Tom Creek are salmon that stayed. They're the ones that didn't make the trip.

"Them lazy-assed, good-for-nothing fish," Link says, "is lost relatives of your Old Man Chinook."

He wouldn't even fish for them.

THE NEXT morning, Saturday after the Reynolds game, I awoke to the tinny drip of rain in the drainpipe. Breakfast smells wafted from downstairs and snaked into the bedroom, but the dry heat in my nest was too good a thing to break. I lay in bed until the screen door banged and the car started up. The car backed out on the crunch of gravel and onto the road. Then it eased off toward town, shifting up and out of earshot.

Time to get up.

In the kitchen, Duncan was grilling hotcakes and eggs. Bacon nested on paper towels by the stove. Mother had taken the car uptown to do some shopping. I sat at the table with the girls. Plenty of hotcakes were piled on the platter, but I waited for a fresh batch. Huckleberry hotcakes. This fall, after a bumper crop at High Rocks, we were having huckleberry everything—hotcakes, muffins, pies.

Duncan, in his apron, talked about last night's football game. Lately he thought I might make somebody a pretty fair small-college quarterback.

"But you have to get mean," he said. "Len Garth says you could play some college ball, the way you can throw. But you have to block and tackle. Punish some people."

I wasn't in the mood for this. With his apron on, waving the spatula for emphasis, Duncan seemed a fine one to talk about throwing my body around. You get the feeling people want you to be what they're not, or should have been.

I cut up the baby's egg and helped her choke it down, while I worked on my own breakfast in silence.

Actually, it bugged me. *Get mean. Punish some people.* This Duncan, my father, was the nicest, most easygoing guy I knew. You'd wait a long time if you expected Duncan to shake anything up, I thought, as he brought the bacon to the table. Duncan's eyes are blue, like Link's, but color isn't the main thing.

On the other hand, there were times I noticed the same blue fire in Duncan's eyes as in Link's. Not often. Not recently.

Once was when a waterskier smashed a beer bottle at the beach below the house. Duncan charged the guy, challenged him. He went berserk. He picked up a ski and held it over this guy's head, made him pick the brown glass shards out of the mud. Surprised the heck out of me.

Another time was on one of Mother's history trips. In fact it might have been the same trip—probably was—that we visited Celilo Falls. We drove back following the Barlow Trail, in thick yellow dust on the east side of Mount Hood. You can still see the rope burns in trees, where they winched the wagons down the steep parts. Duncan was driving slow, of course, on this one-lane mountain road. Behind our car came a red Dodge pickup, honking—which startled us—and Duncan got the fire in his eyes. He wouldn't let the pickup pass. He wasn't about to eat the dust of that pickup. We could've pulled over, rolled up the windows and waited. Instead, Duncan went careening down the Barlow Trail with this red pickup hot on our tail, Mother screaming, Sarah Ellen bawling, Duncan sweating BBs. With his maniac blue eyes on the trail. Crazy, I remember thinking, those eyes.

Link's eyes.

But that was the exception. Which is the interesting part, now that I think about it. Where did that fire go? I mean it's there, somewhere. The Link factor. But normally Duncan's blue eyes have a lakelike calm, a kind of serenity that says not so much he's in charge but that there isn't much left to be in charge of. Ask him about his job or something, and he might look right through you with those cool blue eyes. You'll want to knock to see if anybody's home.

I was a couple bites into my third stack of huckleberry hotcakes when I remembered. Link and Jesse would be watching the World Series. I mopped up the butter-specked maple syrup with a last wedge of hotcake, and excused myself to go across the lake.

"Did you get Link's wood in?" Duncan asked.

"It's in. He's got plenty," I said.

ALONG the path down to lakeshore, the rain had hung silver pearls on the brush. Rising wisps of moisture laced the lake as I rowed across. Morning fog, caught between cloudy water and watery clouds, shifted from the black surface to the low gray ceiling. No fish jumped. No bugs danced the surface. No birds flew. Only the mist fell light and steady to the sound of mill saws in the background.

The ball game on TV was a strange one—Yankees 10, Pirates 0. Bobby Richardson a grand slam, 6 RBIs. So when it was over, I hauled Jesse out of his easy chair and we went to work on Link's wood supply.

Earlier that year, Link had felled a big fir tree up the hill from the bunkhouse. We cleared out some wet brush around the tree so we'd have room to saw.

Jesse took one end of the double-handled crossbuck saw, and I took the other. Link stood by, holding a 7-Up bottle with nail holes through the cap. He sprinkled the sawblade with light oil from the bottle as we chewed deeper into the log. When the upper edge of sawblade slid below the bark, Link slammed a wedge into the cut. Then we got the saw going steady, rocking back and forth.

Which is when it becomes a pleasure, not like work at all. We found a good rhythm, with long smooth strokes. White noodles of raw wood came from the saw's teeth with each stroke, like strips of time. To crosscut an old-growth fir is to pull out these white strips of wood that start as young as me and go back through Duncan and Link and old Gus Schwarz, who claimed this land, and all the way back to Lewis and Clark and John McLoughlin and Robert Gray. And the Indians before that.

We bucked off four or five wheels of tree.

When Jesse quit pulling and collapsed into a thicket of Scotch broom, I started to count the growth rings on one of the hunks we'd bucked off. I quit counting when I could see the tree was over 250 years old. It had been growing before the explorers even had maps for the West Coast. You've seen those old maps, like Sir Francis Drake had? Those old boys had no idea.

"That's why you guys are Indians," I told Jesse. "Everybody was looking for India. West Indies, East Indies. They thought everything they found was India."

Jesse thought about that.

"Good thing they found us," he said. "Or we'd be stuck out here in the woods without any root beer or Oreos or any damn thing."

So Link humped to the bunkhouse to rustle us up some grub. As he stumped away, grumbling about the high cost of labor, his step didn't have its usual spring. I'd been noticing that lately. Link's slowing down. Duncan was his youngest son, after all. Link must be in his seventies. Jesse and I went back to bucking, and it occurred to me Link hadn't taken a turn on the saw, either, which he usually did.

When he came back from the bunkhouse with jerky and pop, and a package of Oreos, we took another break and scarfed down lunch. Once we stopped, though, it was hard to find a rhythm again with the saw. Jesse lost interest. He no longer was pulling his share.

Link reckoned we'd bucked enough, anyway. "Unless we got two winters in a row," he said, "which ain't likely, it ain't happened yet. This ought to do 'er."

We rolled the thick wheels of wood toward the woodshed. Link went to work with the sledgehammer and wedge—

maybe he'd been saving his strength for the fun part—knocking the wheels into halves, fourths, sixteenths. Jesse and I, with double-blade axes, cut these pieces into fireplace-size blocks. The sound of splitting wood echoed off the far bank, where I imagined Duncan—satisfied?—listening from across the lake.

WHEN we finished splitting kindling and stacking wood, Link said it would be all right with him if Jesse and I wanted to clear out the blackberry thicket that had overgrown the south side of the bunkhouse.

"Either that," Jesse said, "or we could go fishing."

Which sounded all right to me, although it was raining. It was a light rain, soundless, the kind you need a dark background to see it fall.

In the bunkhouse Jesse changed to dry clothes and grabbed a rain slicker and his Cleveland baseball hat off the wall pegs. He sat on a bunk to watch me sort fishing gear. Link had a wicker fishing basket, a metal tackle box, and a cardboard box crammed full of hooks, weights, leaders, line, yarn, plugs, spinners, flatfish, swivels, bobs—everything but what you can find when you need it.

"Gonna troll the lake?" Link said.

"You want to go?" I asked him, although he'd made no move to rig up his own pole. "I thought maybe we'd head up Tom Creek."

Link pulled a horrible red hanky from his hip pocket and honked into it, as if that were what he thought about Tom Creek and its lazy fish. He folded up the handkerchief and looked thoughtful, like he might come with us after all.

"You ever fish lower Tom Creek?" he asked. "Below the millpond?"

"Too brushy," I said. "Can't get in there."

Between the millpond and the lake, Tom Creek is so overgrown it would be hard to extend a ball-point pen, much less a fishing pole. And there's poison oak in there, too. I'd walked lower Tom Creek before, just poking around, but never fished it. As far as I know, nobody does. In fact that might be a good reason to check it out. Link might be right.

"Just take a gander up the creek, why doncha," he said. "This time of year, no telling what you'll see."

Jesse rowed us across the lake, where I put on my own dry clothes and rain gear. We picked nightcrawlers from the bait box and changed the moss, which was rank. Then we rowed toward the mouth of Tom Creek. Which isn't far. The creek enters the lake about halfway to the dam, maybe a half mile from our house. I tied the boat to a tree at the mouth of the creek.

We scrambled over rounded gray rocks but it was tough going, upstream. Salal and salmonberry bushes hung low with the weight of fresh rain, and vine maples were so thick we had to wade in the stream bed. The water was icy at first, but I got used to it. Tom Creek flowed only shin deep in the swift parts, knee deep at the pools.

"This ain't workin'," Jesse complained, when he caught the tip of his pole in overhanging brush. He backed up to untangle it. "How are we going to fish here?"

Well, he was right. I had been right. It was too brushy. Why had Link sent us here?

"Let's don't go, and say we did," Jesse suggested.

But now that we were into it, I wanted to keep going. I stashed the poles at streamside. We could come back for them later if we found a place to fish. And then it was more manageable, with both hands free to push brush aside. I took the lead, sloshing ahead of Jesse.

In one pool, I glimpsed a thick dark underwater root. That is, I saw it but I didn't see it. Just peripherally I noticed it, before it saw me.

That root and the whole pool exploded on me. Like an underwater detonation, the pool was afroth with flapping and splashing. Fins and tails broke water on both sides as fish hydroplaned upstream, around a bend and out of sight. It was so sudden, so surprising, I stumbled backward into Jesse. Scared me half to death.

"Holy shit," Jesse said. "What was that?"

"Fish."

When my chest thumped back toward normal, I took a deep breath. "Monster fish," I said.

"Let's get the poles."

"Salmon, I think. Huge. Did you see them?"

"No," he said. "I thought you'd been shot."

"Must be spawners," I said.

"In here?"

Although I'd never seen salmon take the fish ladder at the dam, this was proof they could do it. There's no other way for full-grown salmon to reach Tom Creek. And if they were salmon, it wouldn't do any good to get the poles.

We crept upstream, through the next riffle, wading as if the creek were mined. I watched for dark shadows. But if these were spawning salmon, which they must be, we'd better not walk the stream bed. We took to the brush. We pushed through undergrowth every twenty yards or so to get a look at Tom Creek bubbling through.

At each of the next few looks, we saw nothing. No fish. Just water skippers, skating on skin of water.

At another shallow pool, I pushed brush aside and saw breaks on the smooth surface of the water. What looked at first like a branch tip sticking out was the fin of a salmon. And another. Lots of them, maybe half a dozen, all with their snouts pointing upstream.

Jesse pushed forward to where I was watching.

The fish were idling there, in the drizzle. They looked beat. White bruises blotched their dark backs and sides. Some—the males—were redder than others.

I moved, slightly, to get a better angle. Just that quick, the pool exploded into whitewater. Gray- and red-backed arrows shot forward, upstream. Then the pool settled back to normal.

"Let's get out of here," I said.

But now it was Jesse who wanted to keep going. Somewhere along the way he'd lost his cap. His hair fell wet and lank, and his eyes burned with curiosity, maybe awe. He was right, we couldn't just leave. Those salmon had to stop somewhere short of the millpond, I knew, and we could get another look.

We were far enough up Tom Creek to cut through Hankins' hayfield. A dirt path at the edge of the field returned to Tom Creek just below the millpond.

The pool at the base of the spillway, when we got there, was alive with the backs of fish, all with heads pointing upstream. Most were just idling. But one big red-backed fish drove along the surface, raising a hump of water as he gained speed. He leaped up and out of the pool into the light spray of water off the spillway. Thrashing and twisting into that thin horsetail of water, he rose sad and beautiful, maybe six feet out of the water. But far short of the top. He hung suspended for a moment before gravity and falling water pushed him back to the pool.

This salmon, no longer silvery, was bruised and bumped where he should be sleek. He was gaunt and slack-skinned where he should be taut and springy. And he had grown a hump, back of his head. But these salmon, after surviving the ocean and all the perils of passage, were home now.

And the door was locked.

Another big red took a leap, as proud and pathetic as the last one.

"Ah," Jesse said.

There was nothing you could say.

They couldn't get up there.

At the head of crowded fish in the pool, one or two at a time swam forward and nudged the concrete spillway wall. *Whump*, one butted the wall head on. Like I had seen before, below, at the big dam. She drifted back, dazed and bewildered, into the mass of other fish. Then another tried it—*whump*, a sound I could feel more than hear. The fish wobbled back to recover and to take her place for another hopeless try.

In a small eddy at the pool's far side, fish carcasses swirled in slow circles. White swollen bellies up, they twisted like the tops of screws with no bite to pull them down.

Jesse was beyond speaking. His wet black eyes lost their focus. Before I could stop him, he slid down the dirt bank and waded into the pool. His splash startled fish away from him, but some fiendish pointer kept their heads aimed upstream, where there was no escape.

"Leave 'em alone," I called.

He could only make things worse.

Jesse lunged for a fish, but missed, setting off a mad flurry in the pool. When they settled down, Jesse stood waist deep in the pool, with his back to me. His black hair glistened with rain as he watched the water. He grabbed again, and this time he caught a red male. He scooped the fish from the water and tried—all in one lifting motion—to heave it over the spillway. But the fish slipped from his grip and splashed back to the pool.

Maybe that would work, I saw.

If we could toss them or carry them above the spillway, maybe we could save some. But I wasn't exactly thinking clearly as I slid down the bank to help.

When the pool settled down again, Jesse went for a big dark one. He got her. As he broke the surface, lifting her up, her middle deflated under the pressure of his hands like a squeeze bottle of ketchup. From her underside, the eggs came gushing out. Long viscous clumps of tiny red-orange beads, thousands of them, were held together with milky slime that stuck to Jesse's fingers and to his wet clothes, and then to his hair and face as Jesse dropped the spent fish and grabbed his head.

He was screaming, crying.

FIFTEEN

〜〜〜〜

"You should of left 'em be," Link said.

Which was right. Jesse and I had panicked at the mill-pond spillway. Those fish would die anyway, and some of them might spawn before they did, in lower Tom Creek.

The part that got me, when I had time to think it over, was that these fish went against everything you learn. Darwin's theory and all that. These Tom Creek salmon that made it out to sea and back—the fittest of their breed, you'd think—were the ones that couldn't get past the millpond to spawn.

"Well that's exactly it," Link said. "Them lazy-assed numbers upstream," he said, "been gettin' smaller ever since the millpond went in. Used to be they was a scrappy fish, bigger. Now they don't have to get big. Ain't nothin' gonna bother 'em if they don't leave."

Jesse and I were helping Link clear that blackberry thicket from the south wall of the bunkhouse.

"You're the smart one," Link said. "Figure it out. Them fish at the millpond and up is the ones that survive. They breed more little runts and get smaller and uselesser every year."

Link bent down to gather vines and carry them to the burn pile. But he didn't walk away.

"I don't know much about this here Darwin feller," he said, scratching his ear, "but it looks to me like he's got 'er plumb bass-ackwards," he said. "Plumb backwards. Them that tries, dies."

"UN-natural selection," I said, standing up.

"Survival of the timid," Link said.

JESSE got a car. His license suspension was up, and Reno gave him the money. He skipped school one day and drove up after football practice in a red and white '57 Ford Fairlane—a V-8 with automatic, overdrive, dual pipes. It had scratches on the back right fender, but otherwise it was in excellent shape. The thing is, though, if you skip practice you have to come back with a limp or a dental excuse or at least a sad look on your face. Jesse showed up grinning, revving his engine. He never thought of those little things. Coach Garth—What could he do? We needed Jesse—decided to excuse him, but Coach was whacked off.

I wasn't too thrilled with Jesse myself.

At the barbershop, too, I heard some grumbling. "See that goofy blanket-ass got hisself a Ford Fairlane. That's where your taxes are going, Jake."

"Never worked a day in his life."

The difference between Jesse and the greasers—who had earned it, setting choker or rassling hay bales—was Jesse picked up two traffic tickets in that first week with his car. One was for speeding past the school, which is officially a 25-m.p.h. zone, but nobody observes it. Even log trucks rumble through at 40 or so, and you can't stop a log truck on a dime. But they got Jesse at 45. Not a warning, either, like Miles usually gives out. A ticket.

I say "they" got him. This wasn't just a matter of Miles, the cop, having an eye out for him. Miles discusses all matters of law and order with—and takes his direction from—the barbershop morning coffee crowd.

Jesse's other ticket was for a burnt-out headlight.

But nothing much bothered him. Jesse had money to pay the fines.

Anyway, Jesse'd had his car only about a week when he made his move on Judith Horton. Why Judith Horton? I wondered. Judith was the only daughter of Jonathan Horton, a mill-foreman-turned-real-estate guy. She was a stiff. Aloof. I mean she was beautiful, tall, with a high pompadour wave, but all she did was study. Judith was real quiet and she'd be up for class co-valedictorian if she hadn't got a couple of Bs in P.E. Nobody ever thought to ask her out. Her old man was a blowhard now that he wore suits and sold real estate. The Hortons lived in a split-level cedar house up at Springs with a view of Mount Hood. You wouldn't call her Judy, for example. Judith.

Horton and Howl, she and Jesse had lockers next to each other. Maybe he knew something I didn't.

"It's her posture," he said. "The way she walks. Like she's carrying books on her head."

Now that we had a car with a backseat we could double-date, he said.

So for Saturday night, Jesse had it all arranged. We were to meet Judith in town, outside the Broadway Theater. Which was odd, I thought, until I figured out Judith's folks probably didn't know she was going out. Or not with Jesse. But that was the least of my concerns, because I was taking not Lorna but Rhonda Rheinbeck. This, too, had been Jesse's idea, although I hadn't needed much urging.

Within one class period of my asking Rhonda, of course, Lorna knew about it. When I passed her locker, Lorna gave me a bright actress smile and the old thumbs-up.

"Predictable," she said.

But she was hurt, all right, and I felt bad. I should have at least discussed this with Lorna. But she'd been lost in books since our Friday-night spat, and I didn't get to it. The timing was never right. Or I couldn't think how, exactly, to mention it to her. I mean we didn't have a formal arrangement or anything to break, was the way I explained it to myself.

"For cripe's sake," Jesse said. "Stop worrying about it. Lorna doesn't own you."

Which was right, I guess. I don't know. Anyway by Saturday night I was pumped. I had a boner just walking up to Rhonda Rheinbeck's door that night.

Rhonda wore a pink shift with white polka dots the size of golf balls and a waistband, which showed off her figure, and a big white bow at the neck. Nice-looking outfit. Her blond hair she had in a ponytail, with silver quarter-moon earrings. And lots of perfume, I noticed, as soon as we got in the backseat of Jesse's car. Of the Calamus cheerleaders, Rhonda was probably the second best-looking, after Suzy Barlow, who was engaged. In trig she was lost, but never discouraged, and you had to admire her for taking it.

"You look great," I told Rhonda.

"Thank you. So do you."

Jesse turned around as he was driving. "Both of you," he said, giggling, "look just great."

It was clumsy, all right. I could think of nothing interesting to say. But then I'd had no practice at this. With Lorna you never have to think of anything to say.

Jesse parked on the other side of the theater from the barbershop. Which was thoughtful of him, in case Lorna was on duty that night. Not that I really cared.

We sat in the car and waited for Judith to show up. We were early. Jesse fiddled with the radio and found "Handy Man." Jimmy Jones. "Did you guys know Jimmy Jones is Indian?" he said.

Which was pure bullshit.

"He's a Negro," I said.

"No, I saw him on 'American Bandstand,' " Jesse said. "He's a halfbreed, I think. Or at least he sings like an Indian."

"I think maybe he is," Rhonda said.

It was raining. The Broadway Theater sign bounced reflections off the street. Green and red plumes, neon feathers, rise over the white prow where they put the letters. It's a pretty classy sign, for Calamus. Except they don't have enough Es and Ss and have to mix smaller black letters with the red ones. Which looks kind of bush.

"In Portland," I said, "they'd have enough letters."

Which reminded Rhonda, I guess, of her sister the beautician.

Rhonda had visited her sister over the summer. She had a sister Back East, in Denver, who had an apartment of her own and was engaged to this Air Force guy. She had a swimming pool in the complex, Rhonda said, and her own washer and dryer *right there in the apartment*. They—Rhonda and her sister—had gone shopping for a shower curtain and they walked through the lobby of the Brown Palace. A big hotel, apparently.

"But Roxanne's going back to study nails," Rhonda said. "Nails is where you make it, not just hair."

Rhonda was wound up.

"So she says, 'Why don't you come to Denver, Rhonda, and go to beauty school?' And I says, 'Aw, Rox.' And she says, 'Dad always said you was the pretty one, don't give me that Aw Rox.' And I says, 'Dad did not.' But he did. And Rox goes, 'We could open our own shop, you could go in on it, partners.' And I says, '*Roxanne!*' But I think I will. What do you think?"

All of which I was glad to hear. I hadn't known any of this about Rhonda.

"What I like is someone with plans," I said.

"Stick of Dentyne?" She offered Jesse first, then me.

I took a piece, and she unwrapped a stick for herself.

"You know," she said, "I could have fell off a log when you asked me out."

Now that the wipers were off, color from the theater leaked into shifting streams on the windshield. "Strange," I said, "how you think you know somebody, and you really don't."

"Isn't that the truth?" said Rhonda, full of wonder, as if how could I think of anything so deep.

After Judith pulled up in her family's Buick, we splashed down the sidewalk to the cashier window, where Jesse paid. Inside, a fresh batch of popcorn spilled from the popper, and its buttery aroma expanded into the lobby. I was about to buy popcorn for all of us, but we'd just cut our Dentyne. I could come back later for it. Filled with impending sin, I followed Rhonda's pink polka-dot dress up the ramp to the show room.

Jesse, in the lead, ushered Judith Horton into the back row, right side. The newsreel had started, so it was dark and hard to see. But when my eyes adapted, I could see a pretty good crowd, maybe seven or eight in each row.

When we got settled in, Jesse—beyond Rhonda, on my right—cut loose a loud cackle at a mildly funny thing on the Mr. Magoo cartoon. Just letting people know he was there, I guess. Jesse doesn't often laugh out loud. It was as if the darkness brought out his laugh to replace his grin. An audible grin was what it was, reassuring but a little bit spooky.

The movie—Doris Day and David Niven—was pretty good. Rhonda thought it was great.

"See how they blur on Doris Day?" she whispered. Which was true. The camera did blur on Doris Day's face, unlike the closeups on a doorknob, say. "I read in this magazine," Rhonda said, "where she's got a bad complexion."

I took her hand, which was dry, and laid it on the armrest. A bold move. It being our first date and all. But Rhonda wasn't surprised at all.

Old Lady Briggs, whose son owns the Broadway Theater, paced the center aisle, wielding her flashlight like a .22 pistol. I couldn't see Jesse because he sat on the other side of Rhonda. When Mrs. Briggs flashed the light over there, I guessed it was because of his laugh, which was bound to be unsettling to an old lady. Make her nervous. What a lousy job they gave her, anyway. Mrs. Briggs squirted light wherever it was most needed. I leaned back, peeking past Rhonda's ponytail toward Jesse and Judith. It was too dark to see. I didn't want to be obvious about it, but when a brighter scene came up I glanced over there again.

They were slumped in their seats, and Jesse already had his arm around her. It surprised me, knowing Judith Horton. On a first date. Which, however, gave me something else to worry about.

Tonight, of all nights, I didn't want to be retarded. My hand in Rhonda's grew sweaty as I thought what I should be doing. The flavor was long gone from my Dentyne. I tried to swallow it. It didn't go. It caught on the edge of my windpipe. I fell into a coughing fit and finally hacked it out. The wad thumped into the seat directly in front of us. Which is pretty hard to ignore, although Rhonda kept facing straight ahead.

"Rhonda!" Jesse whispered, loud, when Mrs. Briggs's flashlight found the source of the commotion and lit me up. "Cut that out. You should be ashamed of yourself."

I went to the lobby and brought us back some popcorn. We watched the movie and ate popcorn for a while.

When a kissing scene came on, Rhonda was playing nicely with my hand. My mouth was dry, cottony. So I thought what the hell, now or never, and I swung my right arm around her. But I did it too fast and sort of backhanded her across the left eyebrow. Not hard, but "Ouch," she said. Because I'd clutched, my arm came to rest on the back of the seat, not on Rhonda. Still, she leaned in and put her head on my shoulder. Then it was a more natural thing to bring my arm around her. Except I misjudged it, and my hand came to rest on her right breast.

Rhonda stiffened.

"Sorry," I said.

I pulled my hand back to rest on her upper arm. With her head on my shoulder again, I got a full whiff of Rhonda's perfume. Made me light-headed, dizzy. Lorna doesn't wear perfume. I felt nauseous.

Not that I'd been paying attention to the movie anyway, but the perfume took me completely out of it. When I recovered enough to be sure I wasn't going to throw up, all I could think about was Lorna. Or the un-Lorna-ness of Rhonda

Rheinbeck. Next door to the theater, right through that wall on our left, Lorna was probably serving up sodas and hamburgers—right this minute—unaware of what was going on in this darkened back row.

I felt low as a goddamn worm.

Before long, more than my hard-on was missing. Jesse's cackle was gone. He hadn't laughed for a while. Now that I could look straight over Rhonda's head, I had an easier view, and Jesse was all over Judith Horton. First date or nothing, the two of them were scrunched way down in their seats. They didn't break it up, either, when the old lady's flashlight beam hit them. Mrs. Briggs, baffled, clicked the flashlight as if she were out of ammunition. Finally she walked into the row ahead of us and tapped Jesse's shoulder.

He straightened up, surprised and innocent. But Judith stayed slumped in her seat. And as soon as Mrs. Briggs shuffled down the aisle, they went back at it.

WHEN the movie was over and the lights came on, Judith sat up straight and brushed the wrinkles out of her lap. Sleepy-eyed, like waking up, we spilled out onto the wet sidewalk.

"What do you say we cruise on into Portland," Jesse said, "and see what we can find."

But Judith said she had to get home by midnight.

Which was a relief to me.

We walked up Broadway, away from the barbershop and toward the car. Judith took sideways glances at her own reflection in the store windows. She tried with a sneaky hand to adjust that pompadour back up over her forehead. But with Jesse's arm around her she was happy and even a little bit funny, which was a strange thing to see, Judith Horton laughing. And her walk had improved, too. She wasn't nearly so stiff. She looked almost pretty, not just beautiful.

"Dentyne?" Rhonda offered.

This time I declined.

When we got to Jesse's car, he tossed me the keys. We

couldn't get to Portland and back before midnight, but there was still some time. Jesse and Judith took to the backseat. I drove us up and back through town a couple of times. The car fogged from the rear forward until only the windshield was clear.

I cracked the fly window.

Rhonda, snapping her gum, sat close in the front seat, but I guess she could tell I was out of the mood. "So what about Lorna?" she said. "You guys break up?"

I wished Rhonda wouldn't snap her gum like that.

"Aw, I don't know," I said. "I still like her. But it seems like things get awfully predictable after a while. You know?" It was the best I could think of, under the circumstances. I was anxious for the night to be over, to tell you the truth.

"I know," she said. "You could have knocked me over with a feather when you asked me out."

Which was the end of the evening, as far as I was concerned. It was just a bad idea from the start. Once she got talking about Lorna, I was finished for sure. Lorna's theory of the boxes was making more and more sense to me, as I drove to Rhonda's house and walked her to the door and shook hands.

When I drove back to the Hortons' Buick, downtown, Jesse and Judith were still gasping and heaving in the backseat. The only thing for me to do was walk home. Which I did, even though it was raining and I had no rain gear.

How was I to know—or what would I have done, had I known—that Jesse and Judith Horton were going to stay out all night? They didn't go into Portland, but they did drive out of town and park.

Did I already mention that Jonathan Horton was a blowhard? He blew plenty hard when Judith didn't come home that night. I wasn't there to see it, but I guess they got back to the Buick at about dawn. Her old man met them with a shotgun. You'd think he would've been madder at Judith than at Jesse, but that's not always the way things work. Anyway her old man shot the left rear tire flat on Jesse's car, to show he meant business. He was something of a hero for it at the barbershop.

As if it served Jesse right.

Which was the troubling part. I guess my idea of Jesse was that he had Calamus by the tail, and he could swing it about any way he wanted. Now I got to thinking maybe not, or just the opposite. The way things were set up . . . I don't know. Me, what had always dogged me was the Link factor, that I could never be good enough. Now Jesse was opening this new window where it looked like you could be too good.

SIXTEEN

〜〜〜〜

IN A BROKEN-TOP FIR below the dam, a pair of ospreys took up residence. The ospreys scavenged branches and limbs at riverside and ferried them to the top of the snag. The male was the fetcher. The female was the builder. She stuffed and wedged limbs into place to form a nest that topped the fir snag like an upside-down straw hat.

From the dam, in summer, I could look down on their nest.

Ospreys are fishers. They're a fish hawk, actually, and I liked to watch old man osprey work. He perched motionless on a tree branch overlooking the river. He'd sit there half an hour without rustling a feather. Then he swooped down narrow as an arrow and came up with a trout in his talons. With his beak, he bit through the trout spine behind the head. Then he flapped up to the nest to deliver his prey.

This October, when salmon reached the dam, a bald eagle arrived with them. The ospreys went nuts. They screeched and squawked, scolding this eagle. Faster and more maneuverable than the eagle, the ospreys rose above him and dive-bombed him whenever the eagle cruised near the dam. The eagle couldn't outfly them, so he flipped over and flew upside down—talons up—when attacked from above. It was quite a trick. I never knew an eagle could fly upside down.

They couldn't run him off. The eagle was after dead fish. More a vulture than a fisher, the eagle nabbed salmon that bellied up at riverside. He'd drag a carcass only far enough to take a leisurely meal of it on the rocks. Which is a sorry sight to see, for your National Bird.

WHEN rain comes to Calamus it can hold steady for two or three days, maybe a week. Wind off the Pacific squeezes thick gray clouds against the Cascade Range, and they drain over Calamus like dark sponges. Colors fade, sounds muffle and smoke from the sawmill drapes a sawdust smell over town.

At a Thursday football practice, the field oozed mud. It was brown soup with mud atolls, the outlines of footprints. I had a hard enough time gripping the center snap, let alone throwing the ball with any zip. Gusts of wind did with a football what they wanted. Mud sucked on my cleats.

I was disgusted anyway because Jesse hadn't shown up for practice again. Now that he had his car and the weather turned bad, he'd pretty much lost interest. Football came so easy he saw no reason to practice. The idea of sacrifice, working for it, was foreign to him. Football—maybe Calamus itself—was a big party in Jesse's honor. All he had to do was show up, blow out the candles, and open his presents.

Which was hard to deal with, because he was right. That's the way Jesse's world worked.

The problem was, I began thinking my own world could work that way too, if I could just figure it out. There's no good reason to practice before a Rainier game. It would be a laugher. As we slogged through practice, I thought how stupid it was to come out in this muck when there were dry buildings around.

We should take the day off. Pop popcorn.

When practice was over, we tracked a stream of mud into the locker room. Coach Garth called me aside, into the coaches' room. Where was Jesse? he wanted to know. I had no idea. He'd been in school today, but his car was gone.

"I'll have to suspend him this time," Coach said. "Every member of this football team is a reflection on his community. Its values. I'm at the end of my rope."

"I know," I said.

"This is the last straw."

"You can go to the well," I said, "only so many times."

I guess he expected me to argue Jesse's case. Or maybe Coach confused the fact that I knew Jesse well, and always stuck up for him, with the hope that I could control him. Like you might ask an astronomer to handle a meteor.

"One-game suspension?" I said.

Coach Garth knew as well as I did we could do without Jesse for the game at Rainier, tomorrow. But then we played Seaside the following week. "One game ought to do it," he said. "If you can get through to him. For me it's whistling into the wind."

"I'll talk to him," I promised.

"Atta boy, Wade."

As IF I didn't have enough to worry about, Lorna was at her locker. She'd stayed late with drama, I guess. We were the only two in the hall. My footsteps echoed the hall as I walked toward where she stood, facing her locker. Sometimes it's better if you don't plan what you're going to say. I walked straight up to her and put my hand on her shoulder.

"I had a miserable time at the movie the other night."

"Get your grabby paws off me," she hissed. "Gad."

"No, look," I said. "I just . . ."

Lorna twisted away and turned to face me. Her hot brown eyes shot molten flashes as she looked me up and down. "You and your Sally Rally, Rhonda Rheinbeck," she sputtered. "That cheap tart. That bubble-head floozy."

She snagged her yellow slicker from the locker hook.

When she punched her right arm into the arm hole, I had to take a step back.

"You deserve a cheerleader." Her nostrils flared. "You're just like all the rest." She pursed her lips to cover her chipped tooth. Her hair was a mess. She tossed her head and turned away. "I don't want to talk to you. Leave me alone."

"Hey, calm down," I said. "It was a mistake."

"Oh, right!" she said. "That's great. Fine. You think you can take Harla Hotlips to the show and stay out all night and come running back here when you're . . ."

"Hey, no."

"I said get your grubby mitts off me!"

"I didn't stay out all night."

She narrowed her eyes on me. "Don't lie to me, Wade Curren. Everybody knows. You and that blond bimbo might as well have been on the newsreel."

Lorna stabbed at books on the locker shelf, and took some down. She had trouble catching her breath.

"You didn't?"

"I didn't," I told her. "Jesse and Judith Horton stayed out, but I didn't. I went home after the show. Couple loops through town. Nothing went . . ."

I was thinking, actually, about what Jesse had said. I was probably the only one in Calamus who couldn't get to first base with Rhonda Rheinbeck. But that wasn't going to soothe Lorna.

"Nothing went right?" she said. "See?"

"No, actually it was awful. Nothing went *on.* I'm trying to explain, if you'll just listen. I was in the wrong scene, and I figured it out."

Which was nearly true. Not the whole truth.

Books slid from the crook of her arm and scattered to the hardwood, which infuriated her. She raised both hands over her ears, as if to squeeze her head a size smaller. Then she kicked an algebra text. It scudded across the hall and whanged against a locker.

"You're such a hot ticket," Lorna said. "Go prance

around with Rhonda Rheinbeck and then you think I'll come
wagging my tail like your little puppy. And what I really hate
is you're *right*. I've always just been there."

"Knock it off!" I said. "One stupid time, this was. I said
I was sorry."

I grabbed her and tried to trap her elbows against my
chest, but she was surprisingly strong. I couldn't control her
but I didn't let go. She had just enough room for short, sharp
uppercuts to the underside of my chin. Which was jarring.
And I couldn't talk, for fear of chopping my tongue off.
Maybe because I didn't say anything, she thought she wasn't
hurting me. Her hot wet cheek came against my face, and her
shoulders shook. Lorna was sobbing too heavily now to
shout. I didn't let go of her.

She kicked my shin, which really hurt.

"You're a brat!" I said.

Which sounded about right, as soon as I said it.

A surge of strength came to my arms. "You're a selfish
brat." I shook her as hard as I could. So hard her face—
open-mouthed—went by like a TV vertical gone berserk. "A
brat, a brat, a brat!!"

Unlike Lorna, I lose language when stirred up.

We struggled some more before exhausting one another
and ending up side by side—breathing heavily—in a heap
of books on the floor. I felt pretty good about it, to tell you
the truth. Lorna was still crying. The janitor appeared at
the far end of the hall to see what the commotion was all
about.

"Just leaving," I told him. "It's OK."

She stuffed books back into her locker and gave the door
a testy kick to bang it shut. I walked toward my own locker,
to get my jacket. Then I remembered I didn't have the pickup
today. I'd come to school with Jesse, and now he was gone.

LORNA raised the hood on her yellow slicker as we left the
school. There wasn't much to talk about, now that we'd re-

jected one another. Now that we'd settled how awful and inconsiderate each of us was. It was the opposite of a crowning achievement. We needed a great resounding minor chord, maybe, something to underline the break or to sand off jagged edges so they couldn't fit back together.

I was walking her home.

The sidewalk gave out after a block or two toward the trailer court, across from the mill. Trucks threw up spray from the highway, and my shoes were already wet. We turned in at the mill. At the edge of the millpond, we sat on a log.

It didn't seem possible this was happening. Good-bye? Me and Lorna? In Calamus?

There was the matter of her biology collection. It was in our woodshed, down at the house. I watched rain on the millpond and thought of Lorna's biology collection.

What started it was the rats. They'd ripped a hole in a feed sack, so the woodshed was a popular rat place. Lorna and I used to wait for them. I had the axe. She had the shovel. Waiting for rats to come under our raised tools of death. Which they did. Rats are stupid. Lorna in those days was stronger and quicker than I was, and her shovel came down first. *Whaaaap,* she bashed the lead rat so hard her feet left the ground. *Whaap, whaap,* all hell broke loose in the woodshed while I missed with the axe.

She got the chief rat and another one.

"Gimme that axe," Lorna said one day. We were approaching the shed for another kill. She got four rats that day. Lorna killed a lot of rats. One day Mother saw me shoveling rat parts toward the brush, and she got interested. She couldn't bring herself to go into the woodshed with us, but she stood on a chair outside and watched. Trouble is, the rat population was dwindling. Even rats begin to figure it out. So I went poking around in the wood pile to shoo out a rat, and I uncovered this nest of babies. They were pink and bald, each about the size of a Cracker Jacks favor. Five of them.

"These are mice," Lorna said.

"How could they be mice? These are baby rats."

Lorna put them in a hubcap and we showed Mother.

"They're orphans," Lorna said. I could see her brain at work, how guilty she was.

She and Mother locked eyes, the way women do.

"We'll have to gas them," Lorna announced.

It was the start of a firm friendship between Lorna and my mother, who let Lorna gas the baby rats in the oven. When they were dead, she came up with some formaldehyde and a Ball jar. It was also the start of Lorna's biology collection. I nailed up board shelves in the woodshed. The chief attraction, still, is the five baby rats. Tip the Ball jar, and they'll do pink little dead somersaults in their formaldehyde. But there's also a bat. A bull snake, salamander skins. Pollywogs through frogs, a separate exhibit. Grasshopper jars. Moths, butterflies, and spiders are filed in P through S of a *World Book Encyclopedia*. A dead zoo Lorna's got in our woodshed.

So I mean . . . You see what I mean. What would become of Lorna's biology collection?

Log trucks rumbled off the main road and into the mill, giving up their last loads of the day. Screaming saws cut the soggy air. The huge disk of the main saw whirred so fast it looked toothless, blurred, waiting for the next log. Saw meeting log made a high-pitched whine, and white noodle chips rose in a quick furious arc. Steel arms clapped the log into position for a run at other, smaller, saws. The log slid down the conveyor belt until it came out like French fries—four-by-sixes, this time—for some hideous giant.

Lorna was crying again.

"I'm scared," she said.

It was frightening, all right, the mill saws. But when she didn't continue, I wasn't sure that's what she meant.

"What are you afraid of?" I said.

"Calamus," she said. "Everything."

Her eyes were big pools. She tossed a hunk of bark into the millpond. The ripples disappeared into rain on the water.

"I'm scared of living in a trailer court," she said. "I'm

scared of football uniforms and caulked boots. I'm scared of the mill saws at night." Her voice quavered, but the words kept pouring out. "I'm scared of Jesse's car and the way you are acting," she said. "Calamus is a mean place. I'm so scared sometimes the smell of sawdust sticks in my neck like a sword."

Lorna wasn't one to be afraid of things. Angry, sure. She got mad at stupid things, but I always thought Lorna was above it all. She was the strongest person I knew, except Link. And Link didn't always apply. It was hard to figure. Maybe everybody carries a kind of terror deep in the stomach, like I do, a dark twisted knot that comes from . . . from what?

"I'm scared I'll never get out of Calamus," she said, looking straight ahead. "Wade, we can't get stuck here."

A drip of rain made its way to her chin. It held there. I reached over and flicked it off.

"We?" I said. "We don't even like each other."

"Right."

A load of logs splashed into the millpond, sending waves to lap against the edge. I thought of those dwarfed salmon in the millpond, getting smaller every year.

"Let's walk," I said.

"Not home."

WHICH is not what I had in mind anyway. I just wanted to move. Sometimes it's hard to say what you do have in mind. Things come floating up from deeper than thought, like long-submerged logs. We skirted the edge of the millpond, treading squishy bark. My jacket was soaked through. Lorna's shoes squeaked. Rain hissed against the red-hot screen on the slash burner, and stacks of graying lumber were draped in fog. We were not, I realized, walking aimlessly. We were headed toward the spillway. Something in the the whine of mill saws drew us straight toward the salmon, probably most of them dead by now.

"I know a surprise for you," I told her.

What we could do, maybe, was bypass the spillway. Skip the ugly part. We could cut through the hayfield to check Tom Creek below. Salmon might still be in the lower pools. We could sneak up and take a look.

"A surprise?"

"Jesse and I were down here the other day," I said. "There's something you should see."

Lorna was doubtful. But she let me take her hand and lead her through the hayfield. In her raincoat, she got soaked from below like the wick in a lamp. She pulled up and checked me, quizzically. She ran the tip of her tongue past that chipped tooth.

"Fish," I said. "If they're still here. Salmon."

"Right," she said, rolling her eyes for an I-wasn't-born-yesterday look. But now she had something to wonder about.

When we got close, I whispered to her. "We'll crawl in," I said. "Don't talk. No noise or sudden movements."

Lorna dropped to her knees and forearms when I did. We crept toward a small knoll. A pair of fir trees framed a narrow opening to the creek.

I motioned Lorna to keep her head down.

"Truth," she whispered. "What are we doing here?"

"Sssssshhh."

When we reached the opening between the two firs, I raised my head slowly—very slowly. I saw the dull red backs of a pair of salmon in the pool.

Then I spotted a third.

All males.

I elbowed Lorna to raise her head and look. She did, and the fish didn't bolt. One floated in a slow and lazy arc, circling close to where we lay. The other two idled nervously on the far side of the pool. They twitched and shifted position as if their bus were late. One of them nosed in toward the slow one, who broke from his circle pattern and ran the intruder off, into riffles upstream. But he glided back down and rejoined his skittish buddy on the far side of the pool.

Then I noticed a fourth salmon, where the slow one circled.

This fourth fish was darker, which was why I hadn't seen her at first. Swollen and tired, she lay close to the stream bed. But she was working, too. It dawned on me what we were watching. She wriggled forward, brushing aside pebbles with her belly and tail. When the water settled, she repeated the process, making a troughlike nest.

I wanted to see if Lorna was getting it, but I was afraid any move, even a twist of my head, might catch the eye of that wary old red and break up the whole thing. I could feel Lorna's slow breathing next to me.

Were we right to be watching?

We watched.

Lorna, after a while, eased her head and shoulders back down. My own arms ached from propping me up. Scared we might be noticed, I got my head down OK. Now we were hidden from the pool and the dance of the fish. I could see in Lorna's eyes that she knew what we were watching. She got it.

"This is the end, isn't it?" she said. Lorna had never shown much interest in Link and the salmon.

"The end and the beginning."

We slowly propped ourselves up again, between the two old guardian trees. The male had just made another run at his rivals, so we were in less danger than the first time of being seen. This time the other two reds didn't come back to the pool. The remaining male floated back into his circling pattern. He circled his partner, apparently not even swimming, suspended in water like on a string drawn from up high.

The dark one stopped working on her gravelly nest, leaving one side higher, the side away from us.

It was getting dark.

The male's circles grew smaller with each pass of his partner in the trough. Then he dropped to the bed of the stream and came in alongside her. His head wasn't quite up to hers, but he pressed her sideways into the trough. She shuddered. Both fish shuddered. They vibrated there, a single two-headed fish, and then her body deflated. Though I couldn't see eggs come out, it was the same as what Jesse, not knowing, had done with his panicky and clumsy hands.

The dark one eased forward from her nest, and the red slipped in to take her place. A milky white cloud came drifting from his underside and slipped downstream to disappear in slow current and fading light. With her tail, the dark fish swished up sand and pebbles to drift back and settle over the nest. Which the male, reluctantly, abandoned. He might have preferred to stay and get buried himself.

So I MEAN there we were, Lorna and I, pressed between these two fir trees, watching all this life. The beauty of the unbroken circle. I guess I was pretty worked up. Lorna was, too. We backed down out of sight of the pool and rolled around in the wet grass for a while. Which was nothing new, but it felt especially good.

What was new was when I opened up Lorna's raincoat and this incredibly delicious smell came rushing out. Beyond mushrooms, beyond clams—it was pure steamed Lorna—as if I'd lifted the lid on her pressure cooker when I opened that raincoat. It about knocked me out. I buried my face in Lorna's chest, and her jaws went slack when I kissed her. I thought she was going to swallow me, tongue first, which would have been all right. Lorna arched her back and pressed her hips into me as I fumbled with those hooks to her bra, behind her back. Before I got it all the way loose I felt the juice coming up between my own legs and then the surging release, the warmth spreading inside my pants as Lorna chewed on my ear, and all I could do was kind of bounce on her.

Which I don't know. You never know. I suppose some people can just hop together and make love the first time, like in books and movies, although the scene always fades to a sunset or crashing surf or something, and maybe everybody has trouble with it, how would I know?

Timing.

Anyway I don't mean to complain. Lorna wasn't complaining. I ran my hand down her warm back and under the band of elastic and lace. When I grabbed a handful of her tight buns it was like turning a doorknob. Lorna twisted around and spread her legs, and my hand slid into her hot wet oyster, which closed up on it. She squirmed and yelped and bit me on the knee. With my free hand I got her skirt undone and worked it off her while we rolled around some more in the grass and brush, slithering on and off the raincoat. Lorna started moaning and then launched a shuddering action of her own.

It was too dark to see much. She clamped my head between her thighs when I tried to.

I could've escaped this position but it was better to just lie there, smelling the history of the world. Then I felt my belt buckle go. Lorna rubbed the bulge before she slowly brought the zipper down, and freed my flooded part to the rain.

"Oh my," she said, slipping her fingers around it. "That's a doozy."

Which was generous of her. No doubt she'd never seen one in this condition before. She might have been inspecting fruit.

Since she didn't release her vise grip on my head, all I could do with my arms was hug her buns. Which I did. I felt Lorna's hot ear and wet hair on my stomach, moving down. She put her lips on the tip of my pulsing doozy and rolled her tongue over it, sliding it past her rough tooth. I gripped her bottom and waited for the earth to part and swallow us up.

Which it did, in a way.

As we lay there afterwards and I stared up at the dark outline of fir trees against evening sky, we were a part of those towering firs. We were included, in a way that I thought might be possible but had never known. We were part of the sky, part of the rain falling down and part of the salmon dance in Tom Creek.

If the Great Voice had rumbled overhead and announced, *All right, that's it for you. Now you die,* I would have considered it a square deal. Fair enough.

SEVENTEEN

NATURE IS GREAT, all right. We'd been part of the fir trees, part of the salmon and the rain . . . and part of the poison oak along the bank of Tom Creek.

The thing about poison oak, not everybody gets it. Me, I get it bad. I can pick it up from touching a dog that's been in it, or from smoke off the burn barrel. I'd been laid up a number of times before. Lorna, after our romp at lower Tom Creek, didn't have an itch on her.

The other thing about poison oak, it works its worst revenge—in a delayed reaction—on the thinnest and most sensitive skin. Scratching your crotch isn't all bad, of course. I got off to sleep without thinking much about it. Only when I awoke, on fire, in the middle of the night did I figure out what had happened. Itching spread down my legs, up to my armpits, over the neck, eyelids, everywhere. By morning I was so swollen I could barely walk, much less put on pants.

When she came up to change the sheets, Mother didn't press for more detailed information than she already had, although she'd noticed the condition of my clothes.

"Salmon-watching," she said, shaking her head. She laid

out cotton swabs for the calamine lotion. "Do you feel like anything to eat?"

"Figs me some soub?" I said. In addition to the poison oak, I'd come down with a head cold. "Thangs."

LATE the next night, Jesse appeared in my sickroom. When he switched the light on, I sat bolt upright. The door was closed. I hadn't heard him enter. He wore his black leather driving jacket, all pockets and silver zippers, with the collar up. The sleeves were pushed up his forearms, and he took a good wide stance.

"Faster than a speeding bullet," he said. "Able to leap tall buildings in a single bound. It's . . . *Medicine Man.*"

Beads of rain trailed off his black jacket. His hair, wet, was slicked back. Maybe he had come in the window. He began unzipping his pockets. He pulled out Bayer aspirin, Vicks VapoRub, Johnson's baby powder, cod liver oil, Ex-Lax, Band-Aids, Pez. The pile grew on the bedspread as he unzipped more pockets and unloaded his gifts. An Ace bandage, Smith Brothers cherry cough drops, and a model airplane in its package.

Clorets. Pepto-Bismol.

"Whad a friend," I said.

I wasn't too sick to give him our handshake, which is a no-contact, two-handed sawing motion, back and forth, as if there were an invisible crossbuck saw between us. Jesse had made it up. We'd been using it in football, to celebrate touchdown passes or lesser FGWs.

"Hey, would I forget you?" Jesse laughed. He took a seat at the foot of the bed.

"I'll just have one of your Pez," he said. He snapped the top of the dispenser and offered me one.

"This model airplane here is a genuine Russian MIG-15," he said, holding up the package. "For age ten and up, so I figured you could handle it. Or if none of this other stuff works, you could sniff the glue."

The clock on the dresser said not yet midnight. So it wasn't exactly the dead of the night, although that's how it felt, awakening from deep sleep. I heard a siren uptown, the usual Friday-night stuff. Or was it Saturday? Friday night.

"How you feeling?" he asked.

"Whad habbened at Rainier?"

"They lost it," he said, shaking his head. "Six to six. Fucking mud knee deep and rain all over. I drove over," he said. "Nothing else to do. Henderson couldn't handle the snap, and then the single wing didn't work. Schrenck found a fumble and staggered in, or they wouldn't have scored at all. Glad I didn't have to go out in that slop," he said. "You did the right thing, getting sick."

The siren I'd heard came louder, nearer. Down the lake road. When he stopped talking, Jesse heard it. Ears don't really perk up, but Jesse's eyes widened. He searched the room and settled first on the closet, then on the window.

I stared at the booty on the bedspread. This late at night, the drugstore wouldn't have been open.

"Awww, no," I said. "You didn'd." I flopped back on the pillow. "You dibshid."

Outside the bedroom window, pulsing red light lit the trees. The siren cut off, but the red light kept tracking through tree limbs.

A car door slammed.

"You might want to save these items under the bed," Jesse said, gathering tubes and packages and bottles.

I heard the crunch of gravel, footsteps on the driveway.

When Jesse glanced toward me, I was shaking my head no. I was just amazed how stupid he could be, but I guess he took it as a refusal to cover for him. Maybe he figured I couldn't pull it off, even if I wanted to. Which was probably right. Jesse put his hand on the lightswitch, but he didn't flick it off. His car must be here at the house. And the boat on this side of the lake. He was a gone goose. Jesse sat on the bed and exhaled a great sigh.

"The store was closed," he explained, shrugging his shoulders. "What was I supposed to do?"

Duncan was up and had opened the back door, downstairs. I heard Duncan and Miles speaking down there. Voices, but not the words.

"Is Jesse up there?" Duncan called.

The two of them tromped up the stairs. Jesse opened the bedroom door and extended his arms as if to be handcuffed, which Miles took as a threatening gesture. He stumbled backward in the hall, looking for cover.

When Miles recovered, his left eye twitched. He held his right hand over his holster, not touching the gun but ready.

"There's b-b-b-been a rep-p-p-port of a b-b-break-in," Miles said. "At the Rexall."

JESSE'S arrest was more complicated than you'd expect. In searching his car, Miles found Link's .22 pistol in the glove case. Loaded.

Which is something you never think about. Jesse liked to plunk squirrels or shoot birds off the fenceposts when he was out for a drive. He could do it, too, if he didn't take time to aim. I mean he could hit them from a moving car. Every once in a while. But it was just a .22, for Pete's sake.

Anyway Miles took Jesse in and wrote him up for armed robbery. Which was absurd, everybody knew it. But that didn't quell the excitement. Lorna said they went nuts at the barbershop. Just loved it. Part of the problem is that Calamus doesn't get much in the way of criminal activity. Everybody knows everybody and his dog, so it's hard to pull anything. This business about Jesse burglarizing the drugstore got blown way out of proportion.

Until Link stormed City Hall, as he calls it—the barbershop—that next day. I was still laid up, of course, but Lorna was there.

She says you could hear the last gulp of coffee down

their throats when Link busted in on Miles and his advisers that morning. The door banged behind him. Lorna says Link just stood there in the doorway, breathing blue fire from his eyes and staring them down. Miles said, "L-L-L-Link—" and then Link chewed them like jerky.

I wish I'd been there.

"A lot of it went too fast for me," Lorna said, "but I saved one phrase, in case I might need it: *You lazy-assed, good-for-nothing whistle punks, sorry excuses for coffee-guzzling justicers.* Justicers. I like that. With calluses on their butts. That grandpa of yours filled the room."

I wanted all the details. Lorna told it too fast the first time, but she went through it again.

I guess Link's main harangue was that Calamus was no longer run by loggers but by this group that reminded him of a Key-wanis meeting. Or a sewing circle. He's right about that. The morning coffee crowd is not loggers but Virgil Beasley, the banker. Ed Horton and Howard Wilkins, who has the grocery. Les Farnham. People like that, whose white shins show above their argyles when they sit. It's mainly Friday nights and Sundays that loggers take over the barbershop. Like two different breeds. Loggers wouldn't have been that interested. Anyway Link had learned enough from Jesse—at the barred garage back of the fire hall that passes for jail—to fix it in his mind as a prank. What was the world coming to when you tossed a stupid kid in the hoosegow for wanting to medicate a sick person, his friend?

And since when was a .22 pistol a weapon?

According to Lorna, Link demanded that they fetch Fred Gott—who owns the Rexall—and somebody ducked out to get him. Link sat himself on the corner stool, Lorna says, with his back to the counter, and grilled Gott:

Was any money missing from Gott's till?

Not that Gott could tell.

Was three dollars sitting out on the drugstore counter?

Well, yes, Gott had found that.

That's all the kid had on him, Link says. You got any

complaint if he returns the goods? He might owe you for a package of Pez, Link says.

But Gott didn't think that was quite right, either. Others agreed. They still had Jesse for breaking and entering, didn't they? Gott finally agreed to drop charges in exchange for Link's promise that Jesse would repair the broken window and return the merchandise. When Beasley suggested Jesse ought to at least be kicked off the football team, Link hit the roof again, Lorna says. The way that part was settled—which Link called a compromise—was Jesse would have to agree *not to miss* another football practice.

"That grandpa of yours," Lorna said. "is a genius."

"That's what I've been telling you," I said.

I wish I'd been there.

"Oh, and then Miles," Lorna said. "Miles gauges the tide of shifting opinion and says, 'W-w-w-well, I reckon we can release the p-p-prisoner.' And Link looks surprised and says, 'Let him stew 'til Monday. I reckon you taxpayers can feed and house that varmint a coupla days. I could use me some relief.' "

AFTER football practice one day I came dragging into the house and was surprised to see Lorna. She and my mother had papers spread across the kitchen table, and a cardboard box with Lorna's handwriting on it. COLLEGE, the box said.

"Wade."

"Hi, Wade."

They didn't even look up.

"What do we have here?" I said. You can tell immediately when the conversation was richer before you arrived.

"Research," Lorna said. "Elizabeth is helping me. Pull up a chair."

Lorna is always veering off on some project. I think the mail is her best friend in Calamus, after me. Mail-order catalogs—Sears, Roebuck; Montgomery Ward—were her big thing, but recently she'd found she could write to Chambers of Commerce and they would send her pamphlets. Free. You should have seen all the stuff she got from Savannah, Georgia, for example, including a real pecan. How she picked them, I don't know. Just places, far away.

So now it was colleges.

"A little soon, aren't you?" I said. Lorna was still a junior.

"Now this one," she said to Mother, "is near Philadelphia. Is Bryn Mawr a best?"

"Best," Mother said.

Women together, they had their confidence up. Mother's hands were active and calm, as if she were painting. She sorted catalogs and forms into rows she pronounced best, next best, and common. Mother had gone to a college called Russell Sage herself, a pretty highfalutin place as I understand it. I was surprised she put that catalog in the next-best category. She seemed to know all about it.

I thumbed a couple of catalogs. Bryn Mawr. Smith. "What kind of colleges are these? I never heard of them."

Lorna put her hands on her hips and gave Mother an aren't-we-smart smile. "How would *he* hear of them? Gad. They don't have football teams."

"Now, Lorna," Mother said.

"And it also has Early Admission," Lorna said, capitalizing the last two words and checking that box in her mind. "Let's put Bryn Mawr on top."

"She's actually read these catalogs," said Mother, amazed. Which didn't surprise me. Anything that's ever passed her fingers, Lorna has read.

"Early Admission," I said. "What's that?"

Lorna rolled her eyes. I was slow. "Well, let's see, now, what in the world could Early Admission mean?"

"OK, OK, I'll leave."

But of course I stayed at the table. It turns out some of these colleges will admit you without having graduated. If you're a nontraditional student. "The fine print," Lorna said. She was a sudden millionaire. When I read it, nontraditional sounded like if you were a Zulu or raised by wolves or something. But there was no doubt in Lorna's mind that Calamus qualified her.

"I think it's worth a try," Mother said.

"You're not even a good student," I said. "How could you get into a place like that, even on time?"

"I'll take those SATs," Lorna said.

Lorna is a killer on any test, it's true, but the trouble is— Mother didn't know—she never lifts a finger in school. Just because she's smart didn't make her a good student. Mother had way too high an opinion of Lorna, if you ask me. It was just sickening. Getting Lorna's hopes up like this.

"So now," said Lorna, poofing her hair. She dug deeper into her box for a new batch of catalogs and forms. "We need something for Dumbo, here. Mister good student."

She laid it all out on the table.

Duncan arrived home from his work in Portland. He carried his man bag, his attaché case, and a clutch of mail. He hugged the girls and pecked Mother on the cheek. After saying hello to Lorna, he fixed his see-through blue eyes on the array of papers and catalogs on the table.

"Looks like we're making plans."

We were on the stuff Lorna had collected for me. At least I had heard of these places. Duncan's *Sports Illustrated* had come in the mail, and ordinarily he would have gone to the davenport to nap with it before dinner, but now he stopped at the table. In fact Duncan was interested. He hung up his suit jacket, loosened his tie, and pulled up a chair. Duncan had been Back East in the Navy and thought East was a good place to know about, if not to live.

"What do you think of this Princeton?" I said.

"Top-notch place," he said. Which I took to mean too good. Not for me.

"You'll never know," said Mother, pursing her lips, "if you don't try."

· · ·

Ours, basically, is a family without conflict. Arguments seldom arise. When they do, they are settled by one person acting hurt long enough for the others to give in.

Yet every once in a while there will be something at the Curren house that has to be said. There's a game we play, when that happens, called Trying-To-Say. Or that's what I call it. Not out loud, of course. In Trying-To-Say, the trick is to bring up an uncomfortable topic without actually saying anything about it. The game usually takes the form of a family conference, often at the dinner table. For all I know, this may happen in other families as well, but I can't imagine anyone more proficient at Trying-To-Say than Mother and Duncan. So subtle is Trying-To-Say that it took me years to even recognize when the game was on, let alone figure out how to play.

Duncan finished his dessert well before the rest of us. He folded his napkin neatly beside the bowl and scooted his chair back so he could cross his ankle over one knee. He cleared his throat and said, "You know, Wade, your mother and I have been thinking."

Mother glanced at Duncan and gave him the slightest, barely perceptible nod before turning her brown eyes on me. Meaning, *The game is on.*

We were Trying-To-Say, and I was on defense. On defense, you have to be alert to every gesture of the hands or gentle burp, every raised eyebrow, every shift of tone or veiled glance across the table.

Since it was they who had announced the game, it was up to Duncan or Mother to continue. I took a bite of my dessert—vanilla ice cream with blackberry jam, no nuts.

"We are extremely proud of what you have accomplished in school," Mother began. She smiled. Meaning, *I am extremely disappointed about something, which has nothing at all to do with school.*

"And we appreciate the judgment you normally show," Duncan said. "Your maturity." Meaning, *You've made some dumb choices lately. Grow up.*

Mother pushed her hair behind her ear with a nervous right hand. Duncan, head down, stirred sugar into his coffee.

Let's not rush into this. Let him sweat.

I figured maybe it was about colleges. Maybe it was about Jesse. But it's a mistake to draw quick conclusions in Trying-To-Say. On defense, you want to lay back. The aggressors might be Trying-To-Say something completely different from what you're preparing a defense for.

"Thank you," I said. Meaning, *I need better clues.*

I drained my milk glass, set it back on the table, and watched the white film recede down the inside of the glass.

It was still their move.

Mother wiped the baby's face with a wet cloth. "You two may be excused," she said to the girls. Sarah Ellen, a smart cookie, knew I was in for it. She'd eaten her ice cream too fast, however. Now she was willing the last bite not to melt.

"I'm not finished!" she protested, much too bluntly for Trying-To-Say.

"Finish," Duncan said.

"Aw, Mom," she appealed. Which is the correct procedure, appealing to Mother, but this time she got no help. The girls had to leave the table.

"Upstairs," Mother said.

Which meant only the obvious, that what we were Trying-To-Say didn't concern the girls. It did, however, raise the stakes. Not that anything was going to happen. In Trying-To-Say, there can be no clear winners or losers. No climax. Nothing happens because we never reach a confrontation. We never say.

The three of us and the baby, in her high chair, remained at the dinner table.

Duncan rearranged the knife and fork on his plate. He squared the salt and pepper shakers with the sugar bowl.

Mother poured herself a fresh cup of tea.

"Personally, I have never known Jesse to be anything other than polite and amiable," Mother said.

Which was unusually overt. Mentioning his name, I mean.

"Not that it matters how people talk," said Duncan.

I was furious with them. They were dead wrong about Jesse. Duncan, the ex-logger, with his big desk job and his sincere blue eyes. Mother and her eastern ways. They could go to hell. Jesse was better than the lot of them.

That's how mad I was, not what I said. I didn't say anything.

"We just want you to keep your eyes open," Mother said.

"We like Jesse," Duncan said.

With my spoon I stirred the creamy pink residue of dessert in the white bowl, making narrow temporary valleys that filled into the wake behind the spoon. When I looked up, mother was staring curiously at me. Duncan inspected the light fixture on the ceiling.

A fly buzzed at the kitchen blinds.

"I do keep my eyes open," I said.

Boy, was I mad. But of course you can never reveal how mad you are at Trying-To-Say. That would fracture the whole game and be the same as admitting defeat. Rules are rules, and I understood them.

Mother twirled the tea in her china cup—a family heirloom—and set it back down without sipping from it. Duncan rose and began clearing the table. Trying-To-Say can be over before you know it. That is, the actual playing of the game doesn't last long. It can take a long time, however, to heal.

"We trust you, Wade," Mother said.

Which is a killer. Because I love these people, I really do. But we never say that, either.

EIGHTEEN

≈≈≈≈≈

OF THE THREE THOUSAND or so salmon eggs that hatch from a single spawning pair, maybe half escape the jaws of trout, birds, and streamside feeders. Then they have to make it past turbines at the dam. At the Columbia River mouth, where the smolts feed and adapt to salt water, gulls and pelicans take their toll. In the ocean lurk bigger feeders and the nets of trawlers. If a salmon survives three or four years out in the ocean, he then has to pass seals and fishermen at the mouth before fighting back up the river—in our case from the Columbia into the Willamette and the Calamus—to the dam. And up the fish ladder.

If only two—of the original thousands—make it back to Tom Creek to spawn, the salmon are breaking even. Say five or six get back, from three nests, nine thousand eggs. Pretty slim odds.

One thing in a salmon's favor, though, is coloring. Because a salmon is dark on top, he's hard to see against the dark background of watery depths. Because he's light and silvery underneath, he's hard to see from below, against the sky-lit surface of the water.

Which is no big deal, I guess. You take any wild animal,

he's going to blend with the surroundings. But it depends on your angle, with salmon. I don't know. I just thought it was pretty slick the way that works.

JESSE showed up at every football practice, but the thing about Jesse is when he has to do something—even if the word comes from Link—he loses interest. If it's not fun, why do it? Sometimes you could convince him what he should do was his idea, and then let him invent how to do it. But now that he was sentenced to football, it was as if his football plug had been pulled. He lacked the old fire that would make things happen. He was waiting for practice to be over so he could get out to his car and think something up.

In the Seaside game I overthrew him a couple of times, which had been nearly impossible to do. When he caught a pass in the flat and failed to escape a one-on-one tackle, I knew we were in trouble. On pass patterns that night Jesse zigged when he should have zagged, zagged when he should have zigged. I lost all sense of what he was going to do. Our secret frequency was dead.

I was desperate to find another channel. "Wake up!" I screamed at him, when he came loping to the huddle after another incomplete pass. "Shake yourself!"

Jesse glanced around the huddle. Then he pinched his arm and stood erect. He shook himself. His pads rattled and his helmet flopped. Jesse agitated himself until I thought his parts might come loose.

"OK, that's enough," I said.

Jesse stopped shaking. "Whatever you say, Kemo Sabe."

Which should have been good. This was more like Jesse, and it took the edge off that purple doubt that grips a football huddle when things are going badly. Maybe we even put a drive together after that. I guess we did. The Seaside game is something I'd rather forget.

We should have won that game.

Plus Jesse didn't know how to act after losing. After losing, you have to kind of slink around, like you let the whole town down and maybe they'll not take it too hard. Jesse didn't have an ounce of slink in him. Down at the barbershop after the game he kept playing his new favorite song, "Mr. Custer," on the jukebox. Which is a real annoying thing, anyway—this cavalry guy singing "Please, Mr. Custer, I don't want to go."

When the sounds of arrows pierced the air, Jesse called *Forward Ho!* over the song.

Over at a corner booth sat Frank Jukor with Stub Stevens and Dickie Mills, a crowd of young woods bucks you don't want to mess with. Jukor set his hamburger down and stalked over to our booth. He grabbed Jesse's salmon-vertebrae necklace in his hairy fist.

"If you play that fucking song one more time," Jukor said, "I'm gonna rip your lungs out."

I held my breath while Jesse thought it over.

"He means it," I said.

Jesse slapped at Jukor's hand, which snapped the thong on the necklace and the vertebrae went clattering about the booth and onto the floor. But Jesse stayed in the booth, and Jukor decided not to rip his lungs out then and there.

Jesse didn't play "Mr. Custer" anymore that evening. But did he learn anything?

Shoot.

WHAT I learned, or thought I could see coming, was this rip in his safety net.

Miss Drees, in English, intercepted a note Jesse was passing. When it turned out not only about her but *to* her—My Darling Miss Drees—she'd finally had enough. She sent him to the office with a note of her own. He was flunking English. Which was true. Jesse had stopped handing in papers, even though I always told him what to write. All he had to do was copy it down. It wasn't as if he had to bust his tail.

All he had to do was try.

Coach Garth no longer had reason to excuse Jesse. We'd already lost the Seaside game. "You can't get blood out of a turnip," was the way Coach explained it to me. He kicked Jesse off the team.

What I mean about the safety net rip was I could feel the town turning, like a slow ratchet, against Jesse. A guy with gifts like his could bring out the anger in Calamus. When he was doing his stuff in football, he was exotic and maybe a little suspicious, but he was ours. A natural resource. After he got booted, he was just a dumb Indian.

Jesse had what people called an attitude.

Well, they were right. He did. Jesse hadn't cut his hair since he had arrived in Calamus, and he used too much Brylcreem to slick it back. Although his hair was too long for a proper ducktail, that was the drift of it. Which doesn't help a bit in Calamus. And the black leather jacket, his salmon vertebrae necklace . . .

He was driving us home after school one day and we passed Stub Stevens, coming against us in his El Camino. "See those hubcaps?" Jesse said. Stub had flipper hubcaps, and they looked good. Jesse did a gravel-scattering U-turn by the grade school and took off after him. When Stub pulled into his driveway, Jesse pulled in behind him.

"How much for those hubcaps?" Jesse said, when Stub got out.

"Not for sale," Stub said. He was just off work, and it looked like he'd had a rough day. He set his tin hat and lunch pail on the grass and leaned against the El Camino. It was light green, baby-shit green with yellow trim, but Stub kept his El Camino real sharp.

"I'll give you forty bucks for the set."

"Not for sale. You hard of hearing?"

Charlene came out of the house, carrying the baby. She used to be in our class and they were doing real good. "Hi, Charlene," I said.

"You can get these at Schwab's," Stub said, "for twenty-seven ninety-five. New."

"I'll give you sixty," Jesse said.

Charlene shifted the baby to her other shoulder and twisted her hair with her free hand. She looked at Stub, who hooked his thumbs in his suspenders and scratched at driveway gravel with a caulked boot. What could he do? $60. What he could do was take $60 from Jesse for these hubcaps and then buy a new set for $27.95.

Jesse plucked three twenties from a wad, and we drove off with Stub Stevens' flipper hubcaps.

Stuff like that, it just burned people up. The principle of it. Where did Jesse get his money? From his mother, from the goddamn government, was what people said.

And then he'd filch a bag of popcorn at the show if you didn't watch him like a hawk.

I got on him about it.

"Hey, you have to blend in," I said. "Let 'em sleep."

But I might as well have tried to reason with Coyote. What it boiled down to was Jesse didn't need football. He didn't need school. He didn't need Calamus. "I got more money coming than those suckers will ever see," Jesse said. As soon as he got the rest of his money, he said, he was going to Alaska. He was going to California.

"What I'm going to do," Jesse laughed when I tried to convince him not everybody loved him, that he'd better cool it, "is blow up that dam. Dynamite that sucker," he said, "and bring the fish back. Bring the river back."

THEN there was the matter of the mailbox shootings.

Jesse didn't do it, but he might as well have.

I heard about it at school one morning. I guess there was a stretch up at Springs where all the mailboxes had been shot up. According to Ray Henderson, who lives up there, it was worth driving out to see. Perforated mailboxes.

First thing, I thought of Jesse. That he might've done it.

When I caught up with him, I asked him.

"First I ever heard about it," he said. "Up at Springs?"

And he isn't that good an actor. I can usually tell if he's lying, and I don't think he was.

The important thing, though—and Jesse picked up on it right away—was I'd *thought* he might have done it. Which is just as bad, in Calamus. In fact it would have been out of character for Jesse to shoot up property for no reason. Jesse could be stupid, thoughtless, but not malicious. True, he liked to talk, like how he was going to get back at Judith Horton's old man. But Jesse forgot about it before he could come up with a plan. He never thought that far ahead. It was just talk. Joking around. Like whenever he got in a reflective mood he said he was going to blow up the dam and take off to California. That's about as calculating as Jesse ever got.

"Hey, don't get me wrong," I said, when he gave me that bruised look. "I didn't think you did it."

But the damage was done. I had asked him. Jesse, when he's paying attention, is no fool. He knew what I'd thought. What everybody must be thinking. Whether he did it or not. And I still believe he didn't shoot the mailboxes.

AFTER the last football game, I sat on a bench in the locker room for a while, still in uniform. Lorna had Friday-night duty at the barbershop. She wouldn't get off until midnight, so I was in no hurry to get anywhere. Fred Moore, the cock-eyed equipment manager, built separate piles in front of the drying room for jerseys, pants, shoulder pads, hip pads. Helmets by the door. Whites at the washing machine. It looked like a graveyard, with parts of the victims stacked separately for a more efficient burial.

I lifted my jersey off and threw it on the appropriate pile, then peeled off my gear to shower.

By the time I got dressed and left the locker room, I'd resolved to catch up with Jesse, if I could find him. He hadn't been in school that day, and I had a hollow stomach about it. Maybe Lorna and I could grab him and set him down—tie him to a tree, if necessary—and figure out what was going on.

I checked in at the dance to see if Jesse was there. He wasn't. And his car wasn't at the parking lot. I drove the pickup downtown. At the barbershop I sat at the counter and ate on a cheeseburger and nursed a chocolate milkshake.

"You're not the only one looking for Jesse," Lorna said, as she passed with an armload of dirty dishes.

Mrs. Swenson was on too, and the barbershop was pretty hectic. I had to wait until Lorna called in another order, delivered yet another, and came back with a damp towel to wipe the countertop in front of me.

"Arne Lund came in," she said. "All riled up."

Which was unusual in itself. Arne—a veteran log truck driver with close-cropped silver hair that would hold its part in a tornado—never got riled up. "Says he was down five gallons on his pickup tank, right after topping it off."

An order came up at the kitchen window, and I had to wait for Lorna to come back.

"Saw Jesse driving out that way, earlier," she said. "Siphoning gas is what they think."

"They? Somebody saw him do it?"

"Not exactly," Lorna said. "Arne told Miles, and a bunch of them were talking. I guess Jesse was in the vicinity, after school. I didn't catch all of it," she said. She rearranged the salt and pepper shakers and the menu while Mrs. Swenson passed. "They want to question him."

With Lorna coming and going, it was hard to talk. Although the crowd was thinning, the barbershop was still loud enough that we were actually fairly private. What we had here, I was thinking, was a lot of jumping to conclusions. Anything went wrong, it must be Jesse's fault. So he'd been in the vicinity? He must be guilty. Jesse couldn't even go for a drive in the country anymore.

On the other hand, Larry Wirtz had seen Jesse's red Ford headed out of town, toward Portland. Which wasn't unusual. Where else would he go if he wasn't in Calamus? And Arne

Lund's place wasn't far off the road. But that wasn't the question. No doubt Jesse's car had been spotted out there, but that didn't mean he was stealing gas. Not even Jesse would be stupid enough to steal gas from a logger. Would he?

I worked myself into a sweat about it.

I felt a clap on my left shoulder, and turned that way, as Jesse took a seat on my right. "We got to talk," he said. Which is the way things work with Jesse. Always a step ahead.

"Hey," I said. "What's up?"

Jesse looked up, and seemed to find nothing on the ceiling.

"Where you been?"

"Let's see," he said. "First I shot out power line insulators and poisoned the town water supply. I stole that blue Impala from the Chev Garage, and on my way to Portland I burned the Cliffs store. I robbed a bank on 82nd," he said, ticking the fingers of his left hand, "and raped the teller. With the money I bought a trunkful of dynamite, but I haven't blown up the dam yet. Nothing much," he said, punching me on the shoulder. "What've you been up to?"

"One TD pass, three extra points. Calamus 21, St. Helens 6."

"Good boy," Jesse said.

"Oh, waitress!" he called to Lorna.

She ignored him.

"That chick is dynamite," he said. "Don't think I haven't noticed the change, either," he whispered. I smelled the beer on his breath. "Was I right? Do they all like it?"

"The Grand Poobah would like a cup of coffee," I said to Lorna, when she came by. "Black."

"Two cheeseburgers, giant French fries, and a monster chocolate shake," he said. "I drove all the way from Portland thinking about your shake."

"Kitchen's closed," Lorna said. "Too late."

He spun a full rotation on the stool, and seemed about to fall off it before catching himself. It was not, however, the move of a drunk.

"Dynamite," he said. "If Wade Curren is too dull for you, you know where you can find me."

"Tell you what," I said to Lorna, when she came back. "We'll just take this coffee out to the car. Meet you out there."

"Ten minutes," she said.

Not much of the crowd remained in the barbershop, but nobody left after Jesse came in. The snoops. Gossips. I got him out to his car. He'd been drinking, all right, but he was too alert to have had that much. Jesse was wound up tight, not slowed down. I'd seen him drunk, and it wasn't that.

"This is the end of the FGWs," he said. His laugh was hollow. "Now the FGF."

I waited.

"Fans Get Fucked," he said. There was an edge to his voice, an underlying meanness, that I'd never noticed before. He was acting sneaky, is what it was. Like he had a plan or something. Which was not like Jesse. If Jesse had something up his sleeve, he'd usually roll up his sleeve and show me.

I reached across and turned the key far enough to get the radio on. As I did it, my foot bumped something on the floor. I reached down and picked it up. A section of hose. The smell of gasoline on it was enough to make me sick, just sick.

"What's this?" I said.

Would he tell me?

"Siphon hose," he said. "I needed gas to go get some money and pick up the equipment. Those loggers, they never miss it."

I thought not of Jesse, this poor dumb Jesse, but of Link, how disappointed he would be. Stealing gas from a logger was about the worst thing you could do in Calamus. I sat back in the seat and pictured Jesse's world collapsing around him.

"They think you did it," I said.

But he didn't seem to hear me.

"You're a suspect!" I shouted at him. "They know!"

Jesse seemed strangely unaffected by this. As if he were in a trance. His lips were tight, his eyes straight ahead. He gripped the steering wheel as if the car might rise from the street of its own accord, and he had to hold it down.

"You know what I told you about finding your own special spot?" he said.

"Hey look," I told him. "Don't give me that. You are in deep, deep shit."

He remembered his coffee, on the dashboard, and took a sip from it. But he didn't look at me.

"Fuck 'em," he said.

"Oh, sure. Keep acting like a dope," I said. "They'll put you away. Steal gas from a logger and then come staggering into town like a drunken fool, you think you can—"

"You think I'm drunk?"

"I think you're stupid," I said.

Lorna locked up and came out to the car. I stepped out and let her slide into the middle. She'd brought a grease-splotched brown sack with a couple of cheeseburgers in it. The three of us sat in the front seat while Jesse ate. Which seemed to settle him down a little.

"Smells like gas in here," Lorna said.

"The dumb shit," I said. She gave me a questioning look and I just nodded.

"Gad," she said.

"Fuck 'em." Jesse tossed his empty dinner sack into the backseat. "We got business to take care of."

He started up the Ford and backed out. Everything in town but the Silvertip was closed up. Like bugs to a street-light, cars circled the building and its beer signs. Jesse gunned the motor for the folks inside, and we surged up Main Street. Up on the flat, house lights were out. Only one straggling car passed us coming the other way, and the school slumbered next to the dark football field.

"Better turn yourself in," I said. "Best thing. Maybe they'll . . ."

"What are we doing?" said Lorna. "Where are we going?"

Past the back side of the Entering Calamus sign, Jesse

pulled off to the side of the road. When his car door swung open and the inside light came on, he had this crazed look on his face. "I want you to see this," he said.

We got out and he led us around the mill through Hankins' hayfield. Jesse had a flashlight. He held it behind him, as we walked, so Lorna could see. I followed Lorna. I should have stopped him, I guess. But I didn't. He was leading us toward the spillway. Frogs cut their croaking as we approached. Everything was quiet except the smell of sawdust.

Because it was overcast, I could barely see Tom Creek and the pool below the spillway. But it was seared into my memory from before. This pool of horror. Jesse trying to save the salmon.

"You know what I told you about finding a spot?" he said. He was still in his trance, as if Lorna weren't even there.

"You'll know it when you see it?" I said.

"Right," he said.

"Where you'll hear a spirit or something," I said, mainly for Lorna's benefit. "Is this it? Your spot?"

I didn't get it. This was the dumbest and deafest, least-spirited place I could think of. Of all possible spots, the mill-pond spillway was the anti-spot. The end of the line. The break in the circle.

"Come on over here," Jesse said. He was excited, now. Revved up. "I been working on this all day."

He led us away from the spillway, toward some bushes behind a knoll. I had the flashlight, now, and was looking mainly for poison oak.

"Over here," Jesse said. I played the light that way. He was bent over a small boxlike contraption. With wires. And a handle on top.

A plunger.

Lorna gasped. I tried to stop him, but it was too late. He pushed down on the plunger and there was this terrific explosion. The ground shook. The sky over the spillway blasted yellow-white as high as a church. I pushed Lorna and fell with her behind a tree. Debris from the explosion came raining around us. The smell of explosives hung in the air and was replaced by the sound of the millpond rushing through the gap in its spillway. The first of the logs hit the gap like giant Pick Up Sticks and piled into the opening and down into lower Tom Creek, clearing brush and snapping small trees.

And even as the spillway and its pool were being ripped apart I pictured the logs scouring Tom Creek downstream, where Lorna and I had seen those salmon spawn. Mud over the gravel. Wiping them out. Those eggs. Killing what good there was.

Jesse laughed and whooped. He didn't even know. Trying to help, and he thought he had.

NINETEEN

~~~~~~~

LIKE A WHITE STONE in clear lake, you might float over it and think, *That's pretty, I'll reach down and get it.* But it's deeper than you thought. You can't reach it. Your hand ripples the surface, and then you can't see the white stone anymore. But you know it's there.

CALAMUS was empty without Jesse.

They sent him to MacLaren to finish the school year.

When he left it was like the town's engine was in for repairs. But of course nothing really stops. School doesn't close. The barbershop stays open. Log trucks growl into town, and the mill keeps chewing up logs. They yarded the logs from lower Tom Creek and made a total mess of it, and soon a new spillway for the millpond was going up. Lorna and I got along fine, perhaps because I paid closer attention. Football season moved into basketball season. And basketball moved into baseball. And somewhere in our world—but not in Tom Creek, because Jesse had "fixed" it—salmon eggs hatched into tiny fishlike creatures and slithered up to see what the world had in store.

Before he left, Jesse gave me his car.

"Aw, I couldn't take your car," I said, when he tossed me the keys.

"Don't be a jerk," he said. "You and Lorna keep those seats warm for me. They'll give me a ride over there." As if MacLaren were camp. Which was more or less his attitude. "I'm no jooovenile," Jesse said.

But of course he was—a JD, a juvenile delinquent. I didn't know what would happen when he turned eighteen. Whether they would transfer him to Salem, or what. Jesse would finish the school year at MacLaren, by which time he'd be eighteen. And get his money? Nobody knew. What was clear, at the barbershop and around town, was that Jesse wouldn't be welcome back in Calamus. MacLaren wasn't enough. "Ought to string him from a tree with his long black hair."

People can be so stupid.

MacLaren is what they call a correctional facility, a school and work farm for hoods. Lorna and I drove over to Mac-Laren—down the big valley toward Salem—almost every week. Sunday was visitors day.

The first time we saw it, MacLaren wasn't nearly as grim as I'd imagined. What you see from the road is a high Cyclone fence topped with barbed wire, but once we checked in at the gate it looked like a regular school. The big yellow-brick main building had no bars on the windows. Flat cinderblock dorms surrounded the central building, and a grove of oak trees hid green cottages. Acres of farm and orchard spread behind barns and equipment sheds, beyond which—out of sight—were probably more fence and barbed wire.

The hungry stares Lorna got reminded me what might break Jesse if anything did. No girls at MacLaren.

I guess I'd expected to speak to him through bullet-proof glass. Instead, a nonuniformed, unarmed guard led us to a yellow-walled, windowless room with stuffed chairs and dog-eared *Field & Stream*s on a table.

The guard departed, and we were left alone.

Jesse came bouncing in wearing loose-fitting khaki pants

and a long-sleeved work shirt, but the main thing was his hair. They'd cropped off his hair. He had a brush cut, not well done. It made his ears stick out, his grin even goofier.

"Do they scalp everybody," Lorna said, "or just the Indians?"

"This is what they're wearing." He ran his hand over the bristle. "It's cool over here."

Also his salmon vertebrae necklace was missing.

"Had to check it," he said. "No jewelry. This green badge," he said, fingering the plastic on the pocket of his shirt, "is your status. Those guys with red badges, they can't blow their nose without permission. We got killers, fire bugs. Rapers, burglars, all kinds of talent."

Lorna wanted to know all about it.

So mainly we listened to Jesse talk. He was in good spirits. MacLaren was just another school, according to Jesse. Without cheerleaders. They had a basketball team, but no road trips. Jesse was the star, of course, and he was making new friends. In class they were mainly stupid, he told us, but some were pretty funny. Jesse had to make his bed so tight you could bounce a quarter on it, if he had a quarter. He'd never been much for farming, but that part wouldn't get going until spring. There was too much heat in his dorm. The food was sick.

"It's allowed," Jesse informed us, "to bring in cookies or cakes and stuff. If you think of it next time."

I'd been worried, driving in, that he might try to break out. With all that open space, and orchards for cover, MacLaren didn't even look guarded.

"Looks like you could escape if you wanted to."

"Why would I try that?" he said. "Might as well wait. I wouldn't want one of those red badges," he said. "I got places to go, money to spend." He licked the tips of his fingers and slicked his eyebrows. "I'm practicing good behavior."

Driving away from MacLaren, I was in a better mood. Jesse's spirit wasn't bent, much less broken. Also there was that part about the red badges. It was the first time I'd heard Jesse talk about consequences.

"They don't have a big enough box for him," I said. "MacLaren's not going to package Jesse."

"Maybe not MacLaren," she said.

She shifted in the seat, and we watched the farm country go by. Filbert orchards. Fields of corn stubble. Fencerows and hayfields. The Willamette Valley had a more settled feeling to it than Calamus. Everything organized, parceled off. The biggest trees were in yards.

"So what's going to happen?" she said. "He's got no people, does he? He'll end up a drunk on Burnside in Portland. That's where you see the Indians."

"Not Jesse."

Which was a pretty good question, however. When you come right down to it, Jesse wasn't even an Indian. Not really. He'd grown up at Celilo and all, and he had these stories from the old guys, which didn't make much sense now. It wasn't something you could believe in. What you think of as Indians didn't exist anymore. He was Jesse—however it happened—not an Indian. But then he was, too.

"What's missing is a place," I said. "You take away Celilo, give him money . . . What he doesn't have is a place."

I looked over at her, and Lorna was running her tongue across her chipped tooth. "It's his own fault," she said. "He's speeding down a night road with his headlights off."

When we got to Willamette Falls, just short of Oregon City, I pulled off. The viewpoint is up on a bluff, overlooking where the Willamette River tumbles off a smooth table and comes frothing down. Like Celilo, but more sudden, taller. Now it's paper mills and the smell of bad eggs, but the falls are still there. We sat on the rock ledge and watched the falls for a while.

"You know," I said, "Jesse thinks he died when he was little."

"Huh?" she said.

One thing about Lorna, as smart as she is, you throw her a change-up and she just watches it go by.

"Got killed," I said. "Over at Celilo, he was just a little crawler. A pickup backed over him."

"Jesse?" She sucked her chipped tooth, like the last draft of juice and air through a straw. "Well he didn't get killed too bad," she said.

"Killed him dead, Jesse says. He came back as another person. That's what they believe. Can happen."

A piece of lumber, the shape of an ironing board, came down the river. We watched it take the falls. It *was* an ironing board.

"Bunk," she said. "He's got you buffaloed. Him and his Coyote stories. You believe anything Jesse says."

"I didn't say I believed it. *Jesse* believes it. He thinks he got killed when he was little, and came back." The whole thing seemed more plausible when Jesse told it. "I mean it's sort of like religion, isn't it?" I said. "Faith. A lot of people believe in heaven, that they can go there. Maybe they can, if they believe it."

Lorna gave me her look. She was real disappointed in me.

MY DRIVING Jesse's Ford was the subject of another Trying-To-Say at our house, but I stood my ground. Driving that '57 Ford Fairlane was more than an opportunity. It was a duty. The first dry spell we got, I waxed and polished it, and did the chrome. Jesse had let the white sidewalls go, but they cleaned up bright. I looked forward more and more to our trips to MacLaren, not just to check in on Jesse but also to get out of town. Lorna had always felt that way about leaving Calamus, no matter what the occasion or how short the trip. Now I did, too.

Jesse saw us drive up one time, and maybe that's what got him, seeing his Ford Fairlane all spiffed up. He'd been at MacLaren a couple, three months, now, and he was in a purple funk.

"Put me in the trunk," he said. "We'll drive to Lani Louie's and eat some real food. I been so good."

Nothing we said seemed to cheer him up.

Earlier, on one of our visits, I had knocked on the door of the whatever-you-call-him, the Administrator, to check on Jesse's status. Once he got over his surprise to see Lorna and me, he'd said what a good guy Jesse was and Jesse would probably get out as soon as he graduated, in June. If he toed the line. Which Jesse knew, but now he was having a bad day.

"Well, you got to stick with it," Lorna said to Jesse, "because we got plans. When you get out, we're going to float the river."

"We are?" Jesse perked up.

"Wade and I are building a raft," she said. Which was news to me. Lorna got that filmy look in her eyes like when she gets carried away with her own voice. "It'll be big enough for all three of us," she said, "and we can put in below the dam."

She told him the whole story, our parking story, about how we were going to leave Calamus by floating the river to the Willamette, to the Columbia, and on out to sea. Astoria. Lorna was giddy with the whole idea of it, and I went along. What harm could it do? Cheer him up.

"We'll just let the current take us," I said, "wherever it goes."

Which was just a story, but it turned Jesse around. Jesse loves a story, and this was a good one. His black eyes got their old flash, and he cackled about how we could fish on the way. Sleep on the islands. He must have known it was just a story, not something you'd really do. But it really picked him up.

ON SOME of our trips to MacLaren we took Link, the old drooler, who took a strong liking to Lorna. With three of us in the front seat, me driving, I watched for how long it would take for him to spread himself wide enough to pick up knee contact with Lorna. When she didn't shrink from it, Link was bumping her before we even got out of Calamus.

"Why don't you just sit on her lap?" I said.

"Oh, 'scuse me," he said, all innocence. "Could I?"

"If you take a bath." Lorna laughed.

It stung him. But only momentarily.

"Now that that there scamp Indian has run out on me," Link told her, "you could come live with me. It gets frightful lonesome over there in the woods."

The next time we took him to MacLaren, Link had soaked himself in enough Old Spice to float a boat. We had to crack both fly windows, even though it was raining. Crazy old fart. This time he got all upset about Lorna's hair. She had streaked it, blond. It didn't bother me. I kind of liked it. Whatever Lorna does usually turns out all right. Anyway Link thought her hair was just awful, and he told her.

"Help stomp out natural beauty," Link said.

Which was a high compliment, the way I heard it, but Lorna didn't think so. She pouted.

"Don't get your tit in a wringer, darlin'," he said. "It ain't nothin' but a bump in the road to me. Pull over at that Tastee Freeze there, Wade, my boy. I'll treat this gloomy girl and you to a pop."

"You crusty old fossil," Lorna said. "I'll buy my own."

Link liked Lorna so much he even promised to take her out over the Columbia River bar with us next time. "If I live 'til August," he said.

IN TRIG one day the intercom crackled and Coach Garth's voice came on. He cleared his throat, and then: *"Attention. Wade Curren, please report to the office."*

I don't normally get called to the principal's office, unless maybe it's football season. Coach Garth has these brain-storms and wants to put new plays in. But this was April, not football season. Maybe somebody had a heart attack.

Some kind of emergency. This fear grew stronger when I saw Judge Moore, the doctor, with Coach Garth in the office.

But they were smiling. Positively beaming.

"Princeton Tiger!" said Judge Moore, raising his fat unlit cigar in salute.

"Feast your eyes on this letter, Wade," said Coach Garth. He shoved the sheet across his desk toward me.

"Old Nassaw!" said Judge Moore. Judge was the school board chairman, was why Coach Garth called him in. Because the letter was from Princeton, and I'd been admitted. My hands were busy with the letter, so Coach Garth and Judge Moore shook hands with one another and pounded each other on the back.

Judge lit his cigar. "Boy oh howdy."

"Whatta you say, Wade?"

"Thank you," I said. "I mean amazing. Just amazing!"

And it really was. To tell you the truth, I hadn't given Princeton much thought since filing the application. It was more like Lorna's and my mother's idea. I didn't think I'd get in. I figured Corvallis, Oregon State . . . And what with this big scholarship, too. It was a stunner.

"Two thousand sixty dollars!" said Judge Moore.

"This is the carbon," Coach Garth said. "No doubt the real letter is in your mail." You'd think he'd gone to State. He was real proud. "They run the single wing."

"Woodrow Wilson," said Judge Moore. "The Ivy League!"

"This is a red-letter day," said Coach Garth. "Wade, you're a feather in the cap of the community."

I don't know. I thought they overdid it. It's kind of hard to hold your mouth straight when you're a feather in the cap of the community. Not that I wasn't excited. I was. I caught Lorna between classes, and told her. Lorna about flipped, first one way and then the other. She was happy for me, of course, but she was close to hysteria now about her own chances. She'd heard from two colleges. They hadn't agreed with Lorna's theory about having "exhausted the opportunities available to her in high school." She didn't get in. Get your grades up, they said. Be sure and apply next year.

Lorna was a wreck by the time her letter from Bryn Mawr came, a couple days later. She plucked the envelope like a live grenade from her box at the trailer court. Then she made me drive her up to Day Hill to open it.

"Open it for me," she said.

It was a thin envelope. I didn't want to open it. "Look, it's not the end of the world," I said. "Either way."

She clawed it open. After reading the first couple words, she slammed it on the seat. "Oh!!!" she wailed. "It's not fair!!!"

Lorna's quick eyes darted about the car, looking for a fight. As if maybe it were my fault. Her world had come flying apart. One more year in Calamus was a life sentence. She had nothing left to live for. I got her in a clinch and held her tight. Which she was too hammered to resist.

"It's just . . . not fair!!" she sobbed. "You don't even . . . want to leave," she said. "And I can't!" She pulled away from me and shook her head at the total, complete, reverse-rain injustice of it all. "They take . . . a plodder like you."

ONE OF our trips out of town was to Portland, not to MacLaren. Duncan phoned school. They had to keep his car in the shop overnight, and he wanted me to pick him up at work. Which was a reasonable excuse to miss baseball practice. Not only reasonable but also welcome. Lorna wanted to go, naturally, and we left right after school.

It was one of the first warm days of spring. Trees sprouted new green tips, and daffodils poked up in yards. We headed out of town with the windows down. Lorna rested her head on my lap and hung her bare feet out the opposite window. But she soon tired of that because she couldn't see the road.

"What does he do, exactly, your dad?" she said, straightening up in the seat.

"Hard to say. Procurement and allocation."

"Mmmm."

"Getting things," I said. "Putting them places. A big outfit like NWG, somebody has to procure things. Allocate them. I don't know, exactly."

"People?" she said.

"Things. Contracts and bids. They take bids on things, and it goes through procurement and allocation."

"You don't know what he does?"

"He's a big shot, a boss. Bunch of people work for him."

Lorna fished through her purse and pulled out a bottle of nail polish.

"When we get there," she said, "I'll ask him what he does. And you listen. A person should know what his father does."

Lorna pulled her feet up, onto the seat, and began painting her toenails the color of Pepto-Bismol. This was a change, recently, nail polish. And her streaked hair. You never know about Lorna. The smell of nail polish mixed with honeysuckle from along the road. She blew on each of her freshly painted toes, in turn, and I wondered what more a person could possibly want, to know what love is.

I thought she was going to grill me some more about Duncan, but she'd wrapped that topic and was about to unfurl something else.

"Let me drive," she said.

"Aw, come on," I said.

The Cliffs curves were coming up. The road there cuts close to the bank, and you get the pipes echoing through the turns. Trees close to the road. Glimpses of Calamus River on the left. It's the best part of the drive to Portland. I pulled over at a turnout and we switched places, Lorna driving.

Which made it awkward where I should sit. The place for your woman passenger is snug against the driver. I felt like a fool in that position. I slung my left arm over the back of the seat, but that wasn't right either. Finally I scooted over by the window and put my elbow out to catch the breeze.

Lorna caught a log truck, which slowed us down through the curves. "You know," she said. "There's no real reason for me to stay in Calamus next year."

"Except to graduate, you mean?"

"They have correspondence courses," she said. "Darla Burt got her diploma at home, after she got pregnant. Lots of people do it. It's common," she said. "You mail in lessons and get a diploma. I could get straight A's and then go to college."

The log truck turned into the mill at Cliffs, which gave her open road ahead. She gunned it.

"What I was thinking," Lorna said, "was when you go to Princeton maybe I should go back there, too. I could get a job," she said. "I'll do correspondence courses. Tutor you."

We were getting into some major stuff here. I mean we should at least be parked on Day Hill for this. She passed a Wonder Bread truck. When we got back in the right lane, she looked over at me.

"You mean get married?" I said.

"Gad," she said. She gave me a look that would drive a crocus back into the ground. "Why get married?" she said. "Like a couple of jerks from Calamus?"

I jammed my right foot to the floorboard, but Lorna, too, saw the panel truck pull onto the road ahead of us. She braked in plenty of time. We'd reached the outskirts of city. Shopping centers, warehouses, housing developments. Like a great living thing, the city was spreading toward Calamus. Yellow Caterpillars prowled the hills, and the smell of fresh asphalt snaked into the car.

"Don't they have a rule? I have to live on campus?"

"For crying out loud," she said. She'd read the catalog. She knew the rules. "We wouldn't have to *live* together."

"What about your folks?" I said, thinking about my folks.

She accelerated into a yellow light. I leaned forward and watched for red. She beat it.

"It was just an idea," she said. She poofed her bangs. "You don't have to get so excited about it."

Lorna drove us across a Willamette bridge and into downtown Portland. She found a parking place close to the NWG building—a skyscraper, twelve stories tall. We were early. Duncan would get off at five, and we had half an hour.

"Let's go up," I said, meaning to Duncan's office.

Waiting for the elevator, inside, I said hello to a man in rumpled brown pants. He gave a start and fingered the row of pens in his shirt pocket as if I might have reached for one. It's something I always forget. You don't say hello to strangers in Portland.

The elevator stopped at each floor—we were headed for the sixth—and more people got on. A harelip woman with stringy black hair and thick glasses. A barrel-thighed Negro clutched a packet of fat brown envelopes over his belly— which rolled so far his belt, if he wore one, was hidden. A genius-looking guy with toothpick arms stared at the elevator ceiling, moving his lips, doing long division in his head. A secretary with eyebrows penciled in stepped on, saw the up arrow, and backed off. A bald fellow with high-water pants and Buster Brown shoes had tufts of hair growing out his ears.

If dwarf jugglers had entered at the fifth floor, I wouldn't have been surprised.

We got off with the genius at the sixth floor. Lorna stepped aside and he hurried ahead, his shoulders hunched, his lips still moving.

I'd been to Duncan's office before, but not recently. The thing is, they keep shifting things around. What they call offices at NWG are actually partitions, high enough you can't see over. The sixth floor is a maze, is what I'm trying to say. It wasn't my fault we got lost. Over the gray partitions I heard the clack of typewriters, the thump of a ditto machine, fragments of conversation, the low hum of ventilation. But do you think I could find Duncan's office?

After another couple of turns, I felt panic rising. We were swimming this maze rather than walking it. We were trapped in the millpond.

Lorna found a helpful woman in swirl-frame glasses who directed us to Duncan's secretary, Carla. Carla and I had met before at an NWG picnic. She gave Lorna the once-over.

Duncan heard us and came out from his partition.

"Hey, kids," he said. "You're early." He was glad to see us, glad we came up. Duncan led us around to other partitions and introduced Lorna and me to his colleagues, is what he calls them. Some of them I'd met before, but now I was exhibit A, the chief freak, the amazing Wade Curren who was going from hicksville to Princeton. I felt nauseous. But it wasn't their fault. That's just the way people are, and I should've been happy about it. It was more like this building and the coats and ties and the partitions, the whole setup. NWG.

I couldn't shake the idea of the millpond, landlocked salmon. I was actually having trouble breathing.

"Just a couple things to wrap up," Duncan said, when he'd finished taking us around. "You kids can wait here."

"How about if we . . . meet you outside?" I said. "Down at the park."

In the elevator, I was still drowning. We began our descent, and my stomach bumped to the top of my skull. Out at the park, across from the NWG building, I headed for the water fountain.

"You look terrible," Lorna said. "Hey, I didn't mean to upset you. It was just an idea," she said. She was still on her plan. "We kids don't have to . . ."

"Oh, it's not that," I said.

And it wasn't. Something else was wrong.

We took a seat on a green slatted park bench. Broad-leaf trees shaded the park, but the smell was of city buses and traffic. I didn't know what the hell it was. I couldn't explain it. Like maybe you get a glimpse of white stone in clear lake, and then you reach for it and it's too deep. Your hand ripples the surface and you can't see the white stone anymore.

TWENTY

≋≋≋

IN THE OLD DAYS you could go Out West. Link came Out West. Gus Schwarz, before him, came Out West. Old Huckleberry Finn, for example, he could light out for the territory. The trouble is, Calamus *is* the territory. Calamus puts you flat up against it, geographically speaking. Calamus is where the Oregon Trail petered out and folks bumped up against the Pacific Ocean and filled up the big valley. Dammed the big river, started mowing down trees and organizing things.

Out West still seems the natural way to go. Jesse, I figured, was headed Out West.

I don't know. I guess Out West is more like a way of thinking than a figure of speech. The brain can't quite wrap the idea of going Out East, for example. Or Back West.

JESSE got released from MacLaren in June.

And he'd changed, all right. We did some things together when he got out, but we were forcing it, trying too hard. Even our crossbuck handshake was out of sync. One time we actually bumped knuckles on it. Jesse laughed it off, but his laughter carried a harder edge, a deeper rattle.

I guess it didn't help when right after he got out Jesse wanted to see the raft. What raft? I'd forgotten all about it. "The raft to run the river on," he said. Jesse had believed that story. It had just been a story, to cheer him up. And then, when he found out it wasn't true, it was like Lorna and I had deserted him. Let him down. Sometimes Jesse didn't have a very good grip on the real world. A lot had been going on, what with college coming up and everything. What did he expect?

One change in Jesse, which had nothing to do with me, was he'd come into the rest of his money. In the months he'd been away, Jesse turned eighteen. The trust fund for lost fishing rights at Celilo Falls was now legally his. All he had to do was go to the bank. Jesse bought a new Pontiac Bonneville, in slick dark burgundy. One night he straightened out the Cliffs curves on his way back from Portland. Totalled the car. Next he showed up in a 1958 Cadillac El Dorado.

"I was gonna trade that Pontiac anyway," he said. "Ashtray got full."

Jesse was rich, smart, on top of the world.

"Stupid siwash," was the word at the barbershop as Jesse roared up Broadway in his ice-blue Cadillac. "Gonna get fat and drunk as all the rest of 'em. Squattin' on Burnside."

"If he lives that long."

"Ain't got the sense God gave a dog."

I tried to talk to him. Link tried to talk to him, but we might as well have tried to stay the wind. Jesse didn't have to work, and he was just all this loose energy flying around. Often he'd go off to Portland and Link wouldn't have seen him for days at a time. I worried about him, sure, but he was beyond me. I began to think Jesse and I were pieces to separate puzzles.

Which was not, however, what I wanted to think.

So when Jesse said, "You're looking pale, man. What say we take a drive over to Indian country?" I was ready.

"Just what I was thinking," I said. "That's what I had in mind all the time."

In fact Lorna and I had decided maybe it wasn't necessary for us to wait for a nuclear attack before we did an overnighter. As a matter of principle, however, Lorna said it couldn't be in Calamus. We had to go somewhere.

"You want to?" Jesse said. "You can get away?"

Like I was a prisoner or something.

"Sure," I said.

WE LEFT early Saturday morning. I had fifty-two dollars, and a change of clothes in my green Wilson sports bag. Lorna was waiting at the mailboxes in front of the trailer court. She'd bought a looks-like-leather suitcase, and I set it in the trunk next to Jesse's bag—which was just that, a shopping bag from Wilkins' store. We passed the back side of the Entering Calamus sign to "Ooh Poo Pah Doop" on the radio. I drove. And there's nothing like leaving town, when you come right down to it. Windows down, radio up, in Jesse's big broad ice-blue Cadillac.

I about put them both through the windshield at the Eagle Creek stop sign.

"Jesus!" Jesse said.

"Power brakes," I said. "I'll get used to this."

"Gad. One more mistake and I'm driving."

I smelled the cedar mill before we came to it. And then the strawberry fields, ripe for picking. I was getting the feel for this car, which was an amazing machine. More gadgets. I jiggered the whatnots on the armrest. Windows went up, the aerial down. With another gizmo I put the seat forward and changed the angle with a low-groaning push. I floored it, and the surge pressed us against the seat, which was black leather, like waxed. Lorna slid back and forth on the curves.

"Stick some of this gum on your buns, darlin'," Jesse said. "If you can't sit still."

"Lorna's still immature in a lot of ways," I said.

"Cut the crap."

At Sandy I pulled in for gas at the Flying A. Lorna went in and got a road map. She likes to be sure. We were going to The Dalles, but we would stop off first at his mom's place on the Warm Springs Reservation. It was a variation of the Mount Hood Loop. You can circle to the south and east of Mount Hood to the Columbia River, and then come back toward Portland down the gorge.

The Cadillac sucked at the gas nozzle until the numbers on the pump rolled up five dollars and something. Over five dollars. Jesse let me pay. He took to the backseat when we pulled out. In the mirror, over the left tail fin, the service station attendant pushed his greasy cap back on his head like, *Rich people. How do they do it?*

I stuck my left elbow out the window and steered with one hand. The road swung into a direct line with Mount Hood, straight ahead. The white mountain loomed like Truth itself, or a bad painting, over the purple distance of timberline and between road-hugging firs, crisp dark green.

I was a little concerned that Jesse had let me pay for gas. "Hey, Red Rider. You got any money? Wampum?"

"Money!" Jesse said. "I love it. Lorna. Snatch my sunglasses from the glove box, would you?"

Lorna snapped the glove box door down. There was more money in there than I'd ever seen in one place. Packets of bills, with a band around each stack. I about ran us off the road. Lorna began thumbing it, counting it, while Jesse laughed in the backseat.

"Think that'll get us through the weekend?" he said. "And that's just change," he said. "For the Cadillac."

Which no doubt was true. It just sets you back, is all, seeing that much cash right there in the car.

We hurtled toward the top of the world in this ice-blue Cadillac, up the green shoulder of Mount Hood and into morning sun. Lorna put her hand out the window and hooked the roof, like holding it down.

But Lorna's bladder, when she's excited, doesn't hold

much. I pulled off the highway for her at Toll Gate, a camp-ground. There was a historical marker. Toll Gate was where old Sam Barlow stopped the covered wagons and charged them for using his trail into the Willamette Valley. I knew all about it because of my mother, the history nut. It was one of her favorite things, this last branch of the Oregon Trail.

Lorna got back from her pee and walked straight to the Cadillac driver's side. Which was fair enough. Let her drive.

She peeled out onto the highway. I recalled that family trip, years ago, in the old green Chev. Mother and Duncan, and us kids in the backseat. It was our return trip from Celilo Falls. We retraced the Barlow Trail, even the parts that weren't paved, and never would be . . .

MOTHER had her maps, and she pointed Duncan where we should turn off, coming from The Dalles. This part of the Barlow Trail was a country road of thick brown dust, smooth and straight through dwarf pines. Dust muffled the car.

I heard a loud honk behind us. I looked around and saw a red Dodge pickup, very close. Driving was an angry man who waved over his steering wheel. He wanted to pass.

We'd been clipping right along, but now our car surged forward, faster. Duncan stared straight ahead, aiming us down the single-lane road. His shoulders tensed. His knuck-les clamped white around the steering wheel. Duncan wasn't going to let the pickup pass. I looked back, where the guy was punching at the horn, his face a storm.

Duncan, Mother said. *Don't be silly. Let him pass.*

And eat his dust all the way? Duncan said.

There was more honking. Carol Ann started to cry.

We were really flying, probably as fast as that old Chev could go. Mother leaned over the seat to calm Carol Ann, but she was frantic herself. This was not the way she'd planned to retrace the Barlow Trail, and Mother is no good at sur-prises. I hoped Duncan would keep going, would not budge. This was a very exciting thing.

Duncan, STOP this, Mother shouted, but a deep and secret signal had been switched on inside him.

The CHILDREN! Mother cried.

Duncan ignored her. His jaw muscle bulged below his ear.

The road bent west and up into mountains, getting narrower. We were going fast. The turns got tighter as the grade steepened. Mother was a pale and shaking ghost beside Duncan in the front seat.

We reached the summit, where there was a wide section of road, turnoffs on both sides. Duncan pulled off, rolling up his window to avoid the dust. The pickup screamed past. The horn-blast slid into his own dust like a train whistle into a tunnel.

The bastard, Duncan growled.

He glared at Mother. His eyes were a bright deep blue, Link's blue. A drop of sweat trickled off his bald spot and into the fringe of hair above his ear.

When the dust settled, we could see the pickup pulled off down the trail. The guy was striding back toward us. Duncan got out and slammed the door so hard it rocked the car. Oh, shit, I thought, this guy was bigger than Duncan. They yelled at each other. As they closed in on one another, this guy's steps got smaller and you could see him take in Duncan's eyes. Suddenly he remembered where he had to get to in such a hurry. Duncan jawed him all the way back to his pickup. He kicked out the pickup's left taillight as it pulled out and away.

I thought it was great. As he walked back to our car, I watched Duncan's new blue eyes, those eyes that are always in reserve. Distant. Submerged. It was one of the few times I ever saw that fury in Duncan. It fit with what you hear at the barbershop about Link's youngest son—young stump-kicking, fire-breathing Duncan, they said, who was the wildest of them all.

• • •

"THAT'S a dumb story," Lorna said. "That's not your dad."

Which was the whole point.

"It's not a story," I said. "It really happened. I don't know," I said. "About Duncan. It's like my dad is dormant or something. Or he already happened, and he's through. There was something there that isn't there anymore."

What it actually reminded me of was those land-locked salmon, to tell you the truth, but I didn't mention that.

"Your dad was a logger?" Jesse said. "I never knew that."

"All of Link's sons were loggers," I said. "The others still are, but not in Calamus. It was only after Duncan came back from the Navy," I said, "with Mom, that he left the woods. He'd probably still be a logger but one day he was sitting eating his lunch, out on a site, when a widowmaker fell on a guy sitting right next to him. Killed that man dead. Duncan walked out of the woods for good that day. Went to college."

"That's a better story," Lorna said.

"No, really. That's what happened."

LORNA arched that big blue Cadillac over the highway summit at Government Camp, and down off the other side of the Cascades. Fir trees and rhododendrons gave way to tall straight pines with thick red bark like cracked mud. Undergrowth backed off. Then the pines got smaller, more spaced, and gave way to scraggly juniper and dusty sage. Then there were no trees at all. The road cut straight ahead as far as I could see, in heat squiggles over the curve of the earth.

"Indian country," Jesse said.

Bunch grass and jagged rocks were fenced, although there was no sign of stock or crops. Sorry-looking place. Back from the road sat a low-shouldered shack, slats missing from its windmill. "Gad," said Lorna. "I can just picture those old treaty guys, spreading their maps across a polished oak table in Salem. Olympia. Washington, D.C.," she said. *"We'll give the Indians back all this land. All this country over here."*

Lorna was right. What a deal. On the Flying A map, the Warm Springs Reservation looked far more generous than it was. It was even shaded green.

Jesse said, "Hang a Louie at those mailboxes."

Lorna braked and wheeled us onto a gravel road. We trailed a rooster tail of fine red dust for maybe a dozen miles or so. Jesse's head joined us from the backseat, and he pointed Lorna onto an even worse road. It was a long driveway, with deep dry potholes. At the end of it, a sad cluster of buildings and a broken-down barn came into view. Around the yard lay scattered parts and tires of cars, a refrigerator, a boat trailer, a bathtub, and a Chevy panel truck that looked like it might be in working order.

Lorna pulled up on a bare dirt spot in front of the main dwelling. Our dust cloud overtook the car. All these brown people came spilling from the house, and Jesse was out of the car before Lorna and me, although the Cadillac is a two-door. The older people held back on the porch. Kids went straight to the car as we got out of it, and Jesse banged arms and punched shoulders with a couple guys more or less our age.

We shook hands. The fat one with cowboy boots and a sleeveless T-shirt was Harold Strikes the Heart. The shy one with the beak was Somebody Two Birds. I didn't catch his first name. Everybody was friendly, glad to see Jesse, and looking us over.

"You kids wash this car," Jesse said.

A clutch of them turned their toes in the dust and raced toward the pump to draw water. A committee of yellow chickens came peck-walking across the yard toward the car. Jesse kicked at one, sending it squawking.

"Is Reno around?" Jesse said.

His mother appeared in the doorway. She blinked as if she'd been in a dark place too long, and then she broke into a big wide grin. "Wa-Toosh-Ka," she said, or something like that, and she bounded down the porch steps with that same light grace I'd seen before, hopping puddles in the Calamus rain.

She and Jesse came together with arms extended. They oomphed their arms around one another and danced a little circle in the dirt.

Reno was a stout woman, in spite of the way she moved. She wasn't as young as I remembered, but the colors were right. She wore a tulip-yellow blouse and a one-color orange skirt that set off her dark skin. Her shiny black hair hung straight past her shoulders into a leather-and-bone barrette, before falling on down to her waist.

"Oh! Your hair!" She laughed. She turned him around and inspected his scalp, which had begun to recover from MacLaren but was still short. She flicked his ear. Her laughter bubbled from deep inside.

"These are my people," Jesse said. I thought he was talking to Lorna and me, but he was talking *about* us. He swung his arm proudly in Lorna's and my direction.

Reno pointed her broad smile toward me, first, and I stuck out my hand. She moved right past it and caught me in a hug. "You are welcome here," she said. I felt the warm pillows of her chest against my rib cage. She smelled of damp earth and cedar.

"How are you?" Reno said, holding me at arm's length.

It was a breathtaking question. I mean it was a normal set of words, but the way she said it and the depth of her eyes made me think she already knew the answer. *How was I?* I was basically confused, unworthy, too pale and timid, just stumbling along and picking up hints here and there.

"Fine," I said.

"Yes," she said.

"Wade's going off to Princeton College when the leaves turn," Jesse said, in a mock-Indian way. "Many hills to the east."

If Reno didn't like his tone, it showed only in her fleeting glance Jesse's way, a quick cloud past harvest moon. She turned to Lorna and gave her the same warm welcome.

"Lawrence White Fish, you old buzzard!" said Jesse, moving toward the porch. Lorna and I followed. "Lawrence, you look a hundred years old."

Lawrence White Fish sat apart from others on the porch. He was in a bucket car seat, I think from a Thunderbird, low on the porch. His leather face was a relief map of dry country. In gray-white streaks, his hair was pulled back toward two long braids, one of which fell forward of his left shoulder to the pocket of a washed-out blue-and-gray plaid flannel shirt. His white Converse high-tops hadn't been broken in.

It wasn't clear he recognized Jesse.

"Lawrence White Fish is your bull seal Indian fisherman," Jesse explained to Lorna and me. "The best. At Celilo . . . What's wrong with you, Lawrence?" Jesse said. "This is Jesse Howl. Talking to you."

"Lawrence don't talk no more," said Somebody Two Birds.

"Lawrence never did talk much," Jesse said. "You in there, Lawrence?" He pinched him on the arm. The old man's face was so creased his eyes were nearly closed, and one eye was milky.

"Can he hear us?" Jesse said.

"Don't shout," said Reno. "He can hear you."

IN THE way of old people everywhere, folks on the porch were a little put off by Jesse and his car, but they couldn't hide their pleasure he'd dropped by. What got me was it looked like you had to be under twenty or over sixty to be here. Young or old, nothing in between. An old guy with a single braid stood up and wordlessly pointed Lorna to his chair. She didn't notice. Not wanting to insult him—you never know—I sat in his chair. Which seemed the right thing to do until I did it.

The house was rickety, warped at the edges and porch

rails, like maybe it was salvaged from ancient flood. Inside I could hear the TV on loud. We settled into a wide circle on the floor of the porch. One of the little girls noticed Lorna's chipped tooth and wanted Lorna to show it to her again.

They talked about people they knew. Who's in jail, who screwed up, who's married and got two kids already. Reno stepped into the house for something. The kids yipping and splashing around the Cadillac changed its dust to streaks of mud.

"Heard you got locked up," said Somebody Two Birds.

"Got my money now," Jesse said. "I'm good. Got me these friends, here, and we're headed over to The Dalles."

"Wha'd he get locked up for?" said Somebody Two Birds to Lorna. Maybe he could get a straight answer from her. He lay on his stomach, with his head in the circle.

"He got drunk and dynamited the millpond."

Heads moved in the circle as if a breeze had come up. They exchanged knowing grins. Same old Jesse.

"Heard it was a dam you blew up."

"Sort of a dam. Just a little bitty thing," Jesse apologized.

"Blew up the dam!" said Harold Strikes the Heart. He was quite an admirer of Jesse. When he laughed, his stomach made waves beneath his shirt.

Lawrence White Fish rolled out of his Thunderbird seat. He braced himself against the railing to stand up, and gimped down the porch steps. He listed across the dirt yard toward the barn.

"Did you guys get your dam money?" Jesse said.

"Naw," said Harold Strikes the Heart.

"We won't, either," said Somebody Two Birds. "Them lawyers got it tied up. The Warm Springs is pooling our money to build a lodge." He was bitter about it. "For tourists," he said. "We're supposed to get jobs, but it hasn't started yet."

"Too bad," Jesse said. "Jobs."

Reno and Jesse were Klamaths, not Warm Springs, and

Klamaths were no longer a real tribe. It was sad, in a way, these poor people in this broken-down place and Jesse's car out there with a glove box full of money. The world was so strange sometimes. Different worlds, was what we had. Jesse, with all his money, wasn't in either of them. He was as exotic to these Indians as he was to Calamus.

These are my people, he had said about Lorna and me.

A horsefly settled on my knee and flexed his green wings. We listened to Jesse's laugh, and laughed with him.

Lawrence White Fish came from the barn dragging a pole net behind him.

"What's Lawrence up to?" Jesse said.

"Oh, he does that," said Harold Strikes the Heart. "He gets his net down, and he can't get it up again. Lawrence was a Dreamer," Harold explained. "He's getting worse."

Lawrence dragged the net behind him, sifting dust.

"He wants to go fishing!" said Jesse. "You ever take him fishing?"

Harold Strikes the Heart and Somebody Two Birds looked at each other as if Jesse were the Dreamer. "Where?" said Harold, shrugging his fat shoulders. "Since the dam there ain't no Celilo," he said. "No fishing the old way."

Jesse was already on his feet. "Let's go fishing!" he said. "Lawrence White Fish is the best." He leaped off the porch toward Lawrence White Fish and the net. Jesse picked it up for him.

"We got a rope?" Jesse shouted, checking terrain. "We'll fish off that platform over there. Momma! Get the drums!"

Jesse led the whole crowd of us, everybody who could walk, to a ravine behind the house. There was just a rocky knob, no platform that I could see. And no water, no water within miles of this place. But Jesse was going fishing right here.

And when Jesse gets it going, he gets the whole world going.

Kids brought a rope from the shed.

Jesse tied the safety line around him and Lawrence White

Fish at their waists. "Careful," he said. He shed his shirt and edged out on the rocky knob with the old man and the net. "Watch your step. It's slicker 'n goose grease up here." He toed the rough rock as if it were coated with river spray and salmon slime.

"Lorna!"

He pointed Lorna into the dry ravine, where she was supposed to go. It was about a ten-foot dropoff or so, with a milder entrance off to the left.

"You kids!" he said. "Wade, take those kids and start the salmon run!"

I didn't get what he meant, but the kids did. They followed his point to a clutch of chickens scratching and pecking in the yard. The kids sprang into action, herding chickens toward the ravine. And I joined them. We kept a wide base, sweeping with arms low. I batted a chicken back in line when he tried to escape. Chickens are quicker than you'd think. Chickens squawking and the kids whooping—"Yip, yip, yip"—brought dogs from under the house, and it was quite a wonderful and confusing thing.

"Fishing the wild Columbia!" Jesse shouted. "Come on home, you fish!"

We herded chickens into the ravine and headed them toward Lorna and the suspended net. Reno sat at the edge of the ravine with the drums wedged between her thighs. *Tee-tee pum pum pum, tee-tee pum pum pum,* she played the river crashing over the falls. She was laughing as loud as the drums, with her eyes closed and her yellow top swaying.

"Salmon are running!" Jesse shouted up top. "Hooooooo-eeeeeee! Silvers are coming."

In the bed of the ravine, kids sprawled and dove. Yellow dust rose like spray, high as a church. Some chickens managed to reverse course, but most of them were headed upstream.

Lorna tugged on the dip net, and Jesse jerked.

"Oh, we missed that one!" Jesse whooped.

One little brown girl, naked as sunrise, lunged at a

chicken. She got it by one leg. She shifted her grip to its neck and held it up flapping for Lorna. Lorna grabbed the chicken and flipped it into the waiting net.

"Fish!" Jesse bellowed.

He braced the pole against his shoulder and swung the net. The chicken thrashed and squawked and rained feathers on us.

"This one's a fighter!" Jesse shouted. "Sea lice are still on him! Look at this beauty!"

The net swung out of my sight. He twisted the pole and shook it, nearly forgetting Lawrence White Fish between his arms and the pole. But Jesse kept his balance. Then he swung the net back down into the fishing hole.

Reno drummed. *Tee-tee pum pum pum. Tee-tee pum pum pum.* Old people on the bank began chanting, in strange words. Jesse and Lawrence White Fish caught a lot of fish, Jesse describing each one as he pulled it out.

"A seal bit this one! Look at that scar!"

"A sixteen-pound silver!"

"Look at those scales."

More chickens came herded into the ravine. Some of them had already been caught once. We had a regular assembly line going. The fierce sun made the ravine a narrow, dusty oven. Jesse, up top, glistened with sweat. His Chinook necklace hung from his bare chest, and he was the bull seal Indian fisherman.

Lawrence White Fish wore a kind of half grin. The left side of his face worked and the right half didn't. His laugh was a series of grunts—"Nuh, nuh, nuh."

There came a break in the fish supply, and Jesse looked about shot. But one of the kids came up to the net with big wide eyes, a huge grin, and a mongrel dog yapping in his arms.

"Chinook!" I shouted up to Jesse.

We dumped the dog into the net.

"Chinook!" Jesse yelled, bending at the pole. "Ole Man Chinook!"

Whoops of victory rang across the ravine. The fish chasers stopped to watch Chinook barking and clawing in the mesh of net. "Don't cut *this* one up," said Jesse, as he passed Chinook behind him. "This here's the Last Fish."

Tears of joy ran from the old man's left eye and into the sharp valleys of his cheek.

TWENTY-ONE

~~~~~~~

LINK TALKS ABOUT JUNE HOGS, the huge summer Chinook that used to run the Columbia. He claims he landed a sixty-two-pounder at the mouth of the river. And that wasn't as big as they went. In the old days, a June hog could run you seventy, eighty pounds, Link says.

To me, June hogs were a mythical beast. They were dragons. Centaurs. But I gathered that June hogs really did exist, and not that long ago. Grand Coulee Dam, on the upper Columbia, was what cut them off.

The part I liked was that June hogs *had* to be that big. Salmon don't feed once they return to fresh water, and June hogs had their spawning grounds way up in Canada. Over a thousand miles from the river mouth. They had to pack that much meat and fat to answer their homing call past Celilo Falls, Kettle Falls, and all the way up to headwaters in the Canadian Rockies.

Until Grand Coulee blocked their cycle.

WE WERE back on the porch, shaded from midday sun. Reno had put on a deerskin shawl, fringed at the edges and beaded blue and red. And she'd switched to beaded moccasins. These moccasins had seen some dancing, it looked like. Jesse doused himself at the pump and put on his blue ribbon shirt. With just a word from Reno, the kids went in the house and came out wearing fresh store-bought clothes. Lorna picked up on it and got her suitcase from the car. After she'd changed—to her purple-and-green dress and white heels—I went in to change.

Inside the house, things were tidy. The furniture looked new and there was a Zenith TV and hi-fi record player. On one wall hung one of those velvety, glow-in-the-dark paintings of a bull elk, antlers framed against silver moon. A nice zigzag woven Indian rug draped over the couch. But the porch was the place to be.

Back on the porch, it seemed like we were about to have some sort of ceremony, but we were just sitting around talking, looking good. Which maybe that's all it was, I don't know.

"Do they still have the First Fish ceremony?" I asked Reno.

She was pleased, maybe just surprised, that I asked. "We held it for a year or two after the dam went in," she said. "Too many people moved away. Nobody came, and it wasn't right."

"People still fish at Celilo," said Somebody Two Birds. "But they use boats and setnets. It's lake fishing."

"The sound of the river went away," Reno said. She settled herself on her chair and then leaned forward, with a faraway look in her eye.

"Me and Harold are going up to Alaska, come August," said Two Birds. "That's where the fishing is. Ocean fishing."

"It was an eclipse of the river," Reno said. "Even when we knew the dam was coming, nobody could believe it. It was an eclipse of the river," she said. "Except when the water came up . . . Nobody liked to come to that spot anymore. The First Fish was a dance to no music."

I was sorry I asked.

"The last year of the falls they had Channel Eight there for the First Fish," said Jesse, trying to pick things up. "I was on TV that night."

Lawrence White Fish pulled a pack of Lucky Strikes from his shirt, and Reno went over and shook one out. She lit it for him. She blew the match out and watched the smoke rise in a thin blue trail from the dead stick.

"What was the First Fish ceremony?" Lorna asked.

Which was a good way out of this spot. Reno told what it was all about, about how the first salmon of the season was a visiting chieftain of the people who lived in a great house in the ocean. Whoever caught the First Fish had to treat him right—which was to cook him up and cut him into small pieces so everybody could taste. The bones of this visiting chief had to be placed back in the river, with the right words said over him. Then the fish people saw the bones and knew it was all right to come up the river to Celilo.

"The people thought fish were people?" Lorna asked.

"They *were* people," Reno said, a little too sternly. How would Lorna know? "People who lived in the ocean. They dressed like fish to come up the river."

"You had to believe it," Jesse explained.

Reno nodded, as if that were the trouble.

"People came from all over," Reno said. "Men sat on straw mats in the longhouse. They had their smoke and talk. We grilled salmon over fire barrels," she said, "and people brought berries and roots. Bearskin rugs from the Nez Perce. Ocean shells from the Siuslaw. But that was the old days," she said. "There was dancing and bone games and great joy."

"Big party," said Jesse, his eyes gleaming.

"You guys," said Somebody Two Birds, shaking his head. "Reno remembers better than it was. The last year of the falls," he said, "there was more newspaper guys than Indians."

"That's right!" said Jesse, happily switching gears. "There was no salmon at Celilo yet, and Leonard drove down to Portland to buy some."

Everybody laughed, except Reno.

Over in his Thunderbird seat, Lawrence White Fish had his eyes closed. The cigarette drooped from his lower lip with a long, curved gray ash. When Reno moved to take it from him, the old man stirred as if awakening from a dream. "Nuh, nuh, nuh," he said. Which was his laugh. He was happy about something.

"June . . . hogs," he rasped.

His good eye snapped open. The others on the porch sat stunned, as if lightning had struck from clear blue sky. "Lawrence!" said Harold Strikes the Heart. "Lawrence talked!"

"Hush," said Reno. She put her hand on his arm. "June hogs," she repeated the old man's words.

"Nuh, nuh, nuh," he said. "Billy," said Lawrence White Fish. "Billy got . . . June hog . . . in net."

His voice came from a dry mine shaft.

I looked at Jesse and got the chills.

The old man nodded. His good eye closed. Then it opened again, and the old man told the story. It was long and tortuous, getting it out of him, but Jesse knew the story and helped him tell it. Someone named Billy got a June hog in his net at Celilo. The fish was too heavy. It pulled him in. He slipped off his platform, into the river. "Nuh, nuh, nuh," said Lawrence White Fish. This was a very funny story to him.

"River got Billy," he said, patting his lap for the Lucky Strikes. Reno didn't give him one. She rubbed his arm.

"Try net . . . Billy . . ."

They tried to net Billy but couldn't get him. When Billy went down, the undercurrent looped him back up under the falls. "With fish . . . White bellies . . ." When Billy got flushed out again, they netted Billy. They got him, alive. But that wasn't the end of the story.

"Billy told . . ." the old man rasped. "June hogs . . . sing to him . . ." Lawrence White Fish opened his mouth and put his tongue forward against stubs of brown teeth, as if to make an ess. Out came a high-pitched whistling, like wind in high trees. The sound pleased Lawrence White Fish very much. He did it again, the whistling of salmon underwater.

"Nuh, nuh, nuh," he said.

From under the porch and up through my chair came this idea that if there was something larger than place, maybe Jesse had it. It was a dizzying thought, that somebody could fit the world so well and still have no place. No where. Nothing to do there. It would matter to me, but it didn't matter to Jesse. He could go fishing in a dry ravine, and make the old man talk.

RENO wanted us to stick around for dinner. She was going to fry up some of the fish we'd caught. But Jesse didn't think so. "I got to get these young people over to The Dalles," he said. "They got some business to do at The Dalles."

I don't know. I would have stayed. Lorna would have, too, but Jesse was set about it.

"Just a snack, then," Reno said. She nodded to Lorna, who popped up and followed Reno inside.

Jesse walked to the Cadillac and brought back a fifth of Jack Daniels, about three-quarters full. He unscrewed the cap, took a swig, and set the bottle on the porch in front of Harold Strikes the Heart.

Harold looked at Somebody Two Birds as if he might have stepped on something squishy.

"No booze here," Somebody Two Birds said.

"That's why we're here," Harold Strikes the Heart said.

"What do you mean?" Jesse said. "Is this some kind of *home?*"

"She-Who-Watches," said Harold Strikes the Heart, with a nervous laugh. He nodded toward inside the house. "That's what they call your mother now."

"She-Who-Watches!" Jesse said.

"We don't call her that when she's around."

Jesse took another swig. "Wade, you want to wet your whistle?"

"No, thanks," I said. "Put it back in the car." But there was no telling Jesse what to do, of course.

"She-Who-Watches." He sniffed.

Lorna came out carrying a flat-basket tray, and Reno was right behind her carrying another. They passed fry bread around. They skipped Lawrence White Fish, asleep in his chair. Reno came up short when she saw the bottle. She drew back her foot, as if to kick it. But something caught her, and she didn't. Was Jesse exempt from the rules of this house? She served Jesse and went on to the next person. Reno had great dignity about her, great control. But I could feel the tension rippling off her.

The fry bread had a sweet, donutty taste to it, sweeter than the jam. Which was blackberry, tart.

Reno didn't take fry bread herself. Nor did she sit down. She eyed that bottle of Jack Daniels in front of Jesse as if he had fluted a cobra up on the porch. Her porch. With big, bearlike quickness, Reno swatted the bottle with her open hand, scudding it into a post. Then she kicked it off the porch. When it didn't break, she bounded down the steps, pounced on the bottle and smashed it over a rock.

"Aw, Mom," Jesse said.

Reno stood over the fragments and watched the liquid soak into the earth. Her hands were spread down, in the position she had released the bottle. I half expected her to look upward and deliver a sermon. Instead, she kept her head bowed. "That's just the trouble," she said. Not about Jesse, maybe, but about the world in general.

She wandered across the yard and stooped to pick up the pole net we'd left there. To my surprise, I found myself off the porch and down there with her.

"Let me help you with that," I offered. She was dragging it toward the barn.

"Thank you," she said.

The net was lighter than it looked. We carried it to the barn, Reno in the lead and me separated from her by ten feet or so of pole. There were many times I had wished for the chance to talk to Reno, but now I couldn't think of what to say. Anyway, what business was it of mine?

"You are Jesse's friend," she said.

We were inside the barn, filled mainly with a rusted tractor and old farm machinery. Reno pointed to a high hook, and we lifted the hoop of the net over it.

"Good friend," I said. "That's right."

She fixed the pole so it hung just so, straight down. The barn smelled of old hay and fresh dog.

"The best thing," Reno said, "is to forget the old ways. Not for me," she said, "but for Jesse."

"Jesse likes the stories," I said.

"To Jesse they are just stories," Reno said. "Jesse hears the stories like jokes."

We picked our way from the barn back to sunlight. Reno paused. She fixed the hair in her barrette, as if that helped her look forward. Reno seemed to take in the Cadillac, people laughing on the porch, mountains in the distance, the whole world. She put her hand on my arm. When she looked at me it was as if she were looking through me, deep inside. If I got it right, she was giving me something large and important. She spoke slowly and carefully, picking words from the sky.

"You are Jesse's friend," she said.

JESSE drove. He took the back roads, east and then north, leaving the snow-capped picket of Cascade peaks farther behind. What bugged Lorna about Jesse was he chewed his Lifesavers instead of savoring them. Which was just Jesse, you know. Finish one flavor and pop the next one.

"Your mom doesn't want you over here," Lorna said. "She told me."

"Over where?" Jesse said. "Told you what?"

"On this side," Lorna said. "Said she had a dream. What's that all about?"

"Momma's always having a dream." Jesse laughed. "Ever since they took her river music away, Momma's having dreams. And they're no good. She thinks . . . She dreamed of me falling," he said. "She didn't like those cliffs back of Celilo. She spooked. We came up from the river, up here. But she kept having the dreams."

"Your mother's a powerful woman," Lorna said. "Is that why she let you go to Calamus?"

"She didn't *let* me go to Calamus. She took me to Calamus."

"Yeah, well, that's what I mean. Why?"

"She was fed up."

A dove among vultures, I remembered. Jesse's mother had it backward, if that's what she thought.

"Well, she doesn't seem like that kind of woman," Lorna said. "She likes you a lot."

"Sure!" Jesse said. "That's why. I was the only kid she ever had. But she always wanted kids. We always had cousins and nephews and nieces around. Plus also everybody gave kids to Momma when things happened. Just like now. They still do."

This was making less and less sense, the more he explained it.

"I was her favorite," Jesse said. "She called me Wa-Toosh-Ka."

"Wa-Toosh-Ka?"

"Wa-Toosh-Ka," Jesse said. "Means, 'You-are-a-special-boy-who-will-fly-very-high-and-get-everything-you-want-but-these-other-little-sons-of-bitches-need-a-good-spanking.' "

Lorna got a good laugh out of that, but I'd heard this kind of thing too many times. That's what Jesse does, see? Every time you try to get serious and maybe learn something, he dances away from it. He pulls that Indian stuff on you.

"No, really," said Jesse. "She was real tough on those other kids, but not on me."

"She never had other kids of her own?" Lorna said.

"Just me."

"Twice?" I remembered Jesse had died once.

I think Jesse heard me, but he was off on something else. We'd left the gravel road, and the Cadillac was a quiet blur toward Dufur and brown rounded hills. The land was a loose rug that was buckled and rolled at this end by a giant footstop somewhere behind us. Perhaps I was having the opposite kind of reaction to this hard land from what Jesse said when he got to Calamus. *Jungle here. All these trees. You can't see anything.* Now there was all this land with no trees. Just sky, all over the place, and nothing to see.

"Gad," Lorna said. "You want to know what this reminds me of? This whole thing?"

"No, Lorna. What?"

"Buffaloes."

"Buffaloes!" Jesse said. "Buffaloes are extinct."

"Correct again, Jesse," she said. "Jesse, you're quick."

I nudged her with my elbow. Knock it off. Lorna gave me the sideways eyes. But what I like about Lorna is she doesn't push it. She pulled in her horns.

Jesse didn't seem to have noticed. "Some people said Momma had the gift," he said. "She could hear the wind, and the river talked to her. There was always one or two people had the gift. He-Who-Died had the gift. And Momma might have had it."

"Did she?" I said.

"Maybe she did," said Jesse. "But she lost it. She said, *My nerves are shot.* Nobody has the gift anymore."

The Cadillac nosed down a twisted piece of blacktop between the brown loaves of hills, and the great Columbia River Valley opened ahead of us. The river shimmered blue as it made a wide bend. The town of The Dalles clung to a low bench. On the right, upstream, was The Dalles Dam, a great slab of concrete shutting off the river and releasing it through locks and penstocks.

WE CRUISED The Dalles, which had the look of a very solid old river town. The business part was stone banks and stone-

and-brick stores, and the gray courthouse had stiff grooved columns and wide granite steps. The Dalles wasn't going to burn. Or float away. Some of the houses were stone, too, but in the old section rose tall, pointed-roof, thin-slat wood houses with gingerbread trim and cool green lawns and willow trees in the yards and sprinklers going.

I tried to sear every detail into memory, as this would be the first place Lorna and I ever—technically speaking, in a real bed—slept together.

Downtown we passed the Hotel Bonneville, which I figured maybe Jesse had in mind but he hadn't spoken up. Summer was going full bore in The Dalles. The back of my shirt stuck to the leather seat. We stopped at the Standard station for Lorna to use the bathroom. While we were waiting, I said to Jesse, "Say," I said. "What do you think of that Hotel Bonneville?"

"That's where we'll go," Jesse said. "That's the best hotel in The Dalles."

"Good," I said. "Super." My voice was dry, almost a croak. "Do you think they'll let us in?"

"Just let me handle it."

"Right," I said. "Super."

"For Christ's sake," he said. "Just relax."

"You're absolutely right," I said. "Correct." I elbowed the control console, and my window whirred up until I caught it and reversed it.

"Maybe we should stop at the drugstore," I said.

"What for?"

He knew what for. I hate it when he gives you that look like he's got the goods on you.

Lorna came out. Her purple dress had puffy sleeves and a swishy skirt, small green flowers and a shiny green belt. Which doesn't sound like a perfect combination, purple and green, but it looked good on Lorna with her white high heels. The dry air or something had electrified her fly-away hair, however, and—I don't mean to be critical—she had a kind of Albert Einstein look, with makeup now that made her eyes larger.

Jesse drove us to the Rexall, another stone-block building with large plate-glass windows on a busy corner. "I'll jump in here and get some Lifesavers," I explained to Lorna, who was filing her nails.

Inside the Rexall, it was your normal Saturday crowd, women and old people shopping. And this efficient-looking young woman in glasses at the cash register. It smelled like iodine and Band-Aids. The white-jacketed pharmacist kind of gave me a start, because at first glance he looked like Coach Garth. I cased the joint, checking out the greeting-card section and looking around for where they might keep the condoms. I couldn't see them. I didn't know exactly what kind of package I was looking for. Jesse would know.

I slithered toward the plate-glass window. Jesse and Lorna, in the car, were talking. Lorna had her back to me. Jesse saw me, and I nodded him to come in the store.

Which in a moment he did, barely able to contain his huge glee. He got in line at the cash register. I stood behind him with a roll of multi-flavored Lifesavers in my sweaty grip.

When it was Jesse's turn, he announced loud enough for everyone in the store to hear: "Rubbers," he said. "A pack of Trojans, if you got 'em. Supersensitive and lubricated."

Heads turned all over the store. The young woman at the cash register reached to a sliding drawer behind her and produced a thin three-pack of Trojans.

"Oh, they're not for me," Jesse shouted. "They're for Kemo Sabe, here."

THE HOTEL Bonneville was a three-story yellow brick affair with scalloped concrete trim. Inside, most of the lobby traffic was over at the entrance to the restaurant, Chez Pierre. Prosperous-looking wheat ranchers in their best boots and cowboy hats guided spiffed-up wives toward the dining room. It was a fancy place. Good thing we were dressed up. The hotel reception desk was a long, curved, dark-wood barrier that looked like it had come around the horn.

Jesse whapped the silver dinger, and we waited for someone to appear. When no one did, he slapped it again.

A door marked PRIVATE opened. Out came a frail man with a green visor and armbands and Coke-bottle glasses. "Good evening," Jesse said. "Can we pay in advance?"

No doubt it was to our advantage the man was nearsighted, but he could see the packet of bills in Jesse's fist. Still, he hesitated. He peered out at Lorna and me.

Jesse said, "I heard the Hotel Bonneville has a sixty-dollar suite, is what somebody told us. Is that right?"

Sixty dollars! But money meant nothing to Jesse.

"You in, Al?" someone called from the room marked PRIVATE.

"Yeah, yeah, I'm in," he said over his shoulder. Jesse produced his bogus ID and absently placed four twenties beside it on the desk. The man reached to a row of boxes behind the desk and pulled out a key. "Just one night," he said. "You folks from out of town?"

"Way out of town," Jesse assured him.

"Room Sixteen," he said. He buzzed a buzzer, and a waiter came from the restaurant. The waiter-porter was a tall, serious young man with active eyebrows. Robert was his name. He looked sorry to have been called from Chez Pierre, but he snagged our key off the desk and picked up Lorna's and my bags.

We followed Robert up a narrow set of carpeted stairs to a hallway with a long red rug. Lorna's hair breezed toward the cloth wallpaper, and she got a static shock when her elbow came too close to a doorknob. Robert showed us into Room 16, which was what he called the Corner Suite. Two big poster beds. The room was dimly lit but spacious and rich, old-fashioned, with oval mirrors and a small chandelier. The wallpaper was silvery swirls on light green, which matched the bedspreads.

"Well," said Lorna. She was the riverboat queen. She swanked over to touch the drapes. After Calamus and the trailer court, I guess, the Hotel Bonneville was about right. Certainly no more than she deserved.

"Two beds!" Jesse said.

Robert showed us the marble bath with its lion's-claw legs, and the room service menu. He hovered about the room, fixing windows, as if we might ask him to stay.

"Pay this man a tip," Lorna said.

"Ho!" said Jesse.

"Ah," said Robert, flexing his eyebrows. Jesse palmed him a twenty.

TWENTY-TWO

~~~~~~

THE TROUBLE WITH GOING BACK EAST, in my case, was a sense that I'd already been there. Which I hadn't. Like maybe, when it came time, I should drive the trip backward. Throw the car into reverse and back past Celilo, over the Rockies, in reverse gear. Clean the bugs off the rearview mirror. I'd like to say going Back East was something like the equivalent—a century after they forged the trail—of going Out West. But in fact I couldn't shake this other idea that Back East was the safest of options.

Survival of the timid.

So JESSE got us into the Hotel Bonneville, but there were three of us. And two of us were probably thinking the same thing. "What are *you* going to do?" Lorna asked him. Which was no doubt the way to handle it, straight out. Jesse was never one to think that far ahead, like I said before, and the question stumped him.

"Why don't you come back later," I suggested, "and join us for dinner?" Which seemed only fair. He'd paid for the room and everything. "Room service."

Lorna was checking the view at a window.

"Aw, no," he said. "You guys . . . No, I'll just cruise on out to the drive-in," he said. "Something will turn up." Which was a good possibility, all right, Jesse with his Cadillac El Dorado. There were a lot of Indians around The Dalles. "I'll head up to Celilo for the night," he said. "Somebody will be up for bone games."

After he left, it seemed like the rest of Time was spread out before us, and we took it. Took our time. Or Lorna took our time. We had a good clothes-on bounce on the bed, by which time it was apparent we'd brought the smell of chickens into the room with us from the salmon run, and Lorna said I should take a bath. Her first. But I couldn't stay out of there. I went in the bathroom and helped her undress, as slowly as I could stand it, and then we got in the marble tub together and soaped each other up and had a good time.

So good, in fact, that when the water got tepid and I had fouled it anyway, we drew another bath and did it again.

Which was nothing, however, compared to the feeling of throwing back the covers together and slipping between clean sheets for the first time with someone you've loved a long time. All your life. It was dark by now, and the blue sparks of a mini–lightning storm under the sheets slowed us down getting started. Of the Trojans, there was a timing problem on the first one and another problem you probably wouldn't be interested in. Anyway a three-pack isn't very many. Lorna turned on the lamp beside the bed to help me get *this* one right—they ought to put instructions on these things, it's not all that easy—when there was a knock on the door.

I about had a heart attack. I figured it was Coach Garth or somebody.

Before I could react to the knock, Jesse burst into the room. With his date.

"This is Cheryl," he said. "That's Wade from Princeton I was telling you about. Lorna. Say hello, Cheryl."

Cheryl was as surprised to see us in this condition as we, scrambling for covers, were to see her. "Are we interrupting something?'' Jesse said. He boomed right through it, holding Cheryl by the wrist so she wouldn't bolt. "Hello," she said. She wore a fuzzy short-sleeved yellow sweater and white pants. She was built. Blond cylinder curls.

"I told her about room service," Jesse said. "We just dropped by for dinner."

LORNA and I got dressed and it turned out Cheryl was a college girl, University of Washington, with a summer job as a fish counter at Bonneville Dam. "So how do you *like* Harvard," she asked Jesse, at one point, and he fed her more line about how there was a lot of prejudice at Harvard, even though he was soon to be a chief. Lorna eyed Cheryl like a chipmunk in the same tree with a cat. But Cheryl was an agreeable sort and she knew French, which was a big help with the room service menu.

"You'll love this Poolay Cord On Blue," she said. So I said that sounded good, and Jesse phoned it in. Lorna wanted Chateau Briand, and it wasn't just dinners that Jesse ordered. A white wine. A red wine, 1949. And a selection of desserts.

The food, when Robert wheeled it up, arrived on a double-decker tray. Steam rose as he lifted the dome over each dish and announced what it was. "Mon joo," Cheryl said. It did smell good. Robert whipped a lacy cloth over a folding table he'd brought up. Jesse hawked over him as he arranged the serving tools just so. After fixing a white towel on his forearm, Robert drilled the red wine bottle with a corkscrew, drew the cork—*floop*—and tucked it back into the neck. Then he popped open the white wine bottle and began to pour. But he stopped. Just a little dollop in the glass closest to me.

He stood back to study the plaster swirls on our ceiling.

"Taste it," Cheryl whispered. I don't know why she couldn't taste it herself.

I slugged it down.

"This is excellent wine," I said. Which I guess was the

right thing to say. Robert nodded, and finished pouring wine all around. Then he left.

It was about midnight, and all we'd had since breakfast was fry bread. My dinner was this tender chicken breast, sandwiched around ham and melted cheese with a thin white gravy. Delicious. But everybody's was good, they all said so. Cheryl had organized the dishes so we were eating the right thing in the proper order.

"Now the salad," she said.

Lorna got this look like, Gad, *I* knew that. But she was, in her way, warming up to Cheryl. The wine, maybe, was smoothing Lorna out.

"Bone appateet," said Cheryl, raising her glass for yet another toast.

After which she explained how The Dalles was really *Les Dalles*, French for rocks in the river, and the Deschutes River meant something else. All this French we were learning got Jesse talking about the Indian names for local rivers. Yakima, he explained, was the native word for *Hurry up.* I guess we were on dessert by this time. Mine was chocolate moose, a good rich pudding.

"Now Skamania," Jesse said, "means different things to different tribes." Jesse can be so sincere. "To the Wascos it meant *Ouch*," he said. "You'd sit on a thorn, say, and go *Skamania!*" He sipped from his wineglass. "To your Wishrams, now," he said, "Skamania meant more like, *Knock it off. Get out of here.*"

Cheryl sat spellbound, her fork in her left hand. Maybe she could use this material for a paper. I could see her taking mental notes. Yakima = Hurry Up.

Jesse liked her attitude. Lorna could barely contain herself. "What does Klickitat mean," she prompted him.

Professor Howl emptied his wineglass. He topped off the other three glasses and poured what was left into his own.

"Klickitat," he said thoughtfully. "Klickitat is what your Indian mothers say to the kids. It means," he said, "*Eat your roots.* Like, *Eat your roots or you won't get any berries.*"

I had just swigged some wine, and he caught me in mid-swallow. The wine exploded on me, and I spewed it into my nasal passages and out toward Cheryl, whom I was watching. Jesse pounded on my back. Cheryl rose, inspecting red blotches on her white pants.

The wine spread in my head, into the little chains of bones inside my ears.

"Cold water," Lorna said. I thought she meant for me, but she meant for Cheryl's pants. She dunked a towel in the ice bucket and applied the cold-pack to Cheryl's pants. Which only spread the blotches pink. "You'll have to soak it," Lorna said.

There was this heavy pause, as Lorna looked up.

"Soak those pants in the sink!" Jesse said. He spun the Dom Perignon in the air and caught it by the neck. "It's about time we turned in anyway. I'm bushed."

Cheryl headed for the bathroom. While I blew pink liquid from my nose to a handkerchief, Jesse arranged a night table with four narrow champagne glasses between the beds. "Open that bottle," he told me.

I peeled foil off the neck and worked the twisted wire loose. But the cork stayed in. And Robert hadn't left us the corkscrew.

"Maybe you just twist it out," Lorna said.

I couldn't get the cork to budge. Jesse came over to look at it. I swear, he just looked at it, and the cork started to move. Luckily I didn't have it pointed at him. The cork shot like a thirty-ought-six—Cheryl screamed from the bathroom—and just missed the chandelier before ricocheting around the room. Now I had this green geyser in my hands. Jesse was quick with the glasses. We saved most of it.

Jesse left the lamp on so we could see our champagne. Cheryl came out, and I guess she'd decided to soak her sweater, too. So we all took our clothes off, and Lorna and I were in the window-side bed. We propped pillows against the headboard and sat up, sipping champagne. The sheet didn't reach far enough, but it wasn't cold. In fact everything seemed about right. Jesse told Coyote stories, including one I'd never heard before about how Coyote lost his feathers. Coyote died and came back a number of times.

The champagne was gone, and nobody was sitting up anymore.

I just wished Jesse would shut up.

When he did, however, you could hear everything. I mean four people, two beds, it's kind of hard to concentrate. A bedspring over there was getting quite a workout, and Lorna and I were trying to be quiet about it.

"Skamania," Lorna said, like *Ouch*.

Then she got the giggles.

"Yakima," Cheryl said, from under covers. *"Yakima!"*

Lorna got to laughing out loud and couldn't stop. Then Jesse, too, and me. I mean it isn't even that funny, to tell it, but we laughed and laughed. Sometimes you can't help it. Tears came to my eyes and my stomach muscles ached. After a serious effort I got it more or less under control, and then the pressure came building again in my lungs. I couldn't put a lid on it. Lorna exploded when I did. *"Klickitat,"* Jesse said. We were helpless, two beds shaking. I was finished, jellified. This great, great opportunity slipped further and further away because everything was so funny and right.

LIGHT streamed directly into the south window, so it was late morning. The other bed was disheveled and empty. Lorna lay curled with her back to my front, breathing the slow and rhythmic air of deep sleep. I was just lying there, recalling our feast, when I realized Lorna and I were not the only heat in the bed.

I guess I overreacted.

I whipped up and kicked it—kicked Jesse—out of bed and onto the floor. Which woke them both. Jesse didn't seem to know where he was, or how he got there. No doubt he'd been dreaming, and just wandered in. It was nothing personal.

"OK, campers," I said. "Everybody up for volleyball!"

But you know me, no sense of humor. They didn't appreciate it. Jesse, on the floor, held his head as if I might have broken it.

"Where's Cheryl?" Lorna said.

Jesse jacked himself up off the floor and skulked to his bed. He looked hungover. Or maybe he was just set back that Cheryl had skipped out on him. But if Jesse knows disappointment, it's just a face outside a night window—gone the second time you look. Things happen, and you go on to something else.

"Let's drive up to Celilo," he said.

WE STOPPED at the Piggly Wiggly and bought a couple of chickens off a rotary spit. And a sack of green seedless grapes, a carton of white-powdered donuts and three jumbo bottles of Coca-Cola. Jesse had this island in mind. We were going for a picnic on an island, he said, if he could scare up someone with a boat.

Jesse floored it on the straightaway out of The Dalles, heading east with broad river on our left and bluffs on the right. The road here was a fresh black freeway that made the tires sound wet. Upstream from The Dalles Dam, high hills across the river fell like gold velvet pillows into the gorge, but not all the way to the river. The bank was vertical, a series of lava layers that had cooled just yesterday. The gorge was like a cutaway section in the geography book so you could look in and see the earth in different layers. At the bottom, now placid, lay river so blue it made sky seem yellow.

Famous for wind, the gorge lay breathless today. Its dead river was smooth as glass. Lorna had never seen the real thing, where the old river came bashing and churning through narrow rocky chutes, and the holes boiled with salmon. I wish she could have seen that.

Only a dozen miles or so up the river, Jesse turned off at a green roadsign that said Celilo. The Cadillac bumped over the railroad tracks and onto gravel toward a row of low, wind-blasted houses, fish-drying sheds and campers. Barking dogs greeted the Cadillac at a long A-frame building under construction, and Jesse got out to talk to the builders.

Lorna and I stayed in the car.

Boats sat on trailers with their noses pointed skyward and toward the river. Most had outboard motors, ready to go. Fishing nets and floats were strung like laundry, long since dried.

Jesse didn't seem to know these guys, but they were Indians, after all. It wasn't long before we were out on the Columbia River in a beat-up fiberglass sixteen-footer, white with turquoise trim, and a new 35-horse Evinrude. Jesse doesn't know powerboats, so I ran it. We took off with a great surge, knifing upstream, carving a white curve into the river. Lorna's hair blew straight. The river widened, to maybe a couple of miles across. Jesse pointed to a huge flat-top island, a mesa. Its sides sloped to river like the brim of a broad hat.

We put in at a fringe of low willows, the only plants other than grass out here. The beach was more gravel than sand. This was a big island. I couldn't see the end of it.

We went for a swim, sore-footing it over gravel and slicing —one, two, me-third—into the blue Columbia. The water was clear and a perfect temperature for swimming. I stayed in the river longer than they did, and treaded water. There was slight current, even though the river was dammed.

When Lorna and Jesse started setting the food out, I went up there. The chicken was warm in its wax paper. I don't know when I've tasted anything so good, unless it was last night. We ate both chickens, tearing pieces off with our fingers and mopping up with donuts. And pop to wash it down. I don't know, I suppose it was the place, as much as anything, that made things taste so good. Something about a river. Or this strange wide land, being on an island in it.

What was amazing to me is you could drive half a day and come to a completely different country. Not only that, you could reverse the Barlow Trail and wade through time.

Catch something of the world of Lawrence White Fish. And Reno Howl, with one foot in this world and one foot in another. There was a sense of fullness about it. The world seemed to lay itself out like these layers of lava cut by the great river, exposed for anyone to see.

Lorna allowed herself to be fed grapes, one at a time, as she spread out to work on her belly tan.

A tall tug pushed a double set of barges, with mounds of orange sawdust, from downriver. It floated peaceably over former falls, and chugged on up the river.

"You know," Jesse said. "When I got out of MacLaren, I thought we were really going to run the river. I thought," he said, "like you're always talking about. We could let the river take us, wherever it goes."

"We were just trying to cheer you up," Lorna said.

"Well, you did," Jesse said. He sifted a handful of gravelly sand through his fingers and then flicked the larger pieces into the river. "I was really looking forward to that."

"It was just a story," I said, sounding hollow.

Which reminded me of Reno, what she had said. The trouble with Jesse is he thought the stories were jokes. But she was dead wrong about that. The trouble with Jesse was just the opposite. Jesse was a believer! Stories were Jesse's real world. I'd seen it before. Jesse wasn't like he let on. It was just easier to make a joke of things that were too big or too sad.

"Are you all right, Wade?" said Lorna, sitting up.

I was much more than all right.

"Speak to us," Jesse said.

It was that feeling I'd had with Lorna on the banks of Tom Creek, watching the salmon spawn, that feeling of belonging on earth and being a part of things. In this case we were a part of the wide sky and the tall bluffs on the island, framing the flat blue river. *A dove among vultures*, I thought. *You are Jesse's friend.* Princeton was a slow barge disappearing up the river to the east, something that could be caught up with later.

"We could still do it," I said.

"Do what?" Lorna said.

"We could run the river."

It was all clear to me, a full-blown plan, like a logjam breaking and giving new flow. We could put in below the dam at Calamus and take the river out to sea. I could stay and work for a year. Get Jesse on his feet at something. Wait for Lorna to graduate. What was the hurry? There was more to do out here than anywhere else. By "here," I was thinking not east or west of Mount Hood but west in general, as if I had a moon's-eye view on the planet.

The main thing, the essential thing, would be to ride the river out of Calamus, west. And cross the Columbia River bar. I'd done it enough with Link I should be able to do it alone. "We'll take Link's boat," I said. "Take it right out to sea."

Jesse thought this was great, but Lorna was all confused when I got to the not-going-East part.

"That's the dumbest thing I ever heard!" she said, poofing her hair. Which didn't poof, because it was still wet. "You always wanted to go East."

"*You* always wanted to go East," I said. "You and my mother."

Which shut her up for a moment, trying to think why I was wrong. What occurred to me, then, was Lorna's theory of the boxes. But I didn't want to be too tough on her. Actually, I did want to. I felt like grabbing them both by the neck and tossing them around. I felt real good about this.

"So then what," Lorna said. "Gad. We charge out to sea and then come back to Calamus? That's stupid."

It wasn't stupid at all. "So then what?" I said. "*Anything*. I could work in the woods. Jesse and I could hook up with Harold and What'sizname, Two Birds. Go fishing up in Alaska, earn some money."

When the dust kind of settled, I went for another swim. Let them talk it over. I was right. It was a good plan. There was nothing wrong with it. I felt like a great yoke had been lifted from my shoulders. The river itself was a good friend.

A BREEZE came up the gorge and feathered the river. Yellow hills on the Oregon side turned a deeper honey color. Mare's-tail clouds swept the white top of Mount Hood, and our low willows whispered a new cool. From our low brim of island, we could see only the tip of Mount Hood. Lorna got the idea we should hike up to the bluff and get a better view.

"You two go," Jesse said. "I'll walk up the island and look for shells."

Which was good of him, I thought. But Jesse was skittish about something, a little off, as if he didn't really want to be left alone.

"No, let's all go," Lorna said.

So Jesse took the lead, and we walked the mild slope through tall grass, the tops now waving like blond surf in the breeze. As we approached the base of the rock, the bluff got taller. Something about an island, it throws off your perspective. It would be quite a climb to the top of the mesa. If we could even get up there. Mostly it was guarded by sheer rock, pillared against just such an assault as ours.

We found a place where the bluff had partially collapsed and spilled. We picked across rocks, sharp as broken peanut brittle, and made our way into a shallow draw.

"Could be a little snaky in here," Jesse said.

"Snaky?"

"Rattlesnakes. I don't want to get you nervous or anything."

"Nervous?" Lorna said. Like *Who, me?* She wore a white blouse over her swimsuit, but her legs were bare to her tennis shoes.

"Make noise as you walk, which you palefaces do anyway," Jesse said. "You'll be all right."

I grabbed a couple blocks of rock, one in each hand, and clacked them together as we picked our way up the draw.

Rock walls closed in as we went. Although we were gaining altitude, there was no sign this would lead to the top.

Jesse, a few steps ahead of us, stopped at some writing on the wall. It was drawings. Paintings. Faded and partially covered by lichens, it had been here a long time. There didn't seem to be a story about it, just figures and designs in red paint on black rock. Crude human stick figures, one throwing a spear. I made out an animal with antlers, a deer or an elk. Lorna pointed to a fish with a jawful of nasty teeth. Some of the drawings were just designs—a series of triangles, for example, or a circle with lines coming out like a kindergarten kid might draw the sun. There was one large eye—just an eye—with a pupil the size of a baseball.

"This island used to be a sacred place," Jesse said. "There was a burial grounds down below. And sweathouses."

"Used to be?" I said.

"They dug it all up for the reservoir," Jesse said. "Moved the bodies to a cemetery over by Wishram."

"Seems like they could move bodies but not the spirits," Lorna said. Which is exactly what I was thinking. This place was making my skin crawl.

Jesse didn't seem worried. As we passed the eye on the rock, I looked back toward the slice of river the eye could see. The eye had probably been here when Lewis and Clark paddled by to "discover" this land. The eye would have seen covered wagons creeping the riverbank toward The Dalles. And long before that, Celilo and its falls were where everybody came, if they didn't live here, to trade and pow-wow. If the land had only one eye, this was the place for it, all right.

To me it was sad, if you think about it. People living here ever since there were people. They had it all worked out with the salmon. And then all you read about, what they teach, is these great heroes coming across the plains and over the mountains and streaming into Oregon country. The wagon trains and the savages, and then building the big dams. It made you kind of ashamed of the whole deal. But what could you do? It was just the way things were. It was progress.

"Somewhere up here," Jesse said, "used to be the screamers."

"I think we better head back," Lorna said.

"The screamers," he said, "were supposed to warn people about rapids ahead." Museum people had chipped away the screamers, rock paintings, and removed them, Jesse said. "Nothing's the way it was anymore."

Even as he spoke, there came a high whistling in the rimrock overhead. It came on and faded. Jesse froze. Then it came on again. He cocked his head, listening. The whistling came on like a teapot aboil. No, like . . . Like an old man's whistling of salmon under water.

Lorna grabbed me, and I about jumped out of my skin. The whistling came from the rimrock, a jagged cut against the sky.

"It's the wind," I said.

Jesse scanned the walls behind Lorna and me. His head locked on something and his eyes got wide. I looked over my shoulder. High on the wall was what could only be the screamer. A human face, eerie white against black rock, was all open-gape scream. Her hair was straight up and her eyes were small slits. She was screaming bloody murder.

It all happened so fast. Actually, the white face on the wall was the picture of *Jesse's* scream, a blood-curdling, snake-in-the-sleeping-bag kind of scream that came from his bones and echoed off the high walls and up into sky.

Jesse took off running, or as close to running as you can do across sharp rocks. Lorna and I followed. I didn't let go of her hand, and that slowed us both down.

As soon as we cleared the draw, the wind hit us full force. Whitecaps rolled up the river like surf, and grass lay flat on the wind that came howling up the gorge. Our blanket was wrapped around a willow bush.

The boat was loose!

Jesse, ahead of us, raced up the shoreline parallel to the

boat, upstream. "No!" I shouted, but it was too late to stop him. He flat-dove into a wave that hit him broadside and knocked him to his hands and knees. He came up spouting and waving, but his words flew away on wind and river spray.

He twisted riverward and pushed off into deeper water.

Because of the waves, he had to swim mostly underwater. Which was a terrifying thing to watch, his black head popping up only to get a breath and not being able to see him when he was down. The boat was moving right along, and I wasn't sure he had figured the angle right. We followed him up the shoreline, but there was nothing, nothing at all, we could do.

Finally he reached the boat, and vaulted himself into it. He stood in the pitching boat, bracing himself wide to crank the motor. Not being good with boats, Jesse had all he could do to get it through the angry waves to the island.

I waded out to catch the bow and pull it ashore.

"Get in!" he screamed.

Jesse had lost his mind. He was completely crazed, wild-eyed with terror, like that time he'd picked up the spawner at Tom Creek and squeezed her life all over him.

I tried to argue him back onto the island, but he was ready to leave without us if we didn't get in. Which we did. He hauled Lorna into the rocking boat, and I got in myself and took over at the motor. It was a harrowing trip, but we bucked the river to the Oregon shore, about a mile across, and back to Celilo before dark.

Jesse never, the whole trip, looked back at that island. He was a believer, all right.

TWENTY-THREE

≈≈≈≈≈

DOWN AT THE LAKE one time I came across a flat nest in the brush near shore. In the nest lay a lone egg, speckled, abandoned, about the size of a two-bite piece of candy. I put the egg in the pocket of my green flannel shirt and rowed back toward the bunkhouse.

Link said it was a mallard duck egg. We put the flannel shirt, with the egg in it, over by the fireplace. And a couple of days later we had a tiny brown mallard chick.

Right after he busted out of his shell and dried off, that duckling latched onto Duke, the old German shepherd, and began following Duke around. When Duke roused himself to amble about the bunkhouse, the chick followed. Duke went outside; the chick went outside. I led Duke and the chick down to lakeside, to see what would happen, but neither of them liked water.

The chick pecked at dog food from Duke's tin. Link got the biggest kick out of it. "Fido," he called that chick. "Next thing, Fido will raise his leg to pee."

The sad part, though, was there was no way to teach the chick duckness. This arrangement couldn't work. Fido lasted only three or four days before he disappeared. Probably one of the other dogs got him.

. . .

"OLD WET Shoes," Jesse said. "Wet Shoes was the old man that lived in the river and used to grab little kids that played too close to the water. At Celilo. He lived like a fish most of the time," he said. "But you could hear him walk up through the village at night. In his squishy shoes. Looking for bad kids," he said. "Momma had me scared shitless of Old Wet Shoes. But he couldn't get you," Jesse explained, "if you went to bed on time."

Jesse was sitting at a booth in the barbershop, wolfing down a cheeseburger and telling me things he was scared of. I was trying to figure it out. The screamers and Old Wet Shoes.

Me, it was Walt Disney movies I was always scared of. Captain Hook and the ticking clock. Pinocchio's puppet master. Stuff like that. Why they do stories like that for little kids I'll never know.

Lorna, on duty, brought over a couple of pieces of lemon meringue pie. "If somebody doesn't eat these," she said, "I'm going to throw it out."

"Thanks a lot," I said.

Restaurant pie is awful. I wasn't eating, anyway. I'd just come off work and was having a cup of coffee with Jesse before heading home for dinner. Coffee was another thing I was trying to figure out, why people like it. Lorna sat down to join us. It was slow at the barbershop.

Mr. and Mrs. Farnham came in. Les aimed his twitching mustache and a sour eye our way. I thought it was because Lorna was seated with us, not waitressing. But even as she hopped up, I saw his look directed at Jesse, as if I'd brought a weasel to my booth.

It was a look I became more and more aware of around Calamus. I'm not sure Jesse ever picked up on it. More than a look, it was an attitude. You'd catch it in a short answer to some ordinary question, or the response to a greeting, mumbled then turning away. At the Texaco one time, Gene asked Jesse if he knew where the gas tank was on this Cadillac.

Which I don't know, little things, like even from our friends. Jesse would punch something into the jukebox and I'd see this kind of lowered-head mirthful huddle at the other table, which straightened up when I stared over there.

"Well, what do you expect?" Lorna said, when I mentioned it to her. "All he did was dynamite the millpond. Gad."

"They're jealous," I said.

"Jealous!" she said. "You still don't get it, do you?"

"Of Jesse's car, and being Jesse. Anyway," I said, "he did his time."

She slapped her forehead. I was the dumbest person in the world. She poofed her hair and laid her wonderful speckled-eye sympathy on me. I was beyond help, but she gave it one more try:

"Calamus," she said, "is a vicious place."

Which maybe, you know, I began to think she had something. It was one way to look at it. Except it was mostly subtle, not what you'd call vicious. It wasn't so much what anybody said but the way they didn't say it, or at least around me. There were times I thought I must be imagining things. How could anybody really be mad at Jesse? And other times . . .

The three of us came out of the show one night, and Jesse's aerial was snapped off and hanging from its wires. Like that was some kind of accident, right?

"If I find the son-of-a-bitch that did that," I said, "I'd like to beat the crap out of him."

"Oh great," Lorna said. "You brute." She laughed. "That would help a lot."

THE DINNER was my idea. Mother likes to fix a dinner, and she gets little enough excuse to really do it, with the red table cloth and her good china and the extra leaves in the table and everything. The good silver. What's the use having all these nice crystal waterglasses in the cupboard if you don't use them, was my idea. And mother agreed completely. We'd have Lorna and Jesse down, and root Link from his hole across the lake and have a big old ham dinner. Like it was Easter or something, except just on a regular night.

Truth is, I had kind of neglected to tell Mother and Duncan about my change of college plans. What with one thing and another, I just hadn't got around to it. Not that I was having second thoughts or anything. The timing had never seemed right. I figured it would be better to have this dinner, get everybody together, and announce it. Plus I could get it out of the way all at once.

So that night I picked up Lorna at the trailer court. She had on her purple and green dress, the same one, and her white heels. I'd picked some foxglove and strung it together with Queen Anne's lace to a safety pin as a corsage. But the foxglove lost its starch by the time I pinned it to Lorna's dress. Wildflowers will do that. You shouldn't even pick them.

Down at the house, when we walked in, Duncan was maneuvering the ham from the oven to the cutting board. It smelled just great. Mother brushed her hands on her apron before shaking hands with Lorna. It made me think of the bear hug Reno laid on Lorna and me when we first met her. Mother had known Lorna all Lorna's life, and they were good friends. But here it was a formal handshake. Just a matter of style.

"My, don't we look ravishing tonight," Mother said. Ravishing. She put one hand in the air and did a turning motion with the other, to get Lorna to turn around. Which Lorna did.

"Oh, Mom," Sarah Ellen said.

"What's brown and weighs four tons and sings the national anthem?" said Carol Ann. Carol Ann was in her elephant-joke stage.

"Are you sure this is done?" Duncan asked. He tested the ham. "I'm not sure this is done."

"Is there anything I can do?" Lorna asked. "To help?"

"Oh, no. You're the guest."

"Give up?" Carol Ann said.

"I'm sure it's done."

"Lemme taste that there pig," said Link, coming over the landing from the front room, white head first. "Lorna, darlin'," he said. "If you don't stop rescuin' young bucks out of the Columbia River, you and I'll never get rid of 'em. Give an old man a squeeze," he said, bypassing the ham. He wore his black slacks and a string tie, which clumsified him but didn't slow him down. "I got my Old Spice on."

"How do we want this carved?" Duncan asked. "Thin? Fairly thin?"

"Give up? Does everybody give up? Ella Phantsgerald!"

Link lumbered over toward the table and grazed on olives and celery. Lorna and I moved over there, too, to get out of the way. Link declared how pitted olives were a sign civilization was on the right track, and he hoped he'd be around to see what they thought of next. I told him about the seedless grapes we'd found at the Piggly Wiggly in The Dalles. Not deseeded, but seedless. Which got him speculating how they did that, and what the future of grapes could possibly be, and what the world was coming to and the trouble with kids these days.

"Where is Jesse?" Mother asked. She pulled the rolls from the oven, partly fogging her glasses.

"He's coming," I said.

I didn't know. He'd said he was coming.

"If I waylaid dinner every time that critter said he was coming," Link said, "I'd be skinny as a thermometer."

Mother herded the girls toward the bathroom to wash up. I fixed the baby into her high chair. Duncan carried the ham to the table on a silver tray, and Mother brought the scalloped potatoes. "Careful, this is hot." Fresh peas with a pat of butter melting on top. Salad in the large myrtlewood bowl. Duncan lit the two tall white candles, and we settled around the table.

"This looks like a picture in *Better Homes and Gardens*," Lorna said. Which it did, with Mother's Wade-family crystal and silver on the red tablecloth.

"Duncan, would you say grace, please?"

We bowed our heads and held hands around the table, as we would at Thanksgiving, while Duncan mouthed a short Methodist grace.

Link tucked his napkin into the collar of his shirt. "Father, Son, and Holy Ghost," he said. "Whoever grabs first gets the most."

"Link," Mother said.

"First a toast," Duncan said.

Link was already forking ham to find the right slab, but he set the fork down.

"To Wade Curren and Princeton University," said Duncan, rising. "We're proud."

It wasn't a lot, in terms of words, but Duncan's blue eyes were focused and clear. This was no Methodist grace. Duncan held his waterglass high and said something nice about Lorna, too, and then about the idea of family and how blessed we were. I guess what got me was Duncan saying it direct. I mean I knew they were proud, no doubt about that, but this was quite a departure from our normal Trying-To-Say. It threw me.

We clinked glasses around the table. "To the big river," was all I could think of.

Passing food around the table gave me a chance to get my brain-race under control. I dished out the scalloped potatoes, which were too hot to pass.

"I've got something to say," I said.

"Oh, for Chrissake," Link said. "Let's eat."

"Link!" Mother said.

"Eat," I said. "I didn't mean don't eat. But I have a change in plans."

All eating and conversation stopped.

"Lorna and I . . . ." I began. Which was the wrong beginning. It wasn't Lorna's plan. And the way this came out—too solemn, too large . . . "I have decided," I said, "not to go to Princeton. Not right away."

As if speaking underwater, not really hearing my own words, I told them the new plan. How it was better to wait a year before heading East. East was the wrong direction just now. There were things I had to do with Jesse, and wait for Lorna, and run the river once the water got high enough. Which would be after school started. There were things to do. I could earn some money, work in the woods.

Which I don't know. Somehow my plan had made perfect sense out on the island. Here, it didn't. Mother tried to find a resting place for her hands, and Duncan stared at me like I'd lost my marbles. Even to me, my plan sounded dumb. Maybe I didn't explain it well. The current was much stronger here than in the river. I had expected Link, at least, to back me up.

"You ain't no logger," Link said. "That's plumb crazy."

Mother and Duncan exchanged glances of alarm. She took off her glasses, huffed hot air over the lenses, and wiped them on her skirt. She was Trying-To-Say. "We've always trusted your decisions, Wade," she said.

Duncan wasn't Trying-To-Say. "Have you told Princeton about this?" he said. "How do you know they'll keep your scholarship for next year?"

I hadn't. I didn't. They probably would, wouldn't they?

"It's a well-known fact," Duncan said, "that people who put off college for a year never go."

"I'll go," I said. "It's just for a year. What's the big problem? Whose life is it, anyway?"

And who was this Duncan, this stranger-my-father, actually making an argument?

Lorna squirreled in her seat.

"You'll love it as soon as you get there, Wade," Mother said. Her brown eyes were misty behind their glasses. She turned toward Lorna, her last best hope. "Lorna, what do you think?"

Lorna gave me the sideways eye. But it was all hers. She was on the spot. "I've always thought," Lorna said, locking eyes with Mother, "a person should go to college as soon as he can."

I couldn't believe it.

Lorna followed it up with how she and I had talked it

over and she was sure I *would* go to college, but basically she choked. She swallowed the olive.

Lorna. Gad. My eye fell on a pair of bronzed baby shoes on the china cabinet. My shoes. I guess what you do is you take a pair of soft-worn leather baby shoes and dip them in some kind of bronze solution. Maybe it's done by spraying the shoe. Anyway, it freezes them—wrinkles and stub toes and scuffs and worn heels and all—hard and shiny like a new penny.

"I'm not going," I said.

"He's not going," Link explained. "Now let's eat. If he's not going, he's not going."

"Thank you," I said.

We ate in stone silence, everybody thinking like mad. Sarah Ellen tried to make small talk, but it didn't go. The cuckoo sprang from its clock on the wall and did seven loud hiccups, the first of which startled Lorna and made her jump. A car drove by and I thought it might be Jesse, but it wasn't. The creep. Skipping this wonderful family dinner.

"Well, now," said Duncan, clearing his throat.

We were on dessert.

"I can understand the river part," Duncan said. "If the three of you have something with the river."

He spooned a piece of ice cream onto his pie, then switched to his fork and took a bite. He chewed it thoughtfully. Duncan was the last person I expected to understand the river part. Link stared at Duncan with great interest. I did, too. Duncan was as focused as I'd ever seen him.

"But if you really want to help Jesse," Duncan said, "you ought to get *him* to go to college."

"Oh for crying out loud," Link said.

"No," Duncan said. "Why don't you and Jesse go down to Corvallis for a year?"

Mother, who had been on the verge of tears, finally plunged in.

"COLLEGE!?" Jesse said.

We were out rowing on the lake, trolling for rainbows

and not doing any good. But it was the best way to slow Jesse down and get his attention.

"I couldn't do that," he said.

"Why not? What do you think, you're dumb or something? It can't be any harder than MacLaren," I said. "And college has girls."

"What's Oregon State, the Ducks or the Beavers?"

"The Beavers," I said. "See? You could do that."

Actually it was no trouble at all getting Jesse to swallow the idea of college. I don't know why I thought it would be, or why I hadn't thought of it before. In Jesse's own opinion, he could do anything. And if there was the slightest suggestion he couldn't, it got him all the more interested. College isn't all that common a deal in Calamus. Most people go to work in the woods, where the money is good. Or get married. But if there was any reason Jesse couldn't go to college, it was only in what others expected. They had slots for people, and Jesse's slot wasn't college. In fact it was a lot like Lorna's theory of the boxes, and I had been as guilty of that kind of thinking as the next person. Why couldn't Jesse go to college?

Well, there were reasons. Technical difficulties.

Coach Garth, as principal, pointed out a main one. Jesse hadn't graduated from Calamus High School. We would have to get his papers from MacLaren, and Coach Garth wasn't sure how that would work. Whether Oregon State would take him.

"Jesse isn't exactly . . . ahm . . . college material," Coach Garth said. "This is highly unusual."

The door to his office was open. Coach Garth was in shirt sleeves, not his principal's suit. The school was an empty summer shell of a thing that echoed like inside a drum. He was already bent out of shape that I wasn't going to Princeton. I was no longer a feather—more like a piece of lint—on the cap of his community. I needed a transcript and his signature on the forms for Oregon State. And now this business about Jesse. Coach Garth was having a tough day.

"He's got a C average," I said. "And he earned his diploma from MacLaren."

"I don't see how it's my place to . . ." he said, fingering the application I'd brought him for Jesse.

"Well, if it's highly unusual," I said, "why don't you sign this just in case. Couldn't you write him a recommendation?"

I figured Jesse and I could drive down to MacLaren and get the administrator to do it, too. It just seemed like common sense to me. I was trying to stay cool about this.

"We have our standards," Coach Garth said. "The community . . ."

"Standards!" I said. "Who's going to give a rat's ass if you write Jesse a recommendation? You can help a guy out!"

"Wade, Wade," he said. He stretched back in his chair. It was one of those swivel chairs, on rollers. "Easy does it."

I had to remember who I was talking to. I sat back down. On the wall was a framed cloth and thread-written slogan, WHEN THE GOING GETS TOUGH, THE TOUGH GET GOING.

"Who's going to help him?" I said. "Who's Jesse got?"

"Wade, let me tell you something," he said. Coach Garth leaned forward with his elbows on the desk. He studied a blue and white mug on his desk that held pens and pencils.

"You and your family are special in this community," he said. By special, he meant different. He didn't have to say that. "But there's a lot of resentment about Jesse," he said. "You're asking me to make a travesty of the system. After football. After all we did for Jesse. We bent over backwa—"

"After all you did for Jesse!" I said. "After all he did for YOU!"

A travesty of the system! Next to the pen-holder mug on his desk lay a glass paperweight, the size of a softball cut in half. It looked like it would fit just right in my hand. I pictured myself wiping his desk clean with the paperweight. I saw papers sailing about the office, and the paperweight crashing to the floor with his pens and mug and his IN and OUT box.

Which is not what I did, of course. Once you think about it, it's too late. I wish I had, but I didn't.

Instead, I just looked him in the eye.

"You're a coward," I said.

He was dumfounded. Speechless. It was a satisfying thing. Mildly satisfying. "And Calamus . . ." I said, as I walked out the door. "Calamus is a vicious place."

TWENTY-FOUR

FOR YEARS AND YEARS, they say, Link and one of his sons—it didn't matter which one—won the bucking contest at the timber jamboree. That's what put Link in the sawblade-sharpening business for a time. After that, people swore he was dulling their blades come jamboree time. So Link offered to switch blades. He would use anybody else's saw, as long as he'd been the one to sharpen it. And still he won the bucking, with time to spare. So one year when Link and young Duncan—just a runt kid—won the bucking, a fire-eyed loser wanted to know where Link got his log. In those days, you supplied your own thirty-inch Douglas fir for bucking. Link's log looked like fir, smelled like fir, but this guy wanted to see the stump.

They say Link rowed his accuser across the lake and led him up behind the bunkhouse. Link pointed to a huge virgin fir, still standing. It was six or seven feet across at the base. The guy looked confused. He'd come to see the stump of that thirty-inch fir Link had used. Link pointed up—way up—to where the huge tree rose toward the bushy tops of its neighbors. The tree had been topped. It was the world's tallest stump.

There's thirty-inch fir, and there's thirty-inch fir, is how Link explains it. *The wood up top turns white and fresh and tender, like celery.*

FRIDAY night before the Calamus Timber Jamboree is when the bets go down at the barbershop section of the barbershop. The place was packed.

"Who you bettin' on, Mack, in the buckin'?"

"Bucking!" She spat. "Why, I wouldn't put a plugged nickel on bucking unless Link Curren did, or if the old bastard signed up for it himself."

Silence followed Mack's mention of Link, a silence broken only by a chuckle or two behind vacant eyes. The story about Link and the bucking didn't even have to be told, because everybody knew it. Mack's clippers hummed around Norvis Smith's headband dent, dropping greasy black tufts on the floor.

"I'll take Mike Perry in the toppin', though," Mack said.

"Shee-ut," Norvis said. Norvis can make two syllables out of any short word. "Hay-ul." Which tired him too much to continue, so others took up the argument.

"Perry ain't bowlegged enough for your tree toppin'."

"Won it last year, didn't he?"

"Was a fluke! Frank Jukor was laid up. Frank's ready this year, Frank is."

"Jukor couldn't climb his ol' lady."

"Climb *your* old lady, maybe."

"Shee-ut."

"Frank is strong, real strong."

"Gotta be more than strong, I tell ya. A bull is stronger 'n a monkey, but which one's gonna take your tree-toppin'?"

Jesse showed up. He stood by the plastic strips in the door to the restaurant. He sipped from the straw in a Coke glass, eyeing the crowd.

Mack finished Norvis's haircut and shook out the sheet. He stayed in the chair. Voices rose, and the air was thick with smoke. Odds were shouted, insults exchanged. Mack wrote down bets in her blue spiral notebook.

I worked my way through the crush to Jesse.

"What's coming off?" he asked.

"It's the prejamboree jamboree," I said. "The natives are restless."

"Natives," he said.

Mack mentioned that a guy from Roseburg had checked in at the Silvertip.

"Hay-ul."

Now that the Kiwanis Club had got behind the Calamus Timber Jamboree and made it official—put up prize money— the jamboree was drawing some out-of-town loggers. Outside winners were an ominous possibility. Not that a stranger had yet won anything.

"All's I know is this climber from Roseburg checked in last night," Mack said. "Brought his spikes and strap." She was trying to raise bets as she raised the mystery level, but they weren't going for it. Nobody wanted to bet on a stranger.

Jesse finished his Coke with a loud slurp and set his glass on the linoleum floor. Bets were going down on the logrolling. The jamboree would be tomorrow. Jesse leaned toward me, his black eyes flashing, and asked if logrolling was the one where they spin logs on the lake.

That was it, I told him.

"Hey, Mack," Jesse shouted. "Can anybody enter?"

JESSE showed up the next morning in a pair of Link's old steel-soled caulked boots. Events wouldn't start for another hour, but people came early for the Kiwanis breakfast at the site, a clearcut at lakeside. Fat slabs of bacon sputtered and sizzled on the outdoor grill. Jesse paid, and we got in line. Instead of sitting at the card tables, we took our sagging paper plates to the drop-off and found a stump.

"Where's the old ball and chain?" Jesse said.

"Lorna doesn't go for all this he-man logger stuff," I

said. "She doesn't get it." Which reminded me. "Hey, we have to drive down to MacLaren Monday," I said, "and get your papers filled out."

"Whatever you say."

Jesse pointed to a log lashed against the bank, below us. "That the log?"

"That's the log."

It was a blustery day, cool. The wind kicked up, stopped, came from many directions at once. Billowy white clouds raced around nervously, too few of them to blot out the blue. When the sun peeked through it was warm on the skin, but that lasted only a second or two at a time. Below us the lake lay leaden green, with silvery swirls from gusts of wind. Not your ideal day for taking a dip.

"You don't want to do this," I said.

Jesse's mouth was stuffed with egg and hotcakes, so he could only nod.

"Big guys always win," I told him.

He put down his plate and bounded down the bank. The slope was steep but passable if you were careful. Or if you were Jesse. When he left, I realized I hadn't eaten much. I took a bite, but it was cold already. The food had sponged the smells back into itself. Jesse, down at the log, stepped out onto one end. It barely dipped. Since the log was tethered, he couldn't give it a test spin. He toed the rough bark grooves and danced on it, just playing around. When he scrambled back up the bank, his dark eyes glowed.

"Don't you have to check in or something?"

"Oh yeah," he said, and turned his grin toward the sign-up booth.

By the time the bucking started, the clearing was packed. Many staked their claims on the crest, toward the water. From there they could only hear, not see, the bucking, but they would have a prime view for logrolling, the next event.

Out on the lake sat Link in his boat, eating Oreos. It was strange nobody else thought to do that. The lake was the best place to watch the climbing and logrolling, yet Link was the only one out there except for the official boat that would fish losing logrollers from the lake. Link had an air about him as if he would be the one to give thumbs up or thumbs down. His white hair shimmered whenever the sun shot it up.

After watching a couple of heats of the bucking, I went down the slope and called out to Link. He cranked on the motor—the five-horse troller—and putted over to pick me up. From out on the lake the crowd looked even larger. People sat in trees, even, at the edge of the clearing. The spar tree rose as a huge mast sticking up through the deck of the crowd.

Link was in a foul mood.

"Bunch of candy asses," he snarled. "I told 'em, I sez, them Kee-wanis fellers'd queer the show, I told 'em. Set a spinner log on a flat ol' lake so folks can come out from Portland and go *ooh* and *aah* because a feller got his shirt wet . . ."

He bit into a cookie.

"Used to be," Link snorted, "if you didn't ride that log down the river, you didn't *get* here Saturday night."

I decided to ignore him.

When the bucking was over, the bulk of the crowd spilled over the crest to find places on the slope. Virgil Beasley, the banker, unlashed the log and nudged it with the official boat. He and Coach Garth maneuvered the log out twenty yards from shore and parallel to the bank. Then they swung the boat into shore to pick up the first two rollers.

One was George Burt and the other Od Skinner, an older guy but a good one. They stepped from the boat to the log, one on each end. The log sunk visibly with their weight. George took charge right away, the older man reacting to George's jerks and stutters as he got the log moving first one way, then the other. Od couldn't get the lead back from George, who caught him leaning the wrong way and dumped him. It was a clean win. That is, George stayed on. He brought the log to rest in the water as Od splashed into shore rather than climb aboard the boat.

The crowd loved it, the splash more than anything.

That's what it's all about, the splash, although George had handled the log well. He stepped into the boat and they took him ashore.

Another pair came out, and Jesse wasn't one of them.

Three more pairs rolled before Jesse stepped into the official boat. The fool had taken off his clothes. All he was wearing was his skimpy electric blue swimsuit. Which is bad luck. People had tried it before and never won. And Jesse was barefoot. He'd shucked the caulked boots, too. I didn't see how he could stay on the log without corks.

Link, laughing at the sight of Jesse, pounded on the seat of the boat. "By cracky, that's what I told 'im to do," he said. "Now we'll see somethin'."

Ned Groves was Jesse's opponent. Which was good and bad. Ned never wins, but he's a veteran roller and plenty hefty. When he and Jesse mounted the log, it tilted badly toward Ned. Jesse looked small and naked perched on his end.

Ned was leery. Maybe he expected Jesse to walk down the log and push him in the water. But once he got the log moving, Ned had complete control. With the weight against him, Jesse was on defense. All he could do was flit lightly across the top as the log rocked and jerked under him. I didn't see how he could win unless Ned slipped off. Jesse rode that log, though, as if he'd been doing it all his life. Pantherlike, he kept his balance no matter what Ned did to cut the log from under him. Whenever Jesse seemed about to lose it, he brought himself back with some unlikely twisting of arms and a leg.

Cheering and shouting spread over our boat, echoing as if the crowd were behind us as well as out front.

With time, Ned slowed. He tried changes of pace, changes of direction. But nothing shook Jesse.

Ned stopped, puffing. The two of them stood facing each other, Jesse grinning. Jesse, then, made a couple of moves to take control, but for him the log was anchored in cement instead of floating on water.

Ned found his second wind. Encouraged by shouts from

the shore, he got the log spinning fast. Instead of facing one another, they both faced the bank, running in place. Bark on the log began throwing up spray. And then I saw how Jesse could win. Would win. He had to win. With the log's inertia broken, all he had to do was keep running.

Spray from the log rose higher and higher, blinding them both. Link got so excited I was afraid he might stomp through the bottom of the boat.

Ned tried to keep pace with Jesse on the spinning log, but he tipped slowly backward, still running, and splashed into the water.

It took Jesse a long time to bring the log to rest, to slow its spinning. Which may have been why the crowd acted so strange. During the match, I hadn't noticed the crowd to be either for or against Jesse. It was just a good match. Folks like it. But when Jesse won, the applause was surprised, ominous, cold as the wind. A kind of amplified murmur. No FGWs here. This was something more than a ball game. Jesse was taking on loggers at their own game.

Showing them up.

Link's eyes flashed blue as if Jesse had opened a window to the days of real people. "That'll show 'em," he said. Sweat trickled down the side of his face. "Fling me that there packet of Oreos, Wade, under the seat. That Injun can dive deeper and come up drier than anybody I ever seen."

FOR THE next round of rolling, the scattered clouds called up reinforcements. Short bursts of sun came less frequently, and colors on the bank grew muted, grayer. I watched the next couple of matches without really seeing them, gauging the crowd response against what I remembered from Jesse's win. Jesse was the outsider, all right, the ringer from Roseburg against the town's own. On the other hand, what was there to worry about? There was no way Jesse could get hurt. He could get wet. He could get embarrassed, maybe, but not hurt.

Jesse won his second-round match, too.

In the third round—the semifinals—he drew Frank Jukor, the squat and stubble-bearded tough who was one of the favorites for this event as well as for tree-topping. Frank spat a stream of brown juice into the lake before he stepped onto the log with Jesse. His bowed legs clamped the log like a set of tongs. Frank wore an open-pit undershirt. Kinky chest hair spilled out below his stumpy neck, and his shoulders bulged under blue tattoos. Frank looked like he smelled bad. But worse, he looked impossible to budge off that log.

Frank tested first one way, then the other. Jesse just grinned, without a care in the world. Then Frank started spinning the log, and they both turned to face the bank. Which was a strange move, I thought. Frank must have seen Jesse's first match. The only way Jesse could attack was if the other guy got the log spinning for him. As the log picked up speed, its bark lifted spray, like before.

Then Frank took a running leap up and came down with all his weight, both feet at once, on the rising side of the log. His spikes bit like chisels into a lathe. Jesse, caught in midstride, was thrown into the air when his foot hit the bark. The log flung him forward, up and toward the bank.

Jesse grabbed wildly, hopelessly—even awkwardly—for a handle in the air.

A collective gasp from the bank sucked air off the lake and pinned Jesse in an eerie vacuum as he tried to get a hold on something. He hit the water to a tremendous roar from the mob on the bank.

Frank went in too, of course—you can't just stop a log like that. His sudden brake on the log threw him off balance at the same time it bucked Jesse. But Frank managed two more desperate steps before the log rolled him off. Jesse hit the water first, so Frank was the winner.

Jesse swam quickly to shore.

Frank, when his head bobbed up, vaulted himself into the Kiwanis boat. The cheering was even louder when Frank got to shore. It took folks a while to realize how much they liked it.

• • •

LINK stood in the boat to yank the motor rope. We had drifted enough that we were no longer centered on the action. The motor started on his first pull, sending a blue-white cloud behind the boat that hung close to the surface before wind whisked it away. Frantic white clouds gave way to a heavier gray that was darkest to the west, toward the dam. The smell of rain filled the air. Any minute, the spar tree might poke through the gray tarp of ceiling. I pulled a pair of Army-surplus slickers from under the bow and tossed one to Link, hoping the rain would hold off until after the tree-topping.

Which had already begun.

The spar tree, for topping, was the same one they'd used the last few years, since the Kiwanis Club took over the jamboree. The tree's bark was worn smooth and in fact it was shorter than trees on the edge of the clearing, since it was topped. But the spar tree stood erect and solid in the bursts of wind that caught other trees along the shore and bent them at the tops.

The first few toppers—including the mystery man from Roseburg—were not so hot.

Dickie Mills made a pretty good run. He jammed his boot spikes into the bark and ran up the side of the tree, jerking the leather climbing strap ahead of him and around the tree, to hold him in. But he took too much time getting down. Which, when it's done right, is close to a free fall. You want to slide down the bark face of the tree with the strap held loosely. Tighten it only toward the bottom, to brake in. A couple of years ago Norvis Smith popped both knees on his landing, and they say he's about four inches shorter now.

The worse fate, on the way down, would be to catch a knob.

At intervals between climbs, Jesse's laugh rang full and loose across the lake. He was busy near lakeside, with John Buzhardt and George Burt—Frank Jukor, too—pantomiming his logrolling effort. Others came by to say hello. Jesse had everybody on his side now. After losing, he was everybody's friend. A bottle-shaped brown paper bag passed around Jesse's group. He took a long swig and arched his body back happily. His laughter boomed from the bank.

Well, he deserves it.

Link crumpled the empty package of Oreos and tossed it over the side of the boat.

"Hell, they got that tree all shaved smooth, topped out so the wind don't mess 'er up," he complained. "Got 'er all but circumcised up there and waitin'."

It was true, nowadays, all a topper had to do was stick a hatchet into the top of the spar tree and wave his hand free. But what could you do, without shortening the tree with each climber? The event was still a fair test of climbing, if not actually topping.

Link grumped and farted about it. The only time he'd been himself all day was when Jesse was doing his stuff. It must be hell getting old. I wished I could flash back to see Link in some of his own stories. Or even to look through the window that opened up for him when he watched Jesse.

"Who is Jesse's father?" I asked him. "Do you know?"

I'd tried this before, without learning anything. But what the hell. I just blurted it out.

Link busied himself with the motor and putted us the short, unnecessary distance to get centered.

"I said . . ."

"No," Link answered. "Don't reckon I know. Some nasty wild-man logger, could of been. Ain't nobody knows except Reno. If *she* does."

He understood my question. I waited for him to add something, but Link was busy watching another run up the spar tree. When that had finished, I watched some bubbles wobble up from the lake bed.

I said, "Let me put it this way . . ."

"Ain't nothin' for you to get in a lather about," said Link, cutting me off. "No sense in it."

He rummaged through the duffle bag to see if it was true that the last of the Oreos were gone.

"But what if . . ." I continued. "I mean as far as you know."

"Well, I'll be whizzled," Link said. His eyes danced. "You reckon a creaky old fart like me could of done something that good? Why, my wobbly old dick ain't been stirrin' for twenty years now," he said. "The old lady, she done wore me to a stub. Part of why she kicked off," he said. "There wasn't nothin' left for her to live for."

Link thought about it some more. He laughed and shook his head, but he didn't say anything.

"I guess that's right," I said sadly. "You would've been too old."

Link eyed me sideways.

"Too *old!*" He bit. "Why, you don't know from nothin'." He squirmed on the seat of the boat and went back to watching the events on shore.

"She's gonna cut loose and rain here pretty quick," he said.

Give him a little line, I thought. Don't jerk the hook out of his mouth. That's what Link always taught me. I watched more bubbles ghosting up from the bottom of the lake.

"Oh, I reckon I used to amble over to the dance hall once and again," Link allowed. "Kick up my heels for a spell and break up some fistfights. Them were feistier days, ruggeder nights," he said. His face warmed with the memory of it. "I wasn't the only one to hanker after some dark meat."

"You mean it's possible, at least."

He studied the color of the lake water.

"But there was a number of fine young loggin' men," he said, "would of ripped down trees with their bare hands and built her a house if that Indian girl would of stayed in Calamus and cooked their beans."

Link eyed me carefully.

"Trouble with you is you think you can know everything," he said. "You can go supposin' 'til hell freezes over, but you can't go knowin'. Not until Reno Howl decides to name a daddy. And she ain't seen a need for that yet. Best not to think on it."

. . .

MIKE Perry took the next run up the tree like taking stairs, three steps at a time. The strap skipped ahead of him up the back side of the tree, and his legs pumped smooth where others had been jerky and fitful. At the top he whipped the hatchet out of its sheath, drove it into the top, waved his hand free, jammed the hatchet back into the sheath and shot back down the tree, trailing a thin orange cloud of bark dust on the way down. Perry braked himself only lightly with the strap, which slid all the way without binding on him. He lit holding the side of his face—must've scraped it—but it was a beautiful thing to see, the way he worked that tree.

The time was announced—forty-three seconds. The crowd went nuts. It was a record. A modern record, that is, since they did away with the actual topping.

Jesse and his crowd, still animated but not so comically, were studying the topping. The first large raindrops sliced silver and fat across the bank and plunked the water like marbles, well spaced. I lifted the hood on my slicker.

Frank Jukor was the next climber, probably the only one who could make a run at Perry's time. But Frank wasn't in good form. Probably he was worn out from the logrolling. And stiffened, too, from being in the water. Frank couldn't find his rhythm. He fought the tree all the way.

I looked for Jesse on the bank. This time he was nowhere in sight. My gut tightened as I tried to pick him out among the crowd. He wasn't along the slope, so he must have gone on up on the flat.

"Run me in to shore," I said to Link. "Quick."

Rain came heavier now as Link cranked up the motor. He knew what I was worried about.

"That coyote's too crazy to be that stupid," he said.

I wasn't so sure.

"You ain't gonna stop him anyhow," Link said, "if he gets a mind to give 'er a go."

I jumped from the boat onto the bank, and pushed my

way up the crowded slope. By the time I reached the crest, I was winded. I couldn't pick out Jesse in the crowd. I could only think of the Jesse I'd seen by the lakeshore taking long happy swigs from that paper sack. Of course he would try to climb that tree. And it was just possible they'd let him do it.

Jesse had entertained them well today.

A shout rose from the base of the spar tree and spread outward through the mob. Somebody had started, and the excitement in the cheering was different from what it had been. I couldn't see the base of the tree for all the people. But I knew.

I could push no further through the crowd. Jesse's dark head edged up the spar tree and into sight. He wasn't moving fast. His strap was way too loose, and the boots with climbing spikes looked awkward on him. Jesse struggled more with his equipment than with the tree as he kept going up, steadily but clumsily. Winning was out of the question. The crowd, now, was laughing at him.

There was no way to stop him. I could only stand there and watch him rise, his wet black hair shining. The rain blurred my vision. I tried to think him through this. He'd be all right if he just took it smooth and didn't try anything stupid.

Jesse began to get the feel of the tree. The strap worked better for him as he took larger and smoother steps. I remembered to breathe. He was accelerating now, and no one was laughing. As he grew smaller and smaller, he came more and more in tune with the tree, moving quickly and easily like Jesse can. With each step up the side, he looked more in charge of himself and of the tree, scaling faster still. The hatchet dangled from his belt, and the leather strap skipped up the opposite side of the tree as if he had done this, too, all his life.

Don't chop the strap, I remembered. I may have even mouthed the words as he neared the top.

Jesse did not stop at the top.

He didn't even slow down.

His strap took that last skip—right past the top of the tree and over it—into gray nothing. His body arched slowly up and backward from the top of the tree. All around me came the screams, the thrill and the horror from empty heads. The shrieks issued from hollow drums and were swallowed by gray sky and rain as Jesse fell. He turned to face us, his body extended as if floating through a graceful slow-motion dive for a theater audience.

Jesse's eyes were wide, surprised—Well, isn't this interesting? What will we think of next? I think it's possible that even then, no consequence occurred to Jesse. He got faster, larger, closer until the crowd parted for him. I couldn't watch. But over and over I hear the sound—the unspeakable muffled crunch of bone and flesh against the hard earth, of Jesse's life against death.

TWENTY-FIVE

≈≈≈≈

WHITE.

WHITE is the absence of words on a page.

But white is not the absence of color. What white is, really, is all the colors. It's the whole spectrum, combined and reflected. In science class one time old Weatherby brought out this whirligig machine that spun a disk around to prove it. The disk had wedges of many colors on it before it started spinning. As he cranked the handle, the disk spun faster and faster until the colors blended. Pretty soon the disk got white.

That's what white is. White is nothing from everything.

JESSE'S mother didn't have a phone. Even if she had, I would have wanted to tell her in person. Lorna and I drove over to the reservation. Reno had already dreamed it, or knew in some way, as soon as we drove up. But none of this made it any easier. How do you tell someone? And then the funeral, a couple days later. They had a sunrise service at Wishram, across the river from Celilo, the saddest and best place. The funeral was mostly wind and drums and wailing.

I'll tell you the truth. I couldn't take it.

Sometimes your whole brain can spin white. Nothing

from everything. After Jesse's fall, I was walking around in a white mist, a blizzard, where nothing was distinct. I tried to stick with it, to make some sense of things, but everything melded and mixed together.

The lake seemed about the only place for us. Lorna and I tried other things, anything—a movie, or a drive into Portland. But nothing was right. So here we were, down at the lake again.

As I rowed, ripples of water slipped from the side of the boat. Long rolls of water sent the reflection of each tree trunk into a lazy wiggle. The wiggle worked its way up the tree. A smaller, faster wiggle followed it up, and then tinier and quicker bumps scrambled up the same tree until the reflection vibrated on the lake like a thick and soundless tuning fork. The final glow of day was fading from the sky to the west, but the lake itself was without color. Wisps of vapor rose off the surface like ghostly dancers to an unheard flute before fading into vague air. What I knew to be green was black, and objects appeared only in dark and fuzzy-edged relief.

If Lorna and I had what you'd call a spot, this was it. This lake, this dammed and dead river, this great hole of sadness. The place we are from.

Lorna seemed to be on the verge of saying something, but she swallowed it.

The oars went straight down, breaking the black surface. I brought them slowly and steadily back, not rocking the boat. An oar came out with a barely audible *sssssssslllllppp* over the water, and the oar gave back little drops that hung from the wooden blades, *p . . p . . p . . . p . . . . . p . . . . p.* Rings welcomed the returning drops to the lake, but those rings collided with linear ripples from the side of the boat. Both designs, clean in themselves, got mixed and confused and sloppy.

"Well," Lorna said. It was fully dark on the lake. "We're going to have to get on with it." She sat facing me as I rowed. Her voice sounded choked. This was not easy for her, either. "Jesse is gone," she said. "There's nothing we can do."

She was right, I knew, but it was not so easy.

There should have been some place for Jesse. His was a stupid, unnecessary death. I couldn't get over the idea that I was responsible, we all were, for a world too organized to hold him. Yet there was nobody, really, to blame. Maybe Lorna was partly right, it was Calamus. But there was something inside him, too, that would never have fit, would never have been civilized or comfortable. There should have been some way for us to pull him from the town.

I could have been a stronger friend.

If Lorna's idea was to get me to talk, I guess she did. We talked. Or I talked, and Lorna just listened, mostly, for hours. Some of it even made sense. It was more important just to talk it through, without worrying about what made sense. I talked about Link and our first trip out over the bar. I told her all I could put together about Link and Duncan and the salmon. Lorna didn't interrupt, though there were long pauses and plenty of opportunity for her to do so. We talked about those stunted and lazy salmon at the millpond, the ones who don't take the trip. They are the survivors, fish from the same stock as those battered monsters we had seen spawning below the spillway. Landlocked, selected out. Those are the salmon who stopped at the millpond, fooled there by the crashing of logs into the water and new bugs dropped in with each crash of their artificial surf. Fooled, were they? Or smart. In the millpond there are no blackened heads and bruised jaws, no sea lice and scars and missing fins.

I had long ago stopped rowing. We were just drifting on the lake, sitting on the bottom of the boat with our backs against the seat.

Stars above the lake were bright and close. The sawmill, working through the night, hung the smell of green wood over the lake. A log truck groaned to life. It shifted gears and headed up the river road to start another cycle, though it was still dark. The sound of mill saws in the background carried no special terror. It was a larger, more general kind of fear, this white blizzard in my mind.

When Lorna did speak, it broke a long silence.

"Pick out a star up there and just look at it," she said. "Pick a dim one."

I did it. I had one. I thought we were going to make a wish on it or something.

"Now really concentrate on it. Stare right at it," she said. "The star goes away, doesn't it?"

"Yes," I said. "It does."

"See, you have to kind of look off to one side, not right at the star, if you want to hold it. Sometimes it helps to blink and start over."

We lay in the boat staring and blinking. Lorna and I held each other close against the night chill. And normally you'd feel like a blithering idiot for just crying, sobbing, not being able to say anything to a night sky so deep and strange. But with Lorna it was OK. The crying was our blanket to cover a great, great sadness.

AFTER driving Lorna home, I slipped into the house. Still too brain-white to sleep or read, I poured a glass of milk and took it to the living room. I was sitting on the davenport in the dark when the living-room window just presented itself. Like, remember me?

I hadn't pitched to the window in years.

The living room window at night becomes a mirror, low and wide enough to reflect a pitcher's motion. Take a rolled-up pair of socks and throw it at the window, and the image throwing back is a left-hander. Warren Spahn was the one I used to try for. Whitey Ford I could do better than Spahn. The wind-up, the delivery. The stretch. The pick-off move, the hitch of the belt. Not that this is useful prac-tice, but I used to do it all the time as a kid. Left-handers are more exotic, more unlikely—just more graceful—to watch.

So now I turned on the corner lamp to make the window a mirror. Throwing easy at first, with the rolled-up socks I'd worn into the house, I didn't want to wake them upstairs.

I was working on Warren Spahn.

I don't know. You never know. I guess what happens is you can lose yourself. Before long the left-hander at the window took on the loose-limbed fluid grace of Jesse. Although he did not throw harder, the windowpane began to rattle with each impact of the socks. Thrilled, I kept throwing until a shaft of new light, from up the stairs, brought me to a frozen stop.

"Wade, is that you?" Duncan called.

I stared at Jesse, equidistant from the window, outside. He grinned. It was just a glimpse, just a whisper, that sent a chill up my spine and into my scalp. I gave him our crossbuck handshake, but Jesse returned it out of sync. Perfectly wrong. Plumb backward.

LORNA and I launched the boat from below the dam, after the first good September rain and the Calamus got high enough to sweep us out.

It was Link's boat, the same fourteen-foot Birchcraft he'd always used to test the bar. It had needed sanding and a new coat of paint. Which was a good thing for Lorna and me to work on while we waited for the river to rise. Link helped us get the boat ready. The only hard part was when Link got it in his bushy head that he was going along.

"You're not invited," I said.

I guess it was kind of cruel, this being Link's boat and all. But it was Link's doing as much as anything, what we had to do. Nobody was invited. Lorna and I were leaving Calamus, that's all. We didn't have what you would call plans. We were headed for Astoria, the end of the river. As Jesse would say, *Something will turn up.* I could find work in Astoria, I figured, or wherever. Lorna could work and do her correspondence credits anywhere. Except in Calamus. Later we could catch up with Back East. For now we were headed Out West. Our trip would bust some standards, crush a few rules, but they'd get over it. Or as Lorna was quick to point out, it didn't really matter what anybody in Calamus thought.

"What this vessel needs is a name," Lorna decided. The last coat of white paint had dried and we were doing the red trim. I offered to run up to the hardware store and get a stencil, but she just free-handed it, red letters on white below the bow.

So like I said, we launched the boat below the dam. We loaded it with camping gear and christened the *Plumb Forwards* with a jumbo Nehi orange, my least favorite of the drinks we had packed. Lorna stepped into the boat as I steadied it for her. I pushed off from the bank, tossed the rope over the bow and jumped in, letting the current take us.

Which it did, with a great surge.

We had the 18-horse Johnson on the boat, and the water was high enough to have used it. But the river was also high enough to carry us through the hazards with only my pulling on the oars for direction. It was a fast and delicious high-water trip. The river sliced us through the big bend at Jack Knife and pushed us under the bridge at Cliffs. "Hooooeeeeeee!" I shouted, for Lorna, for Jesse. We were on our way. One of the best parts was when the river lined up with Mount Hood, straight behind us with a fresh coat of white snow. Like the land's own Leaving Calamus sign. And the other best part was just the idea of doing it. Even the danger— especially the danger—of riding the river toward the sea.

Already the river was cutting through my white blizzard. Colors began sorting themselves out, became distinct. Alders yellowed the riverbank, backed by taller and deeper green firs. The high-water river flowed a rich brown-green. There was Lorna's red lettering on the white bow of the boat when we stopped to eat lunch.

The Calamus River grew larger and calmer as it leaned into the big valley and met the wide, slow Willamette. We could have gone farther on the first day. But we were both more interested in getting the tent up than in actually getting anywhere. Air mattresses and goose-down sleeping bags. It all seemed just about right, and there was no hurry.

After hunger drove us from the tent that first evening, we had a wiener roast on the beach. I gathered driftwood for a fire, and Lorna had packed a pair of red candles she stuck in the sand and lit. Ever since I told her about that business with Coach Garth, Lorna liked to think of herself as a travesty of the system. The candles were a nice touch. A candlelight wieny roast.

Because the other way of thinking about Jesse was that Calamus never really got him. It was as if he was too much for the world, which finally coughed and spit him out, dead but unhurt. Jesse never stopped being Jesse, was the way to think about it. This was about the *only* way of thinking about it, here on the flowing river.

For the first time, Lorna and I were able to talk about Jesse, and about us.

I guess we were back in the tent when a Jesse story came in and joined us. "It's not exactly a Jesse story," I said. "It's Jesse's story about Coyote." I told Lorna the story about Coyote joining the night dancers down at the shoreline, and dancing all night, and bloodying his feet. Coyote didn't know the dancers were just cattails, swaying in the wind. He danced and danced. Coyote was a good dancer.

They'll sure be glad I came, Coyote said.

WHEN we rode the gentle Willamette under the bridges of Portland, the next day, Portland didn't even notice. The whole world was on the go, was on a schedule. We had no schedule. No where. Nothing to do there. I hadn't yet fired up the motor, and now it became important not to. Just let the slow river power us, at its own pace. Which was practically no speed at all. I rowed some, but mostly we drifted. Although Portland is over a hundred river miles from the Pacific, we passed monstrous ocean-going ships parked at Swan Island and the high piers of the world's business.

On the far side of Portland, where the Willamette bent lazily into the wider, bluer Columbia, we had a piece of our own business to take care of. Here the waters mixed, part Calamus and part Celilo. I fished the Chinook necklace from the pocket of my shirt. It was the necklace Jesse had made for me, the one I never wore.

"You could, you know," Lorna said. "You could wear it."

Which was generous of her.

I placed the necklace on the water. The ring of white salmon vertebrae hovered between river and sky before the river took it down and away. Very slowly it wobbled and disappeared into obsidian blue, the opposite of a large bubble rising.

The river, here, beyond Portland, was a powerful and soothing thing, flat wide blue between green cottonwood islands and their smooth sandy shores.

"Did I ever tell you about Jesse's vujà dé?" I said.

"What?"

"Vujà dé," I said.

I told Lorna about that time Jesse and I were out rowing on the lake and I tried to explain to him what déjà vu was. Déjà vu was a hard thing to explain if you didn't already know what it was, and I'd thought Jesse didn't get it. But he did, in his own dim-brilliant way.

"Vujà dé, Jesse said, was the opposite."

Lorna was following this closely. She had to change position in the boat because her left arm had gone to sleep. But she was listening.

"Vujà dé," I told Lorna, "is that feeling you're the first one out here. Nobody in the world has ever been here before."

A NOTE ABOUT THE AUTHOR

Robin Cody is a freelance writer. In 1986 he won the Western Writers of America's Silver Spur Award for short non-fiction. He lives in Portland, Oregon, with his wife, Donna.

A NOTE ON THE TYPE

The text of this book was composed in Palatino, a type face designed by the noted German typographer Hermann Zapf. Named after Giovanbattista Palatino, a writing master of Renaissance Italy, Palatino was the first of Zapf's type faces to be introduced in America. The first designs for the face were made in 1948, and the fonts for the complete face were issued between 1950 and 1952. Like all Zapf-designed type faces, Palatino is beautifully balanced and exceedingly readable.

Composed by Creative Graphics, Inc.,
Allentown, Pennsylvania
Printed and bound by The Haddon Craftsmen, Inc.,
Scranton, Pennsylvania
Designed by George J. McKeon